BROUGHTON HOUSE & COLLEGE

AUTIS... ...RNING ...IES

WITH ...

CHALL...

An inter...

and Cli...

to gain ...

require...

commu...

16 – 30...

PATH T...

MAIN HOUSE

COAC HOU...

ECSLS131

No 12 HIGH STREET

COMMUNITY SUPPORTED LIVING

During the programme, young people move within Broughton to increasingly independent living facilities. These planned moves reinforce behavioural improvements and life skills.

Broughton House & College, Lincoln, LN5 0SL

Cambian Education
Meeting special needs

0800 288 9779
All enquiries welcome
www.cambianeducation.com

More Special Needs titles from Lifetime Publishing

If I were ...

The practical introduction to jobs with few or no entry qualifications.

4th edition; Tessa Doe, Helen Evans, Hilary Jones, Debbie Steel

"*If I were . . . every school should have one.*" Careers Education and Guidance

This bestselling pack comprises 155 illustrated leaflets that describe in clear simple terms a wide range of jobs open to those students with few or no qualifications.

£75.00 ISBN: 1 902876 92 X

If I were plus!

An interactive version of our bestselling *If I were* ... information pack. This multi-media CD-Rom includes speech, video clips and allows users to access the information in an easy but stimulating way.

Price: £99.00 + vat ISBN: 1 904979 03 3

If I can ...

A practical, skill-based approach to the world of work

2nd edition; Colette Cassin-Davies, Helen Evans, Debbie Steel, Tessa Doe, Hilary Jones

'*A treasure trove of materials ...with interactive and fun activities that help students to recognise and apply life and work skills*' Newscheck

A colourful, pictorial approach for MLD students to understand what skills are and how they relate to the world of work. Includes photo cards of work situations and job/skill activities with related simple text cards with Widget symbols.

£75.00 ISBN: 1 902876 89 X

Going on Work Experience

3rd edition; Hilary Jones

A very bright and lively card resource to help prepare young people with moderate learning difficulties for work experience.

£24.95 16 Picture cards, users' notes in A4 wallet ISBN: 1 904979 05 X

Going for an Interview

3rd edition; Hilary Jones

A colourful card game about interview skills and preparation. Designed for students with moderate learning difficulties and also used with average ability students.

£24.95 16 Picture cards and users' notes in A4 wallet ISBN: 1 904979 04 1

If I were ... posters

A series of eight full-colour A2 posters illustrating a range of jobs with few or no entry qualifications

£29.95 + vat - set of eight A2 posters; ISBN: 1 902876 74 1

People I Meet posters

Six highly colourful, A2 posters introducing students with learning difficulties to the world of work

£29.95 + vat - set of six A2 posters; ISBN: 1 902876 99 7

View all our resources and download sample pages at: www.lifetime-publishing.co.uk

COPE

Directory of post-16 residential education and training for young people with special needs

Eleventh edition

COPE - eleventh edition

Published by Nord Anglia Lifetime Development South West Ltd, Lifetime Publishing, Mill House, Stallard Street, Trowbridge BA14 8HH

© Nord Anglia Lifetime Development South West Ltd, 2006

ISBN 1 904979 11 4

ISBN-13 978 1904979 111

Printed and bound by Cromwell Press Ltd, Trowbridge

Cover and text design by Jane Norman

Contents

Introduction

This is the eleventh edition of COPE. It has been compiled from information received from the many establishments which provide residential, continuing education and training for young people with special educational needs and disabilities. COPE is a quick-reference guide for professionals and carers involved in supporting and advising such young people.

In COPE we have tried to bring together information about a wide range of establishments, run under many different regimes and philosophies. Their approaches to education and training may vary, but they are all devoted to providing support and encouragement to young people with a variety of special needs.

What you will find in COPE

The information about establishments in COPE has been drawn from materials gathered from them early in 2006. We have used, as far as possible, the original wording of the replies we received, in order to reflect the flavour and stated aims of the establishments.

In this edition we have tried to standardise headings to make it easier to compare establishments. For convenience, we have used the words 'students' and 'courses' in these headings, which may not be the most appropriate terms for some establishments.

(In a few cases, we have been unable to obtain revised information from the establishment itself, so have included information from the previous edition of COPE, with an appropriate 'health warning' that the entry has not been updated.)

We have tried to include not only establishments which provide formal education, but also those whose goals could be summarised as preparation and training for adult life. While we appreciate that many schools offer facilities for their pupils beyond the age of 16, in the context of COPE our criteria for inclusion are that there should be residential facilities available (at least for weekly boarding) and that applications can be accepted from a wide area. We always welcome details of any establishments that we have missed out.

Establishments within COPE are indexed by name, geographical area and specialisation in a particular disability.

The inclusion of an establishment in COPE does not imply a recommendation by us or any judgement of the quality of the education or training provided. We recommend that, if you are investigating training or education for a young person, you should use this book solely as a starting point; it is vital to check details with the establishments themselves. We hope that, in this context, you will find COPE a useful addition to your bookshelf.

Please address comments and suggestions to:

COPE
Lifetime Publishing
Mill House
Stallard Street
Trowbridge BA14 8HH
Tel: 01225 716023
Fax: 01225 716025
Email: sales@lifetime-publishing.co.uk

Explanation of codes

Each establishment's entry is coded according to special needs catered for:

A   Acquired brain injury

B   Attention deficit disorder/attention deficit hyperactivity disorder ADD/ADHD

C   Autism/Asperger Syndrome

D   Blindness/visual disabilities

E   Cerebral palsy

F   Communication, language and speech impairment

G   Deafblind – visual/hearing impairment

H   Deafness/hearing impairment

I   Disadvantage

J   Down's Syndrome

K   Dyscalculia/dyspraxia

L   Dyslexia

M   Emotional disorders/challenging behaviour

N   Epilepsy

O   Learning difficulties/disabilities

P   Mental health

Q   Mixed and multiple disabilities

R   Physical disabilities/impairments

S   Severe learning difficulties/PMLD

T   Tourette's syndrome.

AALPS College (North)

Address: Winterton Road, Scunthorpe DN15 0BJ

Tel: 01724 733777   **Fax:** 01724 733666

Age range: 16-30

Fees: From £2,000 per week

Usual source of funding for students: Social services and health trusts

Aims: To provide a transition service for young people with autistic spectrum disorder to support them through lifeskills, leisure and vocational programmes.

Students catered for: The College provides a service for young people from all parts of the country. They must benefit from a structured environment and may have challenging behaviour.

Premises and facilities
Purpose built buildings over three sites include sports hall, catering kitchen, small animal farm, café, horticultural department, art and pottery rooms and IT suite. An equestrian centre is currently being developed.

Staffing
A high level of highly trained staff, with NVQs 2, 3 and 4, general certificate in autism plus mandatory.

Courses
The College offers lifeskills, leisure and vocational programmes.

Links
Links with North Lincs College; several local charity shops; Scunthorpe.

Other information
Full-time assistant psychologists; supporting consultant psychologist and psychiatrists; speech therapist.

Application procedure
Contact College; visit; request assessment; College places offer.

Acorn Village

Address: Clacton Road, Mistley, Manningtree, Essex CO11 2NJ

Tel: 01206 394124 **Fax:** 01206 391216 **Email:** acornvillage@btconnect.com **Website:** acornvillages.co.uk

Age range: 18 +

Controlled by: Acorn Village Trust

Fees: Variable according to needs. Rising annually

Aims: Acorn Village is a working community for people with learning disabilities. The aim is to create employment and educational skills to enable people to live in an environment which best suits their individual needs. The Village Community offers training towards independent living and residential care.

Students catered for: Registered for residential and independent living. Mixed sexes. Those with learning difficulties. From the age of 18 years onwards.

Premises and facilities

Village Hall on-site for recreational/social/training and public use by special arrangement. Coffee shop run by villagers and staff at Acorn Village as a work skills training facility. Soft toy workshop, weavery studio, woodwork shop. Acorn Village Trust has two shops, one nearby in High Street, Manningtree (providing work for those who wish to take part) and another 20 minutes away in Brightlingsea.

Student accommodation

Six group houses, two independent flats, two single flats at Acorn Village and five houses in the local community.

Staffing

Acorn has a staff of over 200 and employs an NVQ assessor/training coordinator.

Courses

Sessions include horticulture, sports, swimming, music and movement, art classes, computer studies, educational sessions, drama.

Links

Any avenues of work outside the Village Community are followed up. A full social life is encouraged.

Other information

Professional services of physiotherapist, psychologist and speech therapist by referral to the Health Authority. Village registered with Essex Social Services and NCSC.

Application procedure

Apply direct to Acorn Village and, at the same time, notify your social services department of your intentions.

Adolphus Care Ltd

Address: Pentax House, South Hill Avenue, Northolt Road, South Harrow HA2 9BW

Codes: O P

Tel: 020 8939 4695   **Fax:** 020 8938 4696   **Email:** info@adolphus.org.uk   **Website:** www.adolphus.org.uk

Age range: 18-50

Contact for admissions information: Vince Small

Fees: Up to 1:1 support only requires funding

Aims: To empower users by promoting independence through general life education.

Students catered for: Adults with learning difficulties and enduring mental health issues.

Premises and facilities

A comfortable, homely environment including a large garden. A registered service that provides self-contained units for young adults as a stepping stone on to improved autonomy, in line with the Government's strategy. Travel/training promoted as well as house car for longer journeys. PC and internet access available.

Student accommodation

Self-contained units.

Staffing

Generally 08.00 – 23.00 although this may be extended. 1:1 support available in every area of domestic tasks and in accessing external services.
Residents are allocated a key worker who is responsible for the implementation of support plans and to assist each resident in every aspect of his/her life.

Courses

Each client receives culturally- and educationally-appropriate support. Adolphus Care's holistic and structured approach is designed to integrate individuals into the community to experience the variety of social, occupational and educational activities West London has to offer.

Application procedure

Referral form available on request.

Alderwasley Hall School

Code: F

Address: Alderwasley, Belper, Derbyshire DE56 2SR

Tel: 01629 822586   **Fax:** 01629 826661   **Email:** info@alderwasleyhall.com   **Website:** www.alderwasleyhall.com

Age range: 5-19

Contact for admissions information: Headteacher, David Broadhurst Cert Ed, BEd

Controlled by: SENAD Ltd

Fees: Boarding fees from £49,608 per annum (additional fees for enhanced care, education and therapy)

Aims: Alderwasley Hall School is currently the largest specialist school in the UK for students whose special educational needs arise from difficulties in speech, language and communication.

Students catered for: Places are offered to students aged 5-19, on either a day or residential basis and are supported by over 60 LEAs.

Premises and facilities

The School includes primary, secondary and post-16 departments on two sites. A wide range of extra-curricular and leisure activities take advantage of the school's natural surroundings, local facilities and own excellent sports, recreational and equestrian facilities.

Student accommodation

Residential facilities are situated on the two sites, plus a residential house for the oldest students in Matlock.

Staffing

Well-qualified and experienced teachers and therapists together provide a broad, balanced and relevant curriculum, which is based on the programmes of study and assessment arrangements of the National Curriculum. Our team of speech and language therapists enable each class to have a therapist who plans and implements an individual programme for each student and works collaboratively with teachers to maximise all learning opportunities. Therapists work with the whole classes, small groups and individuals and contribute to curriculum planning and development. The school has an occupational therapy team who provide advice to staff and direct intervention for pupils throughout the school.

Courses

The School offers a broad and balanced curriculum with particular emphasis given to English and personal and social development; careers guidance and work experience; academic and vocational education qualifications — GCSE, Youth Award Certificate, Duke of Edinburgh Award; emphasis on developing communication, independence and social skills; inclusion opportunities with local schools and colleges; occupational therapy. Activities are supported by a large group of residential staff, many of whom have expertise or qualifications in relevant areas.

Links

The school has links with a number of local schools and colleges, which provide opportunities for our pupils and students to participate in social and learning activities. Links with a number of community groups also provide access to a wider peer group and activities in the evenings and weekends.

Other information

The school has established an assessment centre on site to provide parents and LEAs with detailed assessment information from educational psychology, speech and language therapy, education, occupational therapy and residential care. Assessments can be requested for placements at the school or for independent advice.

Applications procedure

Normally by referral from LEA.
Email: office@roxbyhouse.co.uk

Beannachar Camphill Community

Address: Banchory-Devenick, Aberdeen AB12 5YL

Tel: 01224 869138   **Fax:** 01224 869250   **Email:** office@beannachar.org   **Website:** www.beannachar.co.uk

Age range: 17-28

Contact for admissions information: Elisabeth Phethean

Out-of-term contact: As above

Usual source of funding for students: Own benefits plus local authority (social services)

Aims: Beannachar is a Camphill Community for young adults with learning disabilities. The cultural, social and economic needs of each one are catered for as part of the community life. Emphasis is placed on mutual help as the basis of the shared lifestyle (inspired by Rudolf Steiner's 'anthroposophy').

Students catered for: Beannachar caters for residents covered by all the codes listed above, plus Prader-Willi syndrome, Fragile X syndrome, Williams syndrome and Angelmann's syndrome.

Premises and facilities

All co-workers, their children and students share a common life in a large 19th century house (now two living units) and two smaller purpose-built houses, in a rural setting just two miles from the city centre. There are extensive grounds encompassing workshop buildings, a walled garden, a small farm, a games room (soon to be built), a playing field and gardens.

Student accommodation

Mostly single rooms, but three double rooms (shared).

Student numbers

22 resident, 10 day.

Staffing

28 staff plus 3 ancillary.

Courses

Further education and training opportunities in farm, garden, laundry, woodwork, weaving, candle making, herb workshop and kitchens.

Swimming, folk dancing, hobby groups, sports and non-denominational service are also offered — all on a weekly basis. Also seasonal activities in drama, painting, music and modelling etc.

Links

Aberdeen College. Work placements occasionally on an individual basis.

Other information

Therapies offered — speech, movement, physiotherapy, counselling, painting.

Application procedure

Please contact Elisabeth Phethean to arrange a visit; then an application form must be returned, and after that a day visit and four-week trial visit may be arranged if felt appropriate.

Beaumont College of Further Education

Code: E

Address: Slyne Road, Lancaster LA2 6AP

Tel: 01524 541400   **Fax:** 01524 846896   **Email:** Macpherson@beaumontcollege.org.uk   **Website:** www.scope.org.uk

Age range: 16 –25

Controlled by: SCOPE

Principal: Mr Graeme Pyle

Contact for admissions information: Above telephone or email

Fees: On application

Aims: As a residential college Beaumont offers students a supportive setting in which to increase their independence and gradually take on greater responsibility.

Beaumont gives students the opportunity to develop as whole people and to become adults. It is a friendly and stimulating place where students can face challenges in realistic situations, develop interests and gradually gain the skills and confidence they need to move on to the next stage of their lives.

Premises and facilities

Students live on campus in a range of well-equipped accommodation, which takes into account both their need to develop independence and their need for appropriate support. This enables students to develop their independence skills in a realistic way while receiving the support they need from a multi-disciplinary team. The level of support given to each student is specified by their individual programme. A restaurant at College caters for any dietary requirements.

Student accommodation

For residential students, accommodation is fully accessible with lift access to upper floors. There are also supported independent living areas within College, as well as shared and single bedrooms, many with overhead tracking hoists. All bedrooms are linked to a computer and telephone network system. Bathrooms and toilet facilities are also accessible.

Courses

The C ollege uses creative arts as a vehicle to teach students of ranging ability to develop communication and independence skills. Inspired by the notion that all people are creative when provided with a supportive environment and facilitated through the person-centred approach, all the courses offer a creative space for personal exploration and growth. The enrichment curriculum supports the development of independence and social leisure skills.

Day students access the same curriculum as residential students and are fully integrated into the student population.

Links

Opportunities are provided for work experience, external college courses and community participation during the college placement.

Application procedure

When applications are received, this prompts the College's assessment procedure. This involves gathering information from a range of sources including parents, schools, physiotherapists, GPs and speech and language therapists. This information is discussed by the College multi-disciplinary team of staff. If a decision cannot be made from this information then the College may possibly ask the prospective student to come in for a more formal assessment. If you are interested in a visit then please contact the College for availability and further details.

Birtenshaw Hall School (Children's Charitable Trust)

Address: Darwen Road, Bromley Cross, Bolton BL7 9AB

Codes: A C D E F J N O Q R S

Tel: 01204 304230   **Fax:** 01204 597995   **Email:** enquiries@birtenshawhall.bolton.sch.uk
Website: www.birtenshawhall.bolton.sch.uk

Age range: 3-19

Contact for admissions information: Ms B Saddington

Out-of-term contact: Mrs P Haton

Fees: Please contact the business manager for current fee structure

Usual source of funding for students: Local Authority/Health

Aims: To provide specifically designed professional education, care and support services that address the needs of each young person, and to provide an environment that is caring, compassionate, respectful, dignified and conducive to personal development.

Students catered for: Young people with severe or profound and multiple learning difficulties, together with physical disabilities, severe medical conditions or autistic spectrum disorders.

Premises and facilities

The facilities include a kitchen area, teaching accommodation and full residential facilities. Some bathrooms are fitted with specialised equipment. Interactive hydrotherapy pool on site. Fully-accessible transport allows for integration into the community.

Student accommodation

A nurturing, homely environment designed to meet holistic needs.

Student numbers

The School caters for up to 43 students (aged 3-19). There are currently six students in the 16-19 department.

Courses

Outcomes are based within the framework of 'Every Child Matters' agenda.
The continuing education provision is staffed by one teacher with additional qualifications in special needs, supported by qualified and experienced care staff.

Links

Young people attend a local specialist college and undertake work experience.

Other information

Experienced and qualified therapists provide occupational therapy, physiotherapy, hydrotherapy and speech and language therapy.

Medical cover is provided by the local GP and there are regular visits from a consultant paediatrician and orthopaedic surgeon.

Application procedure

Formal application usually through sponsoring LEA, social services or careers/Connexions services. Informal enquiries are welcome.

Bladon House School

Address: Newton Solney, Burton on Trent, Staffs DE15 0TA

Codes: B C F J K O S T

Tel: 01283 563787   **Fax:** 01283 510980   **Email:** info@bladonhouse.com   **Website:** www.bladonhouse.com

Age range: 5-19

Controlled by: SENAD

Contact for admissions information: Kate Britt

Out-of-term contact: Vicky Morgan

Fees: £104,000 p.a.

Usual source of funding for students: LEA/Social Services

Aims: A multi-disciplinary and pupil-centred approach to meeting the needs and enhancing the life chances and quality of living for pupils with autism and learning difficulties.

Student catered for: Pupils with autism, SLD/MLD or complex communication disorders are admitted from any area.

Premises and facilities

Bladon provides full educational facilities across two sites. The main School site is for the 5-16 population and includes facilities such as gym, ICT suite, food technology area, sensory and soft play facilities, as well as extensive grounds which provide practical learning opportunities. Post-16 pupils attend the Mickleover site where there are additional catering and horticulture areas.

Student accommodation

Individual house units for up to 12 pupils on the main site. Post-16 pupils have a residence closer to the town centre as do 14+ boys who need 52-week provision.

Staffing

Staff group of 210 plus, includes specialist teachers, speech and language and occupational therapists and healthcare team.

Courses

Access to National Curriculum, assessment and external accreditation to entry level, academic and vocational education, work-related learning and independence development.

Links

Attendance at local FE college possible; strong Duke of Edinburgh programme; extensive use of the community and attendance at community groups.

Other information

Physiotherapy service provided by local health authority; forensic psychologist attends weekly; child and adolescent psychiatrist visits monthly.

Application procedure

Contact the headteacher in the first instance.

Botton Village

Address: Danby, Whitby, North Yorkshire YO21 2NJ

Tel: 01287 660871   **Fax:** 01287 660888   **Email:** botton@camphill.org.uk   **Website:** www.camphill.org.uk

Age range: 21+

Controlled by: Camphill Village Trust

Contact for admissions information: Welfare and Admissions Group

Fees: Available on request

Usual source of funding for students: Local authority

Aims: An international community inspired by the philosophy of Rudolf Steiner. The community aims to enable every individual to lead a dignified and meaningful existence by contributing to the community according to their ability. This is achieved through participation in its working, cultural and social life.

Students catered for: Adults with a learning disability (villagers) who are willing and able to participate in all aspects of our community life.

Premises and facilities

650 acres. Farms, gardens and forestry provide work opportunities, as do the craft and food production workshops (weavery, woodwork, dollshop, candleshop, glass-engraving, papercrafts, creamery, food centre and bakery). Shop, post office, bookshop, giftshop, health centre and coffee bar. Community hall for social and cultural events. Church.

Student accommodation

Villagers, co-workers and their families live together in extended households.

Student numbers

Approximately 130 villagers.

Staffing

Voluntary resident co-workers who live in the community. Long-term co-workers take responsibility for a household and/or one of the workshops.

Courses

Much of the training is hands-on in the workshops. Particular skills are developed accordingly.
'Winter School' and 'Summer School' annually take an inspiring theme which is then worked on by the whole community through talks and artistic activities.
Study groups are variously offered, e.g. literature, biographies, gospel study.

Links

Tools for Self Reliance local group.
FE Colleges at Pickering and Guisborough, offering cookery and horticulture courses.

Other information

Local GP holds surgery in the community's health centre once a week. Visiting professionals include physiotherapist; chiropodist; counsellor; psychiatrist; psychologist; osteopath; advocate; speech and language therapist.

Application procedure

Apply to the Welfare and Admissions Group. Waiting period depends upon available places at point of application.

Broughton House & College

Address: Brant Broughton, Lincoln LN5 0SL

Tel: 0800 288 9779   **Fax:** 020 7348 5223   **Email:** enquiries@cambiangroup.com
Website: www.cambianeducation.com

Age range: 16-30+

Controlled by: Cambian Education Services

Contact for admissions information: Mr Bob Noble CertEd, DipEd

Out-of-term contact: 0800 288 9779

Fees: On request

Usual source of funding for students: LEA/ Social Services/Health

Aims: The College approach is based upon non-aversive positive interventions to manage and understand behaviour and teach alternative more appropriate behaviour.

Students catered for: All of the College's students experience difficulties due to their complex needs and challenging behaviour resulting from autism and severe learning disabilities. Many have communication difficulties.

Premises and facilities

The College is sited in its own grounds on the edge of a rural village with its own local amenities. Access to other community resources is provided by minibus with the towns of Lincoln, Grantham and Newark being close by.

Student accommodation

All students have single ensuite bedrooms either situated in small groups in the main house or in new build semi-detached homes on site or a supported living four-bed detached house and flat.

Staffing

Approximate total multi-disciplinary staff team of 150 with separate care and education and clinical input and therapy teams. A strong emphasis on training to at least NVQ level 3 for all care staff.

Courses

Courses linked to pre-adult entry curriculum framework through Essential Skills. Individual Learning Programmes designed to meet particular needs based on practical challenges and experiences to improve confidence and self esteem.

Links

Link courses to the local FE college and community-based jobs and vocational programmes.

Other information

Access to consultant psychiatrist, GP, clinical psychologist, speech and language specialist.

Application procedure

A formal application by letter from representative of LEA (Connexions), Social Services or Health Authority. Informal visits by parents and professionals always welcome.

Bryn Melyn Group

Codes: I M P and also A B C F N O Q R

Address: PO Box 202 Bala LL23 7RA

Tel: 01678 540598   **Fax:** 01678 540682   **Email:** enquiries@brynmelyngroup.com
Website: www.brynmelyngroup.com

Age range: 10-25+

Controlled by: Independent

Contact for admissions information: Janet Rich

Out-of-term-contact: Janet Rich

Fees: Dependent on service £3,800 - £7,500

Usual source of funding for students: Social services/education/mental health/disability

Aims: To provide an outstanding level of care, therapeutic treatment and education to children and young people/young adults with complex needs who have proved difficult to place in more traditional settings. Includes long-term care with a non-exclusion guarantee, medium-term assessment and transition places, emergency placement service and specialised services for learning disability, autism and sexualised behaviour.

Students catered for: Any student who can benefit from the bespoke packages of integrated therapeutic care and education. Whilst the core population is emotional trauma, the Group has also worked with multiple disabilities, autistic spectrum, mental illness, personality disorder and sensory integration dysfunction in children's residential, young adult and bespoke domiciliary care settings.

Premises and facilities

Students under 16 attend one of the Group's own small specialised schools, registered with DfES in England and WAG in Wales. Each school caters for a maximum of ten students with individual curriculum plans according to their needs and receives therapeutic input/treatment programmes again according to needs identified. Older students attend local colleges or projects with staff support where necessary.

Student accommodation

Accommodation is in single occupancy, shared (dual occupancy) or small group homes in the community with intensive levels of staffing and support. Older residents may live in supported tenancies.

Student numbers

Maximum 40.

Staffing

Students are mostly staffed 1:1, to promote the formation of significant relationships as an aid to achieving therapeutic placement goals. Staffing ratio may be higher or lower depending on assessed need and presenting risks.

Courses

Courses available in English, science, mathematics, PSHE, key skills, motor mechanics, art, ITC and modern languages with access to multiple examination schemes including AQA, ASDAN and GCSE. A full programme of outdoor education is also available leading to Duke of Edinburgh Award. Post-16 young people attend local colleges with support as required, or can continue to benefit from our in-house schooling facilities.

Links

Links with local FE colleges are actively promoted. Programmes of work and work experience are also organised.

Other information

All students undertake personal development work with fully trained therapists and/or psychologists. Work is directed towards childhood abuse and trauma and there are also programmes for young people who have committed sexual offences or are at risk of doing so.

Application procedure

Referral is made using the Application for a Placement or Outreach Service form. However, in the first instance, telephone enquiries are invited to enable an initial screening to take place. All enquirers will be connected to a director or senior manager to discuss their placement needs in detail and in confidence.

Burton Hill School

Codes: A C D E F G H M O P Q R S

Address: Malmesbury, Wiltshire SN16 0EG

Tel: 01666 822685 **Fax:** 01666 826022 **Email:** hdicks@shaftesburysoc.org.uk

Age range: 8-19

Controlled by: The Shaftesbury Society

Contact for admissions information: Harry Dicks, Principal

Out-of-term contact: Above telephone number

Usual source of funding for students: LEA

Aims: To enrich, enhance, educate and provide motivating environment for young people with disabilities, leading to independence and self worth.

Student catered for: Children who have physical disabilities and associated learning difficulties.

Premises and facilities

Burton Hill School is a school for young people with special educational needs. Situated in beautiful grounds in Malmesbury, Wiltshire, it is a co-educational day and residential school for students aged 8-19 years.

Student accommodation

The School can provide residential accommodation for up to 31 students, including part-time and full-time boarding.

Student numbers

Currently 36 students.

Staffing

Over 90 staff including teachers, therapists, carers, feeders, night staff and administrators. The School holds the Investors in People Award for commitment to training and development.

Courses

The school curriculum follows the 'Guidelines for Planning, Teaching and Assessing the Curriculum for Pupils with Learning Difficulties' as drawn up by the Qualifications and Curriculum Authority and approved by the DfES in conjunction with the national curriculum. Burton Hill School is overseen by Ofsted.

Links

Burton Hill School enjoys good relationships with the local community. Students are encouraged to attend groups at the local secondary school, colleges, churches, youth groups and an after-school club.

Other information

With professional and committed staff, the School is able to provide students with the best in education, therapy and care, and prides itself in helping each and every student to achieve their full potential.

Application procedure

Please contact Harry Dicks, Principal, to arrange a visit or for more information.

Callow Park College

Codes: C F K L T

Address: Derby Road, Wirksworth, Derbyshire DE4 4BN

Tel: 01629 823364   **Fax:** 01629 825168   **Email:** info@alderwasleyhall.com   **Website:** www.alderwasleyhall.com

Age range: 16-19+

Controlled by: The SENAD Group

Contact for admissions information: Jane Thorneycroft

Fees: £64,262

Usual source of funding for students: LEA

Aims: To provide an integrated approach through education and speech and language therapy. Providing individualised learning working towards independence and inclusion within the community. Allowing all students to reach full potential, whether academic or vocational.

Students catered for: Students whose needs arise from difficulties with communication, including students with Aspergers, from all areas of the country and abroad.

Premises and facilities

Purpose-built post-16 College with rooms for groups and one-to-one support. Set in beautiful countryside but near to small town. On- and off-site residential provision. Swimming pool, squash courts, climbing wall, tennis courts and multi-purpose, fully-equipped fitness gym.

Student accommodation

Single and double en-suite bedrooms on site. Off-site house to promote independent living in town of Matlock.

Student numbers

46.

Staffing

Teaching staff, teaching assistants, speech and language therapists, occupational therapists, key care workers, school nurse, Connexions service.

Courses

All students have an individual programme. Courses offered include: key skills (application of number, communication and ICT and the wider key skills of problem solving, working with others and improving own learning and performance); Edexcel Lifeskills Programme. The College also offers BTEC and A level courses in applied subjects. Students also have the opportunity to attend link courses in a local mainstream college. All students are supported by a speech and language therapist and occupational therapy is available if required.

Links

Local college links; comprehensive work experience programme; membership of local youth and sports clubs encouraged.

Other information

There is one speech and language therapist to every ten students and an occupational therapy team of four. School nurse available and visiting counsellor and Connexions.

Application procedure

Please contact Jane Thorneycroft. Assessment four days. Referral by parents or LEA. Callow Park College has to be named on SEN statement.

Camphill Blair Drummond

Address: Blair Drummond House, Cuthil Brae, by Stirling FK9 4UT

Tel: 01786 841573   **Fax:** 01786 841188   **Website:** www.camphillscotland.org.uk

Contact for admissions information: The management team

Age range: 16+

Controlled by: Council of Management, Camphill Blair Drummond Trust

Fees: £36,504 – £52,520 p.a. for a 52-week year

Aims: To provide further education and craft training. The broad aim is to enable individuals to improve basic scholastic and manual skills, and mature into stable adults who have learned to work to the best of their ability. Social integration and community living are very important.

Students catered for: From age 16. Both sexes. Mixed disabilities, though primarily those with learning difficulties.

Premises and facilities

Camphill Blair Drummond is one of the therapeutic communities of the Camphill Movement, situated six miles from Stirling and two miles from Doune. Students use local facilities as and where appropriate e.g. shops, swimming pool, horseriding etc.

Student accommodation

There are six group homes on a 17-acre plot of land. Four of the house units are within the walls of a large baronial-style Scottish mansion.

Student numbers

32 students and residents.

Staffing

Camphill Blair Drummond employs a large number of social care staff in both the residential and day-care service. Workshop leaders come from craft backgrounds and receive social care training. Houseparents have a range of qualifications including HNCs, SVQs and RMNs. All co-workers live in houses together with the residents.

Courses

Camphill offers its own extensive training programmes and all co-workers receive ongoing weekly training.

Links

Camphill Blair Drummond has many and varied links with other establishments. Locally, mainly with riding and swimming for the disabled. If appropriate, with local colleges, employers, psychiatric and social services, etc. On a more national level, with other Camphill and Steiner organisations, as well as other bodies.

Other information

Medical care, paramedical care, etc is provided by local professionals as needed.

Application procedure

Applications in writing are sent to the admissions group. As full reports as possible required, particularly of early development. Parents, applicant and relevant professionals are invited for interview. Application and placement must be supported by education or social work departments. A trial period of six weeks is offered; this can be extended if necessary. Waiting time is very varied — but application in good time is advisable. All residents go through a six-monthly review procedure.

Camphill Rudolf Steiner School

Address: Central Office, Murtle Estate, Bieldside, Aberdeen AB15 9EP

Codes: B C E I L M N O P Q R S

Tel: 01224 867935   **Fax:** 01224 868420   **Email:** office@crss.org.uk   **Website:** www.crss.org.uk

Age range: 2½–19

Controlled by: Voluntary independent

Contact for admissions information: Jean Ferries

Out-of-term contact: The Administrator

Fees: £45,500 (standard boarder fee)

Usual source of funding for students: LEA

Aims: The school provides a day, weekly or full boarder service for children and young people with special needs. It offers an inclusive holistic education combining education, care and therapy in a safe community setting seven miles from Aberdeen.

Students catered for: Those with autistic spectrum disorder; those who have been neglected or are physically or otherwise in need.

Premises and facilities
Based over three estates close to Aberdeen set in the country. Swimming pool, playgrounds, two school houses, therapy building, co-worker and pupil accommodation, NHS medical centre, craft workshops.

Student accommodation
Family-style accommodation for ten groups of four to eleven pupils. Bedrooms are single or sharing.

Staffing
All staff are engaged in on-going training and are well qualified. There is a high staff:pupil ratio.

Courses
Students follow the latter part of the Waldorf curriculum which includes work placement, craft activities and life skills. Individual therapies are provided as required.

Links
Good local links to businesses and Aberdeen College.

Other information
Links to Grampian Health Board are good and provide the links above where necessary.

Application procedure
In writing to Jean Ferries.

Care Devon

Address: East Anstey, Tiverton, Devon EX16 9JT

Code: O

Tel: 01398 341252/341292   **Fax:** 01398 341591   **Email:** blackerton@care-ltd.co.uk   **Website:** www.care-ltd.co.uk

Age range: 18+

Controlled by: Cottage and Rural Enterprises Ltd

Contact for admissions information: Saki Hartas/Lisa Dunn

Out-of-term contact: Residential — always open

Fees: £480+

Usual source of funding for students: Local authority

Aims: Care gives support through provision of a range of residential accommodation and work options to people with a learning disability. Work opportunities range from sheltered skill development in areas such as horticulture, catering, IT and mixed crafts, to supported employment opportunities and social enterprise development.

Students catered for: Care operates nationally to support people aged 18+ with a range of learning difficulties.

Premises and facilities

A day service on site with workshops, produce garden, dining rooms, catering kitchens and office accommodation.

Student accommodation

A range of residential provision from bungalows for eight people to group homes providing more independent living and individual tenancies in flats.

Student numbers

50 residential placements plus holiday service placements.

Staffing

Staff are fully trained in all aspects of care and support and are encouraged to develop their full potential. Staff operate in two areas — residential services and day services.

Courses

Care offers NVQ courses for people with learning difficulties.

Links

Partnership arrangements with a wide variety of public and private organisations ranging from local authorities and PCTs to local employers and educational establishments.

Other information

Occupational therapists, music therapists, art therapists, physiotherapists, consultant psychiatrist, community nurses, chiropodists.

Application procedure

Informal visits/open referrals.

Care Ironbridge

Address: 2 Forbes Close, Ironbridge, Telford TF7 5LE

Tel: 01952 432065　**Fax:** 01952 432209　**Email:** careironbridge@freeuk.com　**Website:** www.care-ltd.co.uk

Age range: 18+

Controlled by: Cottage and Rural Enterprises Ltd

Contact for admissions information: Michael Cripps/Jayne Eeles

Out-of-term contact: Residential — always open

Fees: £480+

Usual source of funding for students: Local authority

Aims: Care gives support through provision of a range of residential accommodation and work options to people with a learning disability. Work opportunities range from sheltered skill development in areas such as horticulture, catering, IT and mixed crafts, to supported employment opportunities and social enterprise development.

Students catered for: Care operates nationally to support people aged 18+ with a range of learning difficulties.

Premises and facilities

A day service on site with workshops, produce garden, dining rooms, catering kitchens and office accommodation.

Student accommodation

A range of residential provision from bungalows for eight people to group homes providing more independent living and individual tenancies in flats.

Student numbers

50 residential placements plus holiday service placements.

Staffing

Staff are fully trained in all aspects of care and support and are encouraged to develop their full potential. Staff operate in two areas — residential services and day services.

Courses

Care offers NVQ courses for people with learning difficulties.

Links

Partnership arrangements with a wide variety of public and private organisations ranging from local authorities and PCTs to local employers and educational establishments.

Other information

Occupational therapists, music therapists, art therapists, physiotherapists, consultant psychiatrist, community nurses, chiropodists.

Application procedure

Informal visits/open referrals.

Care Kent

Address: 1 Phillippines Close, Off Hever Road, Edenbridge, Kent, TN8 5GN

Code: O

Tel: 01732 782700   **Fax:** 01732 782701   **Email:** carekent@care-ltd.co.uk   **Website:** www.care-ltd.co.uk

Age range: 18+

Controlled by: Cottage and Rural Enterprises Ltd

Contact for admissions information: David Oguntoye

Out-of-term contact: Residential — always open

Fees: £480+

Usual source of funding for students: Local authority

Aims: Care gives support through provision of a range of residential accommodation and work options to people with a learning disability. Work opportunities range from sheltered skill development in areas such as horticulture, catering, IT and mixed crafts, to supported employment opportunities and social enterprise development.

Students catered for: Care operates nationally to support people aged 18+ with a range of learning difficulties.

Premises and facilities

A day service on site with workshops, produce garden, dining rooms, catering kitchens and office accommodation.

Student accommodation

A range of residential provision from bungalows for eight people to group homes providing more independent living and individual tenancies in flats.

Student numbers

50 residential placements plus holiday service placements.

Staffing

Staff are fully trained in all aspects of care and support and are encouraged to develop their full potential. Staff operate in two areas — residential services and day services.

Courses

Care offers NVQ courses for people with learning difficulties.

Links

Partnership arrangements with a wide variety of public and private organisations ranging from local authorities and PCTs to local employers and educational establishments.

Other information

Occupational therapists, music therapists, art therapists, physiotherapists, consultant psychiatrist, community nurses, chiropodists.

Application procedure

Informal visits/open referrals.

Care Ponteland

Address: North Road, Ponteland, Newcastle upon Tyne NE20 OBW

Tel: 01661 860333   **Fax:** 01661 821830   **Email:** careponteland@btconnect.com   **Website:** www.care-ltd.co.uk

Age range: 18+

Controlled by: Cottage and Rural Enterprises Ltd

Contact for admissions information: Andrea Fox/Tracy Notley

Out-of-term contact: Residential — always open

Fees: £480+

Usual source of funding for students: Local authority

Aims: Care gives support through provision of a range of residential accommodation and work options to people with a learning disability. Work opportunities range from sheltered skill development in areas such as horticulture, catering, IT and mixed crafts, to supported employment opportunities and social enterprise development.

Students catered for: Care operates nationally to support people aged 18+ with a range of learning difficulties.

Premises and facilities

A day service on site with workshops, produce garden, dining rooms, catering kitchens and office accommodation.

Student accommodation

A range of residential provision from bungalows for eight people to group homes providing more independent living and individual tenancies in flats.

Student numbers

50 residential placements plus holiday service placements.

Staffing

Staff are fully trained in all aspects of care and support and are encouraged to develop their full potential. Staff operate in two areas — residential services and day services.

Courses

Care offers NVQ courses for people with learning difficulties.

Links

Partnership arrangements with a wide variety of public and private organisations ranging from local authorities and PCTs to local employers and educational establishments.

Other information

Occupational therapists, music therapists, art therapists, physiotherapists, consultant psychiatrist, community nurses, chiropodists.

Application procedure

Informal visits/open referrals.

Care Shangton

Address: Melton Road, Shangton, Leicester LE8 OPS

Tel: 01858 545401/545402   **Fax:** 01858 546720   **Email:** shangton@care-ltd.co.uk   **Website:** www.care-ltd.co.uk

Age range: 18+

Controlled by: Cottage and Rural Enterprises Ltd

Contact for admissions information: Len Walker/Viv Smith

Out-of-term contact: Residential — always open

Fees: £480+

Usual source of funding for students: Local authority

Aims: Care gives support through provision of a range of residential accommodation and work options to people with a learning disability. Work opportunities range from sheltered skill development in areas such as horticulture, catering, IT and mixed crafts, to supported employment opportunities and social enterprise development.

Students catered for: Care operates nationally to support people aged 18+ with a range of learning difficulties.

Premises and facilities

A day service on site with workshops, produce garden, dining rooms, catering kitchens and office accommodation.

Student accommodation

A range of residential provision from bungalows for eight people to group homes providing more independent living and individual tenancies in flats.

Student numbers

50 residential placements plus holiday service placements.

Staffing

Staff are fully trained in all aspects of care and support and are encouraged to develop their full potential. Staff operate in two areas — residential services and day services.

Courses

Care offers NVQ courses for people with learning difficulties.

Links

Partnership arrangements with a wide variety of public and private organisations ranging from local authorities and PCTs to local employers and educational establishments.

Other information

Occupational therapists, music therapists, art therapists, physiotherapists, consultant psychiatrist, community nurses, chiropodists.

Application procedure

Informal visits/open referrals.

Care Stanley Grange

Address: Roach Road, Samlesbury, Preston, Lancashire PR5 ORB

Tel: 01254 852878/853651   **Fax:** 01254 851154   **Email:** caresgrange@btconnect.com   **Website:** www.care-ltd.co.uk

Age range: 18+

Controlled by: Cottage and Rural Enterprises Ltd

Contact for admissions information: Diane Kirwan/Kelly Livesey

Out-of-term contact: Residential — always open

Fees: £480+

Usual source of funding for students: Local authority

Aims: Care gives support through provision of a range of residential accommodation and work options to people with a learning disability. Work opportunities range from sheltered skill development in areas such as horticulture, catering, IT and mixed crafts, to supported employment opportunities and social enterprise development.

Students catered for: Care operates nationally to support people aged 18+ with a range of learning difficulties.

Premises and facilities

A day service on site with workshops, produce garden, dining rooms, catering kitchens and office accommodation.

Student accommodation

A range of residential provision from bungalows for eight people to group homes providing more independent living and individual tenancies in flats.

Student numbers

50 residential placements plus holiday service placements.

Staffing

Staff are fully trained in all aspects of care and support and are encouraged to develop their full potential. Staff operate in two areas — residential services and day services.

Courses

Care offers NVQ courses for people with learning difficulties.

Links

Partnership arrangements with a wide variety of public and private organisations ranging from local authorities and PCTs to local employers and educational establishments.

Other information

Occupational therapists, music therapists, art therapists, physiotherapists, consultant psychiatrist, community nurses, chiropodists.

Application procedure

Informal visits/open referrals.

Care West Sussex

Address: Eastergate Lane, Walberton, Arundel, West Sussex BN18 0AE

Code: O

Tel: 01243 542714   **Fax:** 01243 544796   **Email:** carewestsussex@care-ltd.co.uk   **Website:** www.care-ltd.co.uk

Age range: 18+

Controlled by: Cottage and Rural Enterprises Ltd

Contact for admissions information: Caroline Fletcher/Sarah Shallis

Out-of-term contact: Residential — always open

Fees: £480+

Usual source of funding for students: Local authority

Aims: Care gives support through provision of a range of residential accommodation and work options to people with a learning disability. Work opportunities range from sheltered skill development in areas such as horticulture, catering, IT and mixed crafts, to supported employment opportunities and social enterprise development.

Students catered for: Care operates nationally to support people aged 18+ with a range of learning difficulties.

Premises and facilities

A day service on site with workshops, produce garden, dining rooms, catering kitchens and office accommodation.

Student accommodation

A range of residential provision from bungalows for eight people to group homes providing more independent living and individual tenancies in flats.

Student numbers

50 residential placements plus holiday service placements.

Staffing

Staff are fully trained in all aspects of care and support and are encouraged to develop their full potential. Staff operate in two areas — residential services and day services.

Courses

Care offers NVQ courses for people with learning difficulties.

Links

Partnership arrangements with a wide variety of public and private organisations ranging from local authorities and PCTs to local employers and educational establishments.

Other information

Occupational therapists, music therapists, art therapists, physiotherapists, consultant psychiatrist, community nurses, chiropodists.

Application procedure

Informal visits/open referrals.

Care Wiltshire

Address: Furlong Close, Rowde, Devizes, Wiltshire SN10 2TQ

Code: O

Tel: 01380 725455/721263   **Fax:** 01380 729030   **Email:** carewiltshire@care-ltd.co.uk   **Website:** www.care-ltd.co.uk

Age range: 18+

Controlled by: Cottage and Rural Enterprises Ltd

Contact for admissions information: Kay Rudge/Christine Smith

Out-of-term contact: Residential — always open

Fees: £480+

Usual source of funding for students: Local authority

Aims: Care gives support through provision of a range of residential accommodation and work options to people with a learning disability. Work opportunities range from sheltered skill development in areas such as horticulture, catering, IT and mixed crafts, to supported employment opportunities and social enterprise development.

Students catered for: Care operates nationally to support people aged 18+ with a range of learning difficulties.

Premises and facilities

A day service on site with workshops, produce garden, dining rooms, catering kitchens and office accommodation.

Student accommodation

A range of residential provision from bungalows for eight people to group homes providing more independent living and individual tenancies in flats.

Student numbers

50 residential placements plus holiday service placements.

Staffing

Staff are fully trained in all aspects of care and support and are encouraged to develop their full potential. Staff operate in two areas — residential services and day services.

Courses

Care offers NVQ courses for people with learning difficulties.

Links

Partnership arrangements with a wide variety of public and private organisations ranging from local authorities and PCTs to local employers and educational establishments.

Other information

Occupational therapists, music therapists, art therapists, physiotherapists, consultant psychiatrist, community nurses, chiropodists.

Application procedure

Informal visits/open referrals.

Chailey Heritage School

Codes: D E F N O R

Address: Haywards Heath Road, North Chailey, Nr Lewes, East Sussex BN8 4EF

Tel: 01825 724444   **Fax:** 01825 723773   **Email:** schooloffice@ chs.org.uk   **Website:** www.chs.org.uk

Age range: 2-19

Contact for admissions information: Mrs P Whiting

Fees: On application

Aims: To provide a stimulating and enjoyable learning experience; to meet the wide range of special needs presented by the pupils; to encourage pupils' personal autonomy to the fullest extent; to be innovative in the development of pupils' communication and mobility; to provide the National Curriculum suitably modified for each pupil to take into account their individual needs.

Students catered for: Chailey Heritage School is a nationally-recognised, non-maintained special school catering for students who have a wide range of physical and learning difficulties.

Premises and facilities

The School has four departments: pre-school assessment unit, primary, secondary and 16+. It operates normal school terms, i.e. autumn, spring and summer.

Student accommodation

Five self-contained, custom-built bungalows which are open for 48 weeks of the year and accommodate pupils for a maximum of 295 nights per year as per the School's registration with the CSCI as a special school.

Student numbers

Approximately 100.

Staffing

Each bungalow is managed by a Team Leader under the direction of the Head of Care. 24-hour cover is provided by the School's care teams as well as nursing staff from South Downs Health Trust.

Courses

Students are offered a learning programme within which personal and social skills can be developed, allowing for individual rates and styles of learning. There are a number of nationally accredited programmes which are offered including ASDAN, Towards Independence, Youth Award Scheme, Lifeskills and the English Speaking Board. Each student has their own programme with elements from some or all of the above programmes as appropriate.

Links

Students are encouraged to prepare for adult life after Chailey Heritage School through experiencing extended education at a college of further education as well as making visits to a variety of future placement options and places of interest in the local community.

Other information

South Downs Health (NHS) Trust provides medical, therapy and Rehabilitation Engineering services.

Application procedure

Contact School, who will be pleased to advise.

Cherry Orchards Camphill Community

Address: Canford Lane, Westbury-on-Trym, Bristol BS9 3PE

Tel: 0117 950 3183   **Fax:** 0117 959 3665   **Email:** cherryorchards@camphill.org.uk   **Website:** www.camphill.org.uk

---

Age range: 18-64

Contact for admissions information: Valerie Sands

Controlled by: Independent; member of Association of Camphill Communities

Fees: On application

Usual source of funding for students: Mainly through social services, some through the health service.

Aims: Cherry Orchards aims to be an integrated therapeutic community.

Students catered for: Adults who want to recover from mental health difficulties. Residents come from all over Britain, and may be aged between 18-64 years old. Mixed sex.

Premises and facilities

Cherry Orchards is on 17 acres of green belt with fields, a little valley with a stream, a vegetable garden and woodland. Residents and co-workers (staff) live integrated with one another and share the burdens and pleasures of domestic life.

Student accommodation

There are two houses which offer a safe, residential therapeutic environment.

Student numbers

12.

Staffing

All staff work as full-time voluntary workers and eight are residential.

Courses

Everyone is included in working activities, within which basic skills are taught as part of the work process. Always the emphasis is on the meaningfulness of any action. Residents spend part of the day in the garden and workshops, and part in artistic activities (including painting, modelling, drawing, craftwork and speech and drama). The Community offers many therapeutic activities including art, candle-making, gardening etc. Residents work alongside the staff and are led to see their work as fulfilling a need in the community. Residents who become able are encouraged to find employment and to grow towards independence.

Links

Individual links can be established according to need. Bristol offers unlimited possibilities for further development. Cherry Orchards could be the base for this.

Application procedure

On request a questionnaire will be sent out. Then an interview can follow. Placement is offered when a vacancy occurs — could be immediately or after waiting for several months.

Cintre Community

Address: 54 St Johns Road, Clifton, Bristol BS8 2HG

Codes: M O

Tel: 0117 923 9979   **Fax:** 0117 946 7842   **Email:** info@cintre.co.uk   **Website:** www.cintre.co.uk

Age range: 16-35

Controlled by: Charity regulated by the NCSC

Contact for admissions information: Martyn Button

Fees: £1,500 plus per week for residential placements

Usual source of funding for students: Government funding for supported accommodation

Aims: Cintre's primary focus is to provide a structured and nurturing environment within a holistic framework and to assist the service users in taking individual steps towards managing their own lives. Cintre believes in each person's potential to achieve his or her own goals in life.

Students catered for: Cintre Community provides residential and supported housing, daycare and outreach services for young people and adults with learning disabilities and challenging behaviour.

Premises and facilities

Cintre provides day care facilities internally and externally. Workshops include arts and crafts, pottery, gardening and woodwork. Cintre also provides outreach support for individuals who have moved into independent housing but require support and guidance. Working within the regulations as set by the National Care Standards, Cintre Community provides full assessment on referral and a choice of homes to meet individual needs.

Student accommodation

Students live in three homes in the Bristol and North Somerset area. Cintre also manages a supported housing unit for six young people wanting to live more independently.

Student numbers

Cintre Community offers residential placements for up to seven people.

Staffing

1:1 support available, minimum two staff on duty.

Courses

Cintre provides flexible individual support packages and care plans; guidance and support of a keyworker; therapeutic intervention; comprehensive staff training.

Application procedure

Full assessment on referral.

Coleg Elidyr

Address: Coleg Elidyr, Rhandirmwyn, Llandovery, Carmarthenshire SA20 0NL

Tel: 01550 760401   **Fax:** 01550 760331   **Email:** colegrhan@aol.com   **Website:** www.colegelidyr.com

Age Range: 18-25

Contact for admissions information: The Administrator

Out of term contact: The Administrator

Fees: In line with the LSC fees matrix

Usual source of funding for students: LSC, Welsh Assembly, social services

Aims: To educate and train young people with learning difficulties, give them stimulation and help them complete their search for identity, develop their potential, acquire vocational skills, gain competence in social skills, and thereby find enough confidence to meet society as people in their own right.

Students catered for: Students from all over the British Isles with moderate to severe learning difficulties, possibly with additional disabilities, e.g. autism, Down's syndrome, cerebral palsy or some communication difficulties.

Premises and facilities

Coleg Elidyr is a Camphill Community set in 170 acres of the Towy Valley. Many of the activities are land based — farming, gardening, forestry and estate work. There are also classrooms and craft workshops (pottery, basketry, woodcarving, carpentry, weavery, green woodwork and candlework).

Student accommodation

Students live together with staff and their families in eight houses run as family units. Each student has a single room.

Staffing

Staff may be short- or long-term volunteers and employees committed to the ethos of a Camphill Community.

Courses

Three-year foundation course (non-accredited) which covers independent living skills, basic skills and a range of work experiences and curricular activities identified according to the needs of the individual.
OCN courses in horticulture, farming, carpentry, forestry, retail and weavery are available for suitable students. Students who progress beyond the third year become apprentices. This allows the student to have a more selective timetable which concentrates on areas of strength and interest.

Links

Where appropriate, students may be able to access some courses at Coleg Sir Gâr (general FE college).

Application procedure

Information pack containing application form available on request. Appropriate applicants will undergo a short residential trial period for community assessment.

Community Solutions

Address: 49 King Street, Thorne, Doncaster DN8 5AU

Tel: 01405 818580   **Fax:** 01405 743110   **Email:** oaasis@hesleygroup.co.uk   **Website:** www.oaasis.co.uk

Age range: 18-65

Contact for admissions information: Mrs S Ekins

Controlled by: The Hesley Group

Fees: On request from the Principal

Aims: Community Solutions aims to provide care and support in a non-institutional setting within the community in a safe, caring and homely environment for all its residents. The principal aim is to develop each resident's independence through 24-hour staff-supported independent living.

Students catered for: People aged 18-65 who have complex and severe learning difficulties; nationwide.

Premises and facilities

49 King Street is situated in the market town of Thorne, approximately 11 miles from Doncaster. It is a five minute walk to local shops and supermarket, post office, health facilities and public transport.

The special nature of Community Solutions' residents entitles them to enhanced effort on the part of the staff to ensure that they have a greater wealth and experience within the home and community than others of a similar age and to enjoy their adulthood. There are planned and organised social activities in the activities room.

An essential part of the daily life of the residents includes evening trips to the local pub to play pool, meals out, walks to the town centre, travelling by public transport and many more educational and leisure activities.

Staffing

The Hesley Group achieved the Investor In People (IIP) Award in 1996 which recognises the significant emphasis the Group places on the quality of its staffing and the associated management processes.

Courses

Facilities enable residents to participate in arts and crafts and IT – i.e. browsing the internet and video links with their families. There are music and movement classes and pottery sessions.

Activities outside the home include keep-fit classes, outings to the seaside and cinema, swimming, shopping, short breaks and other such entertainment.

Condover College

Address: Condover House, Condover, Shropshire SY5 7AA

Tel: 01743 872250 **Fax:** 01743 874815 **Email:** condover@btconnect.com

---

Age range: 18-24 education; 24-65 community

Controlled by: Independent specialist college (LSC and CSCI)

Contact for admissions information: Pauline Carmichael/Vikki Pryce

Out-of-term-contact: Steve McGill/Vikki Pryce

Fees: Individual needs assessed

Usual source of funding for students: LSC, Welsh Assembly, Social Services

Aims: To provide a quality transition between school and adult life. To enable students to participate and contribute fully in all aspects of community life.

Students catered for: Priority will be given to students with a visual impairment who may also have severe learning difficulties and multiple and complex needs and may be wheelchair dependent.

Premises and facilities

Residential accommodation is located in the heart of rural Condover village. Students live as part of the community. Education facilities are currently located at Whitchurch, sharing a small friendly campus with a general FE college. The College is looking to acquire independent premises closer to Condover.

Student accommodation

One period house and three dormer bungalows. Accommodation is adapted providing single bedrooms, some en-suite and some suitable for dependent wheelchair users.

Student numbers

Registered for 19 currently but seeking registration for 28.

Staffing

Dedicated and specialist qualified education staff. Experienced care staff who support students in all educational environments both on and off campus.

Courses

'Design for Living' aims to equip students with appropriate skills to enable them to make decisions about their lives. To develop skills to become contributing members of the community in a supported living environment and to direct their carers. A range of teaching styles, resources and environments are used to provide a challenging curriculum which enables students to fulfill their potential.

Achievements are recognized through accreditation by OCR and in-house college certification.

Links

Telford College of Arts and Technology, Walford and North Shropshire College of Horticulture and Agriculture, RDA (Riding for Disabled), church groups, youth and leisure clubs, local employers.

Other information

Physiotherapy services, mobility and orientation specialist, functional vision specialist, educational psychology, massage and reflexology, speech and language therapy.

Application procedure

Telephone/letter enquiry. Pre-entry application form to be completed by the student. Visit by education/care staff to current provider (education and care). Overnight visit to Condover College.

The Croft Community

Address: Gawain House, 56 Welham Road, Norton, Malton, North Yorkshire YO17 9DP

Code: O

Tel: 0845 4582178 **Fax:** 01653 600102 **Email:** paton23@gmail.com **Website:** www.camphill.org.uk

Age range: 19-60+

Contact for admissions information: Andy Paton

Controlled by: Camphill Village Trust

Fees: On application

Usual source of funding for students: Local authority

Aims: To assist adults with learning difficulties towards independence and integration within the community by providing a home, work, further education and general care.

Students catered for: Each case considered individually — no automatic exclusions. Wide ability range.

Premises and facilities

A working community located in small friendly market town. Music classes are run by local friends. Variety of indoor and outdoor activities.

Student accommodation

Six houses within the local community.

Student numbers

16 males, 15 females at present.

Staffing

16 co-workers.

Courses

This is a working community with activities offered in the garden, bookshop/café, weaving, papermaking, woodwork, candle making, cooking and housework. Some adult education is carried out in the evenings, and there is a rich and varied cultural life including drama, eurhythmy, dance, study groups, and celebration of Christian festivals. Evening classes are attended locally. Some people attend local college one day a week.

Links

Good links with local community. Residents attend churches and evening classes. Possibility of open employment outside the Community.

Applications procedure

Apply to Andy Paton at the address above. After interview, a two-week trial working holiday is offered, followed by a pause for reflection. Waiting period approximately one year.

Croft House

Address: Bolton, Appleby, Cumbria CA16 6AW

Codes: B C K M O

Tel: 017683 62580/62589   **Fax:** 017683 62580   **Email:** crofthouse@prioryhealthcare.com
Website: www.prioryhealthcare.com/edengrove

Age range: 16-19

Controlled by: Principal, Eden Grove School

Contact for admissions information: Miss S Mullen

Out-of-term contact: Open 52 weeks

Fees: More information from Miss S Mullen

Usual source of funding for students: Local Authorities/Education/Health

Aims: Croft House's purpose is to promote independence to each young person offering opportunity and choice to give fulfillment towards their future citizenship. It offers an holistic approach to encompass the reality of being part of the community and gaining the necessary skills to be successful.

Students catered for: Young men with special needs including: autism/Asperger; emotional, educational and behavioural disorders; ADD and ADHD and more.

Premises and facilities

Croft House is the 16+ off-site facility of Eden Grove School. It is situated in the centre of Bolton Village which nestles in between the beautiful Eden Valley and the Lake District fells. Croft House is an old farmhouse and three converted farm buildings.

Student accommodation

Single bedrooms in all houses. Houses are divided to accommodate independent, semi-independent and supported students.

Student numbers

12 males.

Staffing

High ratio of staff to students, including special needs educational coordinator, educational tutor, house manager and a team of dedicated, motivated professionals.

Courses

Individual education plans are written for each student including the core curriculum, ASDAN/Certificate for Working Life for schools, key skills in numeracy and literacy, GCSE maths and literacy.

Links

Local FE colleges (full and part-time courses) and work experience with local employers, giving each individual the chance to fulfill their potential.

Other information

On-site nurse; speech and language therapist; counsellor; play therapist and links to all Priory resources.

Application procedure

Initial home visit; visit to Croft House; funding discussed with authorities; assessment period set; placement agreed.

Daldorch House School & Continuing Education Centre

Address: Sorn Road, Catrine, East Ayrshire, Scotland KA5 6NA

Code: C

Tel: 01290 551666   **Fax:** 01290 553399

Age range: 5-21

Controlled by: National Autistic Society

Fees: Individually calculated

Usual source of funding for students: Social work and education

Aims: To provide the highest quality fusion of education, care and supported living to enable young people with an autism spectrum disorder to learn and develop to their full potential in all aspects of learning and life experience.

Students catered for: A UK-wide resource for young people with an autism spectrum disorder, the School caters for a wide range of individual needs and abilities.

Premises and facilities

Two campuses provide excellent opportunities for pupils aged 5-16 and students aged 16-21. Formal classroom/tutor rooms, PE hall, music, cooking facilities as well as outdoor areas provide a broad range of venues to develop learning.

Student accommodation

On the junior campus young people live in houses for four. On the senior campus terraced houses provide flexible accommodation either in bedsits or shared supported living accommodation.

Student numbers

32 residential and four day (junior campus); 27 residential and eight day (senior campus).

Staffing

Staffing is assessed in relation to the individual needs of the pupils. Normally one-to-one support is provided, with greater (or lesser) support as required.

Courses

A broad and balanced curriculum following the Scottish Curricular Guidelines is provided. Young people can specialise and develop their particular interests further in the post-14 age group. National qualifications from Access to Intermediate level are offered, along with ASDAN and the Caledonian Award.

Links

Catrine Primary, Auchinleck Academy and Kilmarnock College of Further Education provide links for young people as appropriate. Work experience is encouraged for all young people as they progress through school.

Other information

The school has medical support provided by Ayrshire and Arran Health Board, e.g. paediatrician, school nurse, community dentistry, podiatry, dietetics and occupational therapy. The school employs a speech and language therapist.

Application procedure

Formal referrals must be made by the funding agency. Parents and professionals may visit the School and Continuing Education Centre prior to referral.

The David Lewis School

Address: Mill Lane, Warford, Nr Alderley Edge, Cheshire SK9 7UD

Tel: 01565 640066   **Fax:** 01565 640166   **Email:** enquiries@davidlewis.org.uk   **Website:** www.davidlewis.org.uk

---

Age range: 7-19

Controlled by: The David Lewis National Epilepsy Centre

Contact for admissions information: Deborah Good, Head of Education

Out-of-term contact: Alison Sutherland, Education Services Support Manager

Fees: On application

Usual source of funding for students: Tri-partite (Education, Health and Social Services)

Aims: To maintain and further develop expertise in educating and caring for young people with complex neurological needs.

Students catered for: No geographic restrictions. The David Lewis School is a small, very specialist school catering for pupils, aged 7-19, whose neurological impairment is their primary difficulty.

Premises and facilities

There are six classrooms for key stage 2, 3 and 4. Most classrooms have their own or shared kitchen facilities. 16+ has five classrooms including an independent living room/careers room. Specialist rooms for PE, School hall, sensory teaching, speech and language therapy and soft play.

Student accommodation

The School has eight residential houses which are the homes for the resident pupils.

Student numbers

32 boys and 27 girls.

Staffing

14.6 wte teachers; 2.2 wte unqualified teachers; 21.4 wte qualified teaching assistants; three therapy assistants.

Courses

All pupils have particular individual needs. They all have an entitlement to access the National Curriculum and religious education and through this the school aims to teach a broad and balanced curriculum. Pupils at key stage 4 complete the ASDAN Transition Challenge. 16+ students follow the Essential Skills Curriculum.

Links

The school has links with local FE colleges and industry links through Team Enterprise.

Other information

The school has a full-time speech and language therapist and part-time OT and physiotherapist. It has a visiting dentist and dental nurse, chiropodist and dietitian.

Application procedure

Formal referral required from young person's leading funding authority, usually the local education authority. Informal visits arranged.

Deafway

Address: Brockholes Brow, Preston, Lancashire PR2 5AL

Code: H

Tel: 01772 796461   (**minicom:** 01772 652388)   **Fax:** 01772 654439   **Email:** info@deafway.org.uk
Website: www.deafway.org.uk

Age range: 18+

Controlled by: Chief executive, David Hynes

Aims: Working to provide equality of access and opportunity for deaf people in all areas of life.

Students catered for: Deaf people locally, nationally and internationally who require care, rehabilitation or independent living skills training.

Premises and facilities

Services and projects include: residential care and rehabilitation for deaf people with a range of needs, community services, deaf awareness and British Sign Language training, information and advice on a variety of issues related to deafness, the provision of premises for sports and social clubs for deaf people in Preston and Lancaster, research projects, deaf and sign language arts development projects. On the site in Preston, there are meeting rooms, a restaurant and catering facilities and a social club that can be hired for meetings and functions.

Courses

The areas of activity presently being undertaken are: educational and technological opportunities; employment training opportunities; individual rehabilitation programmes; individual packages of care and community support work.

Links

Deafway will work in partnership with other organisations to create new services tailored to specific needs in all parts of the UK and partnerships, and has links with projects with deaf organisations in Nepal.

Applications procedure

Referrals can be made by local authorities, probation or health authorities in respect of individuals. Following initial assessment, appropriate time-limited care plans or rehabilitation programmes are negotiated.

Delrow College

Address: Hilfield Lane, Aldenham, Watford WD25 8DJ

Codes: O P

Tel: 01923 856006 **Fax:** 01923 858035 **Email:** email@delrow.newnet **Website:** www.camphill.org.uk

Age range: 21+

Contact for admissions information: Jane Brumwell

Controlled by: Camphill Village Trust

Aims: Delrow provides assessment, further education and practical help for those with mental health problems, learning disabilities and other special needs with the intention of rehabilitating them towards life in one of the Camphill Villages or open employment, based on individual capabilities.

Students catered for: Those with mental health problems, learning difficulties and other special needs; mixed sex.

Premises and facilities

Delrow is built around a Jacobean mansion set in 11 acres on the outskirts of Watford. There are workshops for needlecraft, basketry, baking, weaving, and pottery. Everyone shares in the daily life of their household, eating and socialising together. Delrow has a vegetable garden and smallholding in addition to the parkland it occupies that provide a variety of work. In addition to the residential opportunities offered by the college there are a number of day places.

Student accommodation

The development includes ten extended-family households, and three two-bedroomed apartments for supported living.

Staffing

Delrow (as part of the Camphill Community) is run on a sharing basis as a community with no wages being paid.

Courses

The College follows a Camphill Community lifestyle, dividing the week into two college days, three workshop days and weekends. Subjects available for study include art, drama, modelling, music, creative writing and needlecrafts. Residents are encouraged to develop their own interests. There are also lecture and discussion groups and remedial education and craft training.

Links

Some students also attend nearby colleges to gain formal qualifications.

Other information

Therapies include speech, painting, massage and counselling. (All therapies are prescribed and assessed by Delrow's medical consultant on a two-week basis.)

Application procedure

Apply to the College.

Derwen College

Address: Oswestry, Shropshire SY11 3JA

Tel: 01691 661234   **Fax:** 01691 670714   **Email:** david.kendall@derwencollege.co.uk   **Website:** www.derwen.org.uk

Age range: 16+

Controlled by: Independent charity with a Board of Governors

Contact for admissions information: David Kendall, Director

Out-of-term contact: David Kendall, Director

Fees: LSC banded

Usual source of funding for students: LSC

Aims: To promote the vocational, educational and personal development of young people with a wide range of learning difficulties and disabilities. To provide further education in its broadest sense leading to a maximum degree of independence.

Students catered for: The college offers expertise in supporting students with a wide range of learning difficulties and disabilities.

Premises and facilities

The single storey accommodation is of the highest quality and designed to provide for the diverse needs of the students. Indoor heated swimming pool, fitness suite and large multi-purpose sports hall with adjacent tennis and basketball courts. A modern medical centre with qualified nursing staff and a physiotherapy department.

Student accommodation

Accommodation is modern, spacious and well appointed, providing a comfortable, sociable and pleasant environment. There are also supported living opportunities within the community.

Student numbers

240.

Staffing

Teaching staff hold/are working towards teaching certificates. College offers a dynamic professional development programme; specialist teaching and support qualifications for students with learning difficulties.

Courses

Independent living skills; basic skills; personal development; catering; creative arts; horticulture; hospitality and housekeeping; office skills; practical skills; retail.

Links

Close links with local sector college. Work experience within real work situations through work-based training, internal and external work placements.

Other information

Medical officer, Connexions, social workers, chiropodist.

Application procedure

Prospective students are assessed on their curriculum and support needs. Funding applications are undertaken by Connexions or Careers Wales.

Dilston College of Further Education

Address: Dilston Hall, Corbridge, Northumberland NE45 5RJ

Code: O

Tel: 01434 632692   **Fax:** 01434 633721   **Email:** yvonne.ball@dilstoncollege.com   **Website:** www.mencap.org.uk

Age range: 16-25

Controlled by: MENCAP

Contact for admissions information: Mrs Lee McDonough

Out-of-term contact: MENCAP National Office, 4 Swan Courtyard, Coventry Road, Birmingham B26 1BU. Tel: 0121 707 7877.

Fees: From £24,000-£66,000

Usual source of funding for students: Learning and Skills Council

Aims: The aim of the college is to support young people with a learning disability in the progression and transition to adult life. It provides them with a range of opportunities, experiences and skills which will be of value to them in the future and will provide access to full community participation as adults.

Students catered for: Male and female, with moderate to severe range of learning disabilities.

Premises and facilities

Established in 1971, Dilston College is close to both Corbridge and the pleasant market town of Hexham and, with Newcastle within easy reach, there are good rail and road links to all parts of the country.

Student accommodation

Accommodation is either in single or twin-bedded rooms, in flats, cottages and houses. There are four self-contained units in the main college building, four cottages within the college grounds and six community houses in Hexham.

Student numbers

62 residential and a number of day students (currently 15).

Staffing

110 staff – educational, administrative, care and ancillary.

Courses

Access and achievement: Inclusive learning covering daily living skills, personal development, practical & vocational skills and community & leisure, personal care. This provides access to NVQ level 1 in several vocational areas, and a number of other nationally-accredited qualifications (C&G, LCCI, National Proficiency Tests Council). Basic Food Hygiene Certificate, RSA CLAIT.

Vocational areas include horticulture, estate maintenance, catering and domestic services. Work experience is arranged for students as appropriate and students also have access to physical pursuits, the performing and creative arts and leisure facilities. Towards independence and employment: Certain core skills are addressed to help students develop their self-confidence and self-awareness. Dilston offers each student opportunities for personal growth, development of general employability skills, acquisition of specific vocational skills, and increased independence and maturity.

Planned courses and educational support, monitoring and review of progress, and the recording and measuring of outcomes and achievements are essential elements of each individual's learning programme.

Links

Links with NATSPEC, MENCAP Further Education Colleges, Newcastle FE College; work experience placements with local employers; local community education.

Application procedure

Visit college, complete and return application form. Additional information collected by college (school reports, social reports, etc.). Prospective student invited for assessment if appropriate. Place offered if successful.

Doncaster College for the Deaf

Address: Leger Way, Doncaster DN2 6AY

Codes: F H O

Tel: 01302 386720   **Fax:** 01302 361808   **Email:** enquiries@ddt-deaf.org.uk   **Website:** www.deaf-college.co.uk

Age range: 16-65

Principal: Alan Robinson

Contact for admissions information: Mrs Pat Innes, the Admissions Office. Tel: 01302 386721 or email: admissions@ddt-deaf.org.uk

Fees: On request

Usual source of funding for students: LEA, LSC, DWP, private

Aims: The College provides a wide range of academic and vocational courses. The majority of the students are trained entirely on campus.

Students catered for: Students aged 16 to 65 who are deaf and/or have additional communication difficulties.

Premises and facilities

There is a sports complex, with a bar and social area with pool table, a TV/video with large screen facility, internet access and an area of relaxation. The bright and spacious main library resource centre, with friendly, helpful staff on hand to help students study and learn in a relaxed atmosphere, has a wide-range of non-fiction and reference books related to college courses, and fiction books with modified language to help students enhance their literacy skills. Daily newspapers and deaf journals help students keep up-to-date with current affairs. The centre also includes a computer-based careers guidance section. Internet and email facilities are in a separate computer room. There is also a TV/video for subtitled educational programmes. Doncaster town offers a shopping centre, a leisure complex, cinemas, a civic theatre, a museum and art gallery, libraries, parks and a wildlife nature reserve.

Student accommodation

The accommodation has recently been refurbished to a high standard, and is allocated according to the individual needs of each student. The facilities and routines aim to encourage personal maturity and independence. Residential life is structured and incorporated within an 'Independent Living Programme'.

Student numbers

180.

Staffing

College staff are highly qualified and experienced in delivering a curriculum within a 'total communication' environment. The team comprises experts in vocational subjects and occupations, including language specialists, teachers of the deaf, student support workers, medical and audiology professionals, an educational psychologist and a speech therapist. A team of Student Support Workers offer students individual and group advice and guidance including a full range of programmes aimed to meet their independent living and cultural needs. The Employment Liaison team offers students a comprehensive local and national placement programme.

Courses

An extensive range of courses offering nationally-recognised and accredited qualifications in: business studies and office technology; catering and hospitality; construction and motor vehicle engineering; design and technology; foundation skills; health and social studies and sport, recreation and leisure. A substantial number of students find jobs as a direct result of participation in work experience placements. All courses are work-related and offer realistic job prospects at the end of their training.

Application procedure

Enrolment is anytime during the academic year. Details of open days are on the website. Informal visits can be arranged by contacting Margaret Moran, Marketing Officer by telephone: 01302 386709 or by email: mmoran@ddt-deaf.org.uk

Dorton College of Further Education

Code: D

Address: Seal Drive, Seal, Sevenoaks, Kent TN15 0AH

Tel: 01732 592602 **Fax:** 01732 592601 **Email:** dcfe@rlsb.org.uk **Website:** www.rlsb.org.uk

Age range: 16+

Controlled by: Royal London Society for the Blind

Contact for admissions information: heather.bullough@rlsb.org.uk

Out-of-term contact: dcfe@rlsb.org.uk

Fees: Dependent on individual needs

Usual source of funding for students: LSC or RTU

Aims: Dorton College offers a unique opportunity for people with a visual impairment to study, with a focus on inclusion and integration. The College works to develop the independent learning and living skills of young people to enable them to be integrated into society on the basis of parity of esteem with their sighted peers.

Students catered for: Young people and adults with a visual impairment. In addition some students may have other physical disabilities and/or learning difficulties.

Premises and facilities

The College opened in 1989 in attractive buildings specifically designed to provide a learning environment for people with a visual impairment. Teaching rooms at the College and base rooms in mainstream colleges are fully equipped with specialist equipment with extensive computer network/internet available through access technology software. Specially adapted accommodation including radio station, swimming pool and multi-gym.

Student accommodation

Residential accommodation consists of units varying in size from four to ten individual study bedrooms. Each unit has a shared lounge, kitchen/diner and bathroom.

Student numbers

80-100.

Staffing

A well-established staff team comprises tutors, classroom support, residential support staff, therapists, mobility officers and admin support. All staff have specialist v.i. qualifications or are working towards them.

Courses

A model of inclusive education is based on a syndicate which includes Dorton College and local sector colleges. This provides access to a full range of courses from entry level (pre-foundation courses) to level 3 (AS/A2 and advanced courses). As a student-centred organisation,

the College also offers individual programmes, based on the Dorton campus. Students at Dorton therefore have over 150 different course programmes to choose from.

Links

Numerous links include local employers and three local mainstream colleges.

Other information

Additional services in adaptive technology, Braille, mobility, disability rights, job search, on-site health services, occupational therapy, speech and language therapy, physiotherapy, ophthalmology, counselling and career guidance.

Application procedure

Contact Heather Bullough from Student Services who will arrange an individual visit to the College.

Doucecroft Further Education Department

Address: 86 High Street, Kelvedon, Colchester, Essex CO5 9AA

Tel: 01376 570203   **Fax:** 01376 570203   **Email:** acp@essexautistic.org.uk

Code: C

Age range: 16-19

Controlled by: Essex Autistic Society

Contact for admissions information: As above

Usual source of funding for students: LEA and Social Services

Aims: To provide a service dedicated to offering a 24-hour curriculum that will promote the development of independent living skills in young people with autistic spectrum disorders.

Students catered for: Students aged between 16 and 19 with a diagnosis of an autistic spectrum disorder. Preference given to those from Essex/East Anglia but consideration given to out-of-county applications.

Premises and facilities

The College is situated in Kelvedon, within easy reach of public transport services to Witham, Chelmsford, Colchester and Braintree. The building has a large garden, which offers students the opportunity to learn how to grow vegetables and maintain their environment.

Student accommodation

A well-resourced provision can accommodate eight weekly boarders and four day students. All bedrooms are single occupancy with shared bathroom facilities.

Student numbers

12 students.

Staffing

Dependent on needs.

Courses

The 24-hour curriculum is planned so that it gives a three-year programme designed to develop and enlarge upon the skills needed to live as independently as possible, post-19. The students learn to access community activities via public transport, practise money-handling skills and interact appropriately in a wider social arena. The College undertakes, where feasible and desirable, to get work experience for students, and work with the students, their families and involved agencies in planning for their future post-19 provision. Students can gain OCR Adult Numeracy, Literacy and ICT; Accreditation for Life Award; ASDAN life skills qualification; Trident Gold.

Links

Cross-college links with Braintree College, Colchester Institute etc. Membership of local youth clubs. Work experience arranged with local employers and Trident.

Other information

We have access to the services of a specialist behavioural psychologist.

Application procedure

Through the auspices of LEAs.

Easter Anguston Training Farm

Code: O

Address: Peterculter, Aberdeen AB14 0PJ

Tel: 01224 733627   **Email:** info@easteranguston.org.uk   **Website:** www.easteranguston.org.uk

Age range: 16-25

Controlled by: VSA

Contact for admissions information: Alison Brook

Out-of-term contact: All-year service

Fees: From £365pw residential, from £155pw training

Usual source of funding for students: Social Services

Aims: To provide a range of social and vocational opportunities for young adults with learning difficulties in a working farm environment.

Students catered for: Young adults with a learning disability.

Premises and facilities

Easter Anguston is a 70-acre working farm, located on the outskirts of Aberdeen. Training is provided in horticulture, agriculture and rural skills (including the environment and conservation issues).

Student accommodation

Accommodation can be provided in a core and cluster complex in the nearby village of Peterculter.

Student numbers

12 residential/18 day placements.

Staffing

Farm – six full time and one part time; residential – two full time and six part time.

Courses

Attendance at the farm is not for a fixed duration. Through a system of annual progress reviews, the sponsoring local authority and Easter Anguston staff make a decision as to whether the placement continues to be a benefit to the individual.

Links

Good links with local college and community placement team. Some work placements available with local businesses.

Application procedure

Social work departments should forward SSA and any additional assessments of need after initial discussions and enquiries.

Enham

Address: Eastleigh Community Enterprise Centre, Unit 3, Baton Park, Eastleigh SO50 6RR

Codes: O R

Tel: 02380 687710   **Fax:** 02380 687714   **Email:** info@enham.org.uk   **Website:** www.enham.org.uk

Age range: All ages

Controlled by: Independent charity

Aims: Enham offers people with disabilities the opportunity to make real choices in life. Access to worthwhile employment, decent accommodation, high quality care, relevant training and a fulfilling social life are all fundamental to anyone taking their place in life. Enham's programmes open up opportunities and a fuller lifestyle. Choices for living options provide short and long-term solutions for all accommodation needs. Choices for work give real work opportunities for real life.

Students catered for: Adults with disabilities or long-term health issues.

Premises and facilities

Enham offers individuals help in finding accommodation and employment in the community, but also provides residential training at Enham Alamein village in Andover.

Student accommodation

Residential trainees can expect individual accommodation in self-contained, fully equipped studio apartments, together with leisure facilities and opportunities both on site and throughout the wider community to provide for personal and social development.

Student numbers

90 village residents.

Courses

Enham residential training programmes open up opportunities for worthwhile employment in computer-aided design, IT maintenance and commercial and amenity horticulture. Programmes are personally tailored, with clients' learning and support requirements assessed prior to the design of their individual training programme. This approach has enabled Enham's trainees to enjoy success in both the achievement of nationally recognised qualifications and progression into employment.

Fairfield Farm College

Address: High Street, Dilton Marsh, Westbury, Wiltshire BA13 4DL

Code: O

Tel: 01373 823028   **Fax:** 01373 859032   **Email:** fairfieldoppfarm@hotmail.com

Age range: 16-23

Controlled by: Independent charity: Fairfield Opportunity Farm (Dilton) Ltd

Contact for admissions information: Principal: Janet Kenward

Fees: Assessed via LSC Matrix

Usual source of funding for students: Learning and Skills Council (LSC)

Aims: The College aims to provide students with opportunities to learn new skills to prepare them for adult life in the community.

Students catered for: Local/national catchment. Students with learning disabilities who wish to undertake a course of pre-vocational training in land-based subjects and increase their independence skills.

Premises and facilities

The College is situated on a 25-acre site in the village of Dilton Marsh. It offers well-equipped facilities for its students to learn pre-vocational skills in catering, engineering, farming, horse studies, horticulture and house maintenance skills. Students also work on daily living skills, communication, literacy and numeracy.

Student accommodation

The College has five student houses in the village each accommodating five to six students. The houses are a short walk from the College site.

Staffing

The College has pre-vocational tutors who all have a strong practical background in their vocational subject area. The support staff have experience of working with people with learning difficulties.

Courses

The course starts with an induction programme where students try all the vocational options for one term. After this extended assessment period they are able to work with staff to determine the balance of their programme. An element of daily living skills is compulsory throughout the course. All students follow a Skills for Life programme either as a discrete subject or embedded into the curriculum. Each student's programme is planned and reviewed according to individual need.

Links

All students undertake regular work experience during their course, with an appropriate level of staff support. Some students follow short courses at other colleges.

Other information

The College is unable to offer places to students with physically challenging behaviour. The College can offer speech and language therapy and occupational therapy assessments.

Application procedure

Potential students telephone the College for an information pack. They then visit the College informally with their parents/carers. All students have a five-day assessment at the College before being offered a place.

Farleigh Further Education College, Frome

Address: North Parade, Frome, Somerset BA11 2AB

Tel: 01373 475470   **Fax:** 01373 475473   **Email:** ffecadmissions@priorygroup.com
Website: www.prioryeducation.com/farleighfrome

Age range: 16-22

Controlled by: The Priory Group

Contact for admissions information: Kally Brown

Fees: Learning and Skills Council Funding Matrix

Usual source of funding for students: Learning and Skills Council

Aims: To provide support in mainstream academic and social situations, helping students to develop strategies for managing the difficulties associated with Asperger's Syndrome.

Students catered for: Students have a diagnosis of Asperger's Syndrome, the ability to cope with a mainstream course and an aspiration to become an independent adult.

Premises and facilities

FFEC has fully equipped learning resource centres which enable students to work independently on assignments and course work. Leisure resources include pool, table tennis, PlayStations.

Student accommodation

FFEC has a range of residences, from halls of residence as at university, to family-style homes. Most students have single rooms.

Student numbers

50 students.

Staffing

Teachers, therapists and learning support workers are trained to provide a high level of support to students on an individual basis.

Courses

All FFEC students undertake an individual programme of independence training.
Academic/vocational courses are delivered through partnership arrangements with mainstream colleges of FE. Hence a comprehensive range is available. Work-based learning courses are also available.

Links

Partnerships with general colleges of further education allow us to offer a comprehensive range of academic and vocational courses.

Other information

Staff include a speech and language therapist, occupational therapist, art therapist and counsellor. An educational psychologist acts as a consultant.

Application procedure

Students' papers considered. Appropriate students invited for full day's assessment. Place offered; Connexions adviser notified. Connexions adviser negotiates funding with local Learning and Skills office.

Farleigh Further Education College, Swindon

Address: 105 Bath Road, Old Town, Swindon SN1 4AX

Code: C

Tel: 01793 484031   **Fax:** 01793 529541   **Email:** ffecadmissions@priorygroup.com
Website: www.prioryeducation.com/farleighswindon

Age range: 16-22

Controlled by: The Priory Group

Contact for admissions information: Kally Brown

Fees: Learning and Skills Council Funding Matrix

Usual source of funding for students: Learning and Skills Council

Aims: To provide support in mainstream academic and social situations, helping students to develop strategies for managing the difficulties associated with Asperger's Syndrome.

Students catered for: Students have a diagnosis of Asperger's Syndrome, the ability to cope with a mainstream course and an aspiration to become an independent adult.

Premises and facilities

FFEC has fully equipped learning resource centres which enable students to work independently on assignments and course work. Leisure resources include pool, table tennis, PlayStations.

Student accommodation

FFEC has a range of residences, from halls of residence as at university, to family-style homes. Most students have single rooms.

Student numbers

23 students.

Staffing

Teachers, therapists and learning support workers are trained to provide a high level of support to students on an individual basis.

Courses

All FFEC students undertake an individual programme of independence training.
Academic/vocational courses are delivered through partnership arrangements with mainstream colleges of FE. Hence a comprehensive range is available. Work-based learning courses are also available.

Links

Partnerships with general colleges of further education allow us to offer a comprehensive range of academic and vocational courses.

Other information

Staff include a speech and language therapist, occupational therapist, art therapist and counsellor. An educational psychologist acts as a consultant.

Application procedure

Students' papers considered. Appropriate students invited for full day's assessment. Place offered; Connexions adviser notified. Connexions adviser negotiates funding with local Learning and Skills office.

Finchale Training College

Address: Durham DH1 5RX

Tel: 0191 386 2634   **Fax:** 0191 386 4962   **Email:** enquiries@finchalecollege.co.uk   **Website:** www.finchalecollege.co.uk

Age range: 18+

Controlled by: Independent charity

Contact for admissions information: Principal, Dr D Etheridge

Usual source of funding for students: Students are sponsored by the DWP and usually attend under Work Based Learning for Adults or Work Preparation, but other sponsors can be accommodated.

Aims: To provide vocational rehabilitation and training for people with disabilities and special needs and help them regain confidence through employment.

Students catered for: All disabilities except severe sensory disabilities. UK-wide.

Premises and facilities

A residential training centre with residential, classroom and workshop accommodation of a high standard, so that people with disabilities are able to care for themselves with maximum independence.

Staffing

Training staff are experienced personnel from commerce and industry. The staff: student ratio in training is 1:15, some classes are even smaller.

Courses

Courses offered include those leading to NVQs in horticulture (amenity and commercial plus lift truck and pesticides training), wood occupations, computer technology, office skills, distribution and warehousing operations with lift truck training. Also CISCO Systems – this course involves up to 36 weeks training to achieve the CISCO CCNA certificate. The College also offers CISCO Networking Academy IT Essentials, and also training to Association of Accounting Technicians levels 2 and 3, the European Computer Driving Licence and basic construction skills, as well as other business and IT courses. Additional support is given in numeracy, literacy and ITC plus dyslexia support where needed.
Training is continuous except at bank holidays, and for approximately ten days over Christmas and New Year.

Other information

There are nursing, welfare and counselling facilities, and trainees are encouraged to organise their own leisure activities.

Application procedure

Apply through the local Disability Employment Adviser. Application should be accompanied by full medical reports.

The Fortune Centre of Riding Therapy

Address: Avon Tyrrell, Bransgore, Christchurch, Dorset BH23 8EE

Tel: 01425 673297   **Fax:** 01425 674320   **Email:** education@fortunecentre.ac.uk   **Website:** www.fortunecentre.org

Age range: 16 - 25

Controlled by: Independent

Contact for admissions information: Mike Cromie, Head of Admissions Direct dial 01425 673297 admissions@fortunecentre.ac.uk

Out-of-term contact: main switchboard as above

Fees: LSC matrix

Usual source of funding for students: LSC/Social Services

Aims: The FCRT is a residential specialist college of further education for horse-motivated young people. Through the horse-based curriculum, students are, for example, taught life, social and independence skills, personal health and development, literacy, numeracy, and money management to improve confidence, maturity and self esteem. All students work to an Individual Learning Plan.

Student catered for: Students with learning and behavioural difficulties may come from any location in the world, subject to funding.

Premises and facilities

The FCRT is situated on three sites in the New Forest, two of which have indoor and outdoor arenas. Work tends to be of a practical nature, but there is a library and various tutorial rooms.

Student accommodation

The three residences at the FCRT are regularly inspected by CSCI. There are a variety of study/bedrooms.

Student numbers

45.

Staffing

Full- and part-time staff, including physiotherapist, nurses, occupational therapists, teachers, assistants and so on.

Courses

All students follow the Further Education Through Horsemastership course. All students have an Individual Learning Plan. Staff are not divided into 'teaching' and 'care' situations, but work across the board at all sites, including the residences, in order to deliver the extended curriculum.

Application procedure

First contact/initial visit/one-day assessment/7-day residential assessment. It is recommended that first contact and applications are made well in advance.

Fourways Assessment Unit

Codes: A R

Address: Cleworth Hall Lane, Tyldesley, Manchester M29 8NT

Tel: 01942 870841   **Fax:** 01942 875958

Age range: 18+

Controlled by: Wigan Council Adult Services

Contact for admissions information: Manager, Christine Pilling

Out-of-term contact: Manager available all year

Fees: Current fees available from Wigan finance department

Aims: To assess support for independent living, employment, training etc and to provide activities and experience aimed at helping people with a physical disability, acquired brain injury or sensory impairment.

Students catered for: Physical disabilities/acquired brain injury/sensory impairment and associated problems, provided there is no need for nursing care beyond that which would be provided in their own homes or by a community nursing service.

Premises and facilities

The facilities at the unit include a day centre with IT suite and a developing outreach service.

Student accommodation

Refurbished 18-bed residential accommodation, with six of these beds for short breaks.

Staffing

Experienced and qualified staff including manager, day service manager, four assistant accommodation managers, three instructors, around 25 support workers, 5 full-time night care assistants, administration staff, domestics, cooks, drivers, physiotherapy/occupational/ speech therapy sessions, consultant. Referrals can be made to other services for additional assessments.

Courses

The assessment and rehabilitation supported programmes aim to identify short- and long-term personal objectives of people using the service. Service users can stay for up to two years. Specific guidance in social/life skills/computer aided learning.
At Fourways: individual tuition. Individualised assessment and rehabilitation programmes.
Fourways IT suite: attached to Fourways providing short courses covering wordprocessing, ECDL, spreadsheets, desktop publishing and systems management.

Application procedure

Informal visits by arrangement. Access to services via social worker referral.

Fullerton House School

Codes: C S

Address: off Tickhill Square, Denaby, Doncaster DN12 4AR

Tel: 01709 861663 **Fax:** 01709 869635 **Email:** fullerton@hesleygroup.co.uk **Website:** www.hesleygroup.co.uk

Age range: 8-19

Controlled by: The Hesley Group

Fees: On request

Aims: To develop the skills that students will need to cope with everyday problems and situations. The School assesses individuals' abilities across a wide range of educational activities so that it can target the skills they need.

Students catered for: Fullerton House School provides accommodation, education and therapeutic services for people with severe challenging behaviours resulting from autism or severe learning difficulties.

Premises and facilities

The School is situated in the village of Denaby near Doncaster. It is a 52-week co-educational school for children and young people. The school provides a safe, comfortable home and stimulating school environment for students — with the added advantage of being in the heart of the local community. Students benefit from a wide range of recreational and therapeutic facilities at the school including soft play area, snoezelen, fitness gym, art therapy, music therapy and a sensory corridor.

Student accommodation

All bedrooms are for single occupancy, are well furnished and decorated. The accommodation is divided into several distinct homes.

Student numbers

Fullerton House offers accommodation for 36 boys and girls.

Courses

Based on assessment, the School develops individual 24-hour learning programmes linked to the National Curriculum, with focus on the key areas of communication, social development and personal hygiene. Positive, non-aversive strategies are used to change or reduce the severity and frequency of challenging behaviours.

Education for the majority of students is provided on-site, but all post-16 students attend the School's own vocational training centre at nearby Mexborough in addition to attending local colleges and work experience outlets.

N.B. *This entry has not been updated by the establishment for this edition. Please check details.*

Garvald Centre Edinburgh

Address: 2 Montpelier Terrace, Edinburgh EH10 4NF

Code: O

Tel: 0131 228 3712 **Fax:** 0131 229 1468 **Email:** admin@garvaldedinburgh.org.uk
Website: www.garvaldedinburgh.org.uk

Age range: 17+

Controlled by: Garvald Training Centre Ltd

Contact for admissions information: Administrator (re Day or Accommodation service) — Tuesday to Friday

Out-of-term-contact: Same

Fees: Details on request

Usual source of funding for students: Local authority; some ILF

Aims: Inspired by the ideas of Rudolph Steiner, Garvald Centre Edinburgh provides day and accommodation services to people who have a learning disability. In striving to build a community together, the Garvald Centre recognises and values the uniqueness of each person and seeks to create a quality of environment, activities and social relationships which foster the realisation of individual potential.

Students catered for: The Centre offers a therapeutic environment in which individuals with a range of learning disabilities can take steps in their development towards maturity, and can be supported in finding their place in relation to the wider community.

Premises and facilities

Day services premises, care home and supported tenancies. Premises are situated in the south west and central areas of Edinburgh.
Use is also made of local facilities with support to foster integration and inclusion.

Student accommodation

Registered care home for eight residents.

Student numbers

As well as users of the day services, 34 tenants are supported in their own tenancies and there is a care home for eight residents.

Staffing

Garvald Centre has over 100 staff.

Courses

Day activities include: bakery & confectionery; joinery; pottery; painting/glasswork; puppet-making/puppetry; metal work and Tools for Self Reliance; weaving; education; speech therapy; eurythmy.

Links

Links with other organisations whose work is based on the ideas of Rudolf Steiner, including other Garvald ventures around Edinburgh and the Borders.

Many community based facilities including local libraries, swimming pools, horse-riding and FE colleges, are used on a daily basis.

Other information

Visiting professionals include: anthroposophical medical doctor; speech and language therapists and physiotherapists from the local Primary Care Trust; occupational therapists from Health & Social Care.

Application procedure

Contact the Admissions Administrator.

Garvald West Linton

Codes: B C F J K M N O Q S T

Address: Garvald House, Dolphinton, West Linton EH46 7HJ

Tel: 01968 682211   **Fax:** 01968 682611   **Email:** info@garvaldwest.fsnet.co.uk   **Website:** www.garvald-wl.org.uk

Age range: 16+

Controlled by: Independent

Contact for admissions information: Robert Crichton

Fees: £674 p.w.

Usual source of funding for students: Local Authorities

Aims: To provide residential care, day care (training and further education) based on the principles of Rudolf Steiner, with the aim that each individual achieves growth and development. Garvald West Linton strives to create a social structure that encourages individual growth and development.

Students catered for: Adults with a wide range of learning disability and challenging behaviour.

Premises and facilities

Garvald has a beautiful rural location, 25 miles south of Edinburgh. It has recently developed its workshops and many are now in purpose-built buildings. It has many large public rooms which lend themselves to a variety of uses.

Student accommodation

There are four residential houses with space for eight residents in each house. Each person has a single room with shared kitchen and dining room etc.

Student numbers

32 resident, 40 day.

Staffing

There are 52 staff, many qualified to SVQ level 3. Specialists are employed for many activities and there are also staff employed in therapeutic activities.

Courses

Training is available in the following areas: horticulture, woodland and estate work, baking and confectionery, cooking, woodwork, crafts and pottery. Also available are painting and artwork and music.

Links

Partnership with Borders College on a skills accreditation programme.

Other information

Garvald West Linton also works in partnership with the local NHS Learning Disability Service.

Application procedure

Please contact the manager for further information.

George House

Address: Swalcliffe Park School, Swalcliffe, Nr. Banbury, Oxon OX15 5EP

Code: C

Tel: 01295 780302   **Fax:** 01295 780006   **Email:** admin@swalcliffepark.co.uk   **Website:** www.swalcliffepark.oxon.sch.uk

Age range: 15-19

Controlled by: Board of Trustees/Board of Governors

Contact for admissions information: Caroline Daniels/Melissa Fazackerley

Usual source of funding for students: Children's Services

Aims: To encourage a high level of independence, personal growth and the acquisition of life and vocational skills working towards real social inclusion.

Students catered for: Students primarily with ASD.

Premises and facilities

A purpose-built unit situated in the grounds of Swalcliffe Park. Completely independent from the main school, has its own high standard of accommodation and equipment, and a high staffing ratio. It is designed to allow either group living or, for those who are capable, independent living.

Student accommodation

Six of the rooms are single bedsit type, fully-furnished with toilet and shower en suite and one of these is designed to accommodate a disabled person. The remaining rooms are shared by two boys. Some meals are prepared either by staff or boys in one or more of the three fully-equipped kitchens. Laundry is done in commercial machines situated within the building. A student common room, bathroom and staff flats complete the complex.

Student numbers

11/12.

Staffing

Care leader; deputy; assistant; teaching-unit teacher; access to, and use made of, specialist teachers from main school.

Courses

An emphasis on lifeskills and independent living. Linked to school practice in general subjects. Local technical college courses. Work experience.

Links

Links with Oxford & Cherwell Valley College and other local colleges.

Application procedure

Individual interviews.

The Grange Centre

Address: Rectory Lane, Bookham, Surrey KT23 4DZ

Tel: 01372 452608   **Fax:** 01372 451959   **Email:** info@grangecentre.org.uk   **Website:** www.grangecentre.org.uk

Age range: 19+

Controlled by: Council of Management (Volunteers)

Contact for admissions information: Gillian Nicholls (Assistant Director —Residential & Training)

Fees: On Application

Usual source of funding for students: Local authority funding/benefits/private funding

Aims: To maximise independence for each individual, according to their abilities, through independent living skills training and support in individual accommodation or small group living with care, together with skills training in life skills, horticulture, creative textiles, catering and work experience placements.

Students catered for: Adults with physical and/or learning disabilities, nationwide, provided that the home county can guarantee funding for the duration of the placement.

Premises and facilities

15-acre site with three purpose-built bungalows and on-site swimming pool.

Student accommodation

Small group living in bungalows, and supported living in flats on and off site. Each bungalow contains five bedrooms with French windows to the garden, a living room and a kitchen. An additional bungalow is due for completion in November 2006, containing five individual flatlets, living room and assisted bathroom. There are 29 self-contained flats on site, four in Bookham village, with plans for further flats in the community during 2007-9.

Student numbers

52, including day placements.

Staffing

Director, two assistant directors, three secretaries, 20 care/support staff (non-medical), twelve tutors as well as maintenance and administration staff.

Courses

The Grange Centre offers training for clients in horticulture and creative textiles. It provides skills training involving work skills, life skills and living support, which gives continuing assistance to clients in their own flats. For staff there is also the opportunity to obtain NVQs and other qualifications and courses run annually for members of the public in dressmaking and soft furnishings.

Links

North East Surrey College; Treloar College; Derwent College; British Legion Industries, Leatherhead.

Other information

Physiotherapist visits monthly; fitness and aqua-aerobics instructor visits weekly.

Application procedure

Forms from the Grange Centre. Informal visits welcomed. One-day assessment followed by two-week assessment, including weekend.

Grange Village Community

Address: Littledean Road, Newnham on Severn, Gloucestershire GL14 1HJ

Code: O

Tel: 01594 516246   **Fax:** 01594 516969   **Email:** grange@camphill.org.uk

Website: www.camphill.org.uk/guide/grange/grange.htm

Age range: 20+

Controlled by: Camphill Village Trust

Contact for admissions information: Annette van der Ulist

Out-of-term contact: Judy Wakeman

Fees: £550 per week

Aims: Grange Village aims to assist adults with learning difficulties by offering a home in an extended family living situation. The Village offers meaningful work, adult education, general care and opportunities for personal development within a vibrant, life-sharing, working community setting.

Students catered for: Adults with learning difficulties.

Premises and facilities

The site, with views of the River Severn, comprises: eight extended-family houses; three flats; a magnificent hall; a health centre (where health checks are carried out by a visiting nurse); a gift shop and several workshops.

Student accommodation

Between four and seven residents live in each family house with co-workers and their children.

Student numbers

40 men and women, plus co-workers and their children.

Courses

No courses as such are provided, the Village being a community within which each resident can be assisted to individual independence and social adjustment. Work realms include a wood workshop, a basket workshop and a pottery, a biodynamic and organic farm, an estate team (responsible for the general upkeep of the estate) and a village bakery. On-the-job training is offered within all work areas.

Festivals are celebrated and there is a very wide range of evening activities: study groups, lectures, dancing, games, music, acting, reading etc.

Links

Royal Forest of Dean College, and several others according to individual needs.

The Grange Village Community has close ties with the local village and other Camphill Communities.

Other information

Visiting therapists etc according to needs.

Application procedure

Applications to The Admissions Group at the above address can be made at the age of 20 onwards. The particular needs of each applicant are considered. The waiting list is only made up of those who have had a successful trial visit. Visits are arranged as soon as possible after interview, usually for a fortnight initially, then for a three-month period when accommodation is available.

Grateley House School

Address: Pond Lane, Grateley, Andover, Hants SP11 8TA

Codes: B C

Tel: 0800 288 9779 **Fax:** 020 7348 5223 **Email:** enquiries@cambiangroup.com
Website: www.cambianeducation.com

Age range: 11-19

Controlled by: Cambian Education Services

Contact for admissions information: Claire Chester

Out-of-term contact: 0800 288 9779

Fees: £112,434.20 per annum (basic fees)

Usual source of funding for students: LEA

Aims: Grateley House is a 38-week termly residential school, with a post-16 community, offering supported education for students with Asperger Syndrome, ADHD and similar conditions. The School aims to prepare them for adulthood by giving them confidence and the necessary academic and social skills.

Students catered for: Students (male and female) who have a diagnosis of Asperger Syndrome and associated disorders.

Premises and facilities

The School is set in a large country house and eight-acre grounds. There is a wooded area and hard court surfaces for recreation. Students live in house bases. Educational provision extends to an ICT suite, specialist food technology, CDT and art rooms. Numeracy, literacy and careers taught in a dedicated room.

Student accommodation

Single bedrooms, communal kitchen, living and dining rooms, bath and shower facilities similar to family-style living.

Student numbers

Up to 12 in the post-16 unit.

Staffing

Full complement of teaching and care staff to meet the needs of students; a minimum of 1:3. All staff receive thorough and on-going training.

Courses

Access to mainstream college courses in the locality. AQA adult literacy, numeracy, basic skills. Food hygiene, first aid, lifeskills programme, GCSEs — ICT, maths, English, science (by agreement). AQA — entry level certificate English and maths (by agreement).

Links

Links to Salisbury College, Cricklade College, Sparsholt College (agricultural) and part of Trident work placement scheme.

Other information

On-site therapeutic services team including consultant psychiatrist, clinical psychologist, speech and language therapist, occupational therapist. Regular opportunities for leisure and sporting excursions.

Application procedure

Contact the post-16 coordinator for an informal discussion about the application process.

Grenville College

Address: Bideford, North Devon EX39 3JP

Tel: 01237 472212   **Fax:** 01237 477020   **Email:** registrar@grenvillecollege.co.uk   **Website:** www.grenvillecollege.co.uk

Age range: 2½-18

Contact for admissions information: Headteacher, Mr Andy Waters

Controlled by: Woodard Corporation

Fees: per term £5432 max (full boarding and tuition); £4073 max (weekly boarding and tuition); £536 (special English tuition)

Aims: To help all pupils, including those with specific learning difficulties/dyslexia, to achieve their potential academically, and in other ways via extra-curricular activities, and to provide a broad education founded upon a sound moral basis.

Students catered for: A full secondary curriculum is provided for boys and girls aged 11-18. Entrants, including those with specific learning difficulties/dyslexia, may join at sixth form level.

Premises and facilities

Co-educational boarding and day school for pupils aged 2½-18. The College has a recently-built science and library block, a language laboratory, well-equipped design and technology workshops, art rooms and a music school. A modern assembly hall/chapel provides not only a centre for worship but also has excellent facilities for dramatic and musical productions. The School has extensive playing fields and excellent sports facilities. Special emphasis is placed on club activities and the school is one of only four in the south west to have its own Operating Authority Licence to issue awards for the Duke of Edinburgh Award Scheme. It also has a thriving rowing club.

Courses

A course brochure is available on request. GCSE and Advanced level courses, including Applied A level courses in business are also provided.

Dyslexic 6th form students have an adviser from Grenville's long established dyslexia department who will be able to offer support and advice. If necessary, lessons can be timetabled with the adviser for specific work in areas such as study skills, reading techniques and spelling. Re-take English GCSE is available. The student is also welcome to make use of the dyslexia department during private study periods and to benefit from the computer facilities. Advanced level teaching is carried out in small groups by staff with long experience and expertise in teaching dyslexic students. Finally, the pastoral system is carefully designed to be of help to the dyslexic student. Tutor groups are small and they meet regularly.

Links

Grenville maintains informal links with FE colleges and universities. A considerable number of dyslexic pupils go on to higher education.

Other information

All sixth formers receive guidance and advice on their choice of higher education courses and careers as part of the weekly timetable. In addition they have access to a wide selection of reference books in the careers library.

Application procedure

Parents of dyslexic applicants are asked to submit an educational psychologist's report prior to a child's interview and testing at Grenville. All entrants are expected to be of at least average intelligence and capable of following academic courses to GCSE level. Relevant GCSE passes at grade C or above are necessary for entry to A level courses. Enquiries to the Registrar.

The Helen Allison School

Address: Longfield Road, Meopham, Kent DA13 0EW

Tel: 01474 814878   **Fax:** 01474 812033   **Email:** helenallison@nas.org.uk

Age range: 5-19

Controlled by: The National Autistic Society

Aims: To provide education modified to meet the specific needs of children and young adults with autism and Asperger Syndrome in a safe and structured environment to enable them to reach their fullest potential and to prepare them for adulthood.

Students catered for: Diagnosed as being on the autistic continuum.

Courses

The Jubilee Unit provides continuing education with a programme appropriate for pupils with autism and Asperger Syndrome.

Application procedure

Applications via local education authority. Selection panel — principal and senior management team.

N.B. *This entry has not been updated by the establishment for this edition. Please check details.*

Henshaws College

Address: Bogs Lane, Harrogate, North Yorkshire HE1 4ED

Tel: 01423 886451   **Fax:** 01423 885095   **Email:** admissions@hsbp.co.uk   **Website:** www.hsbp.co.uk

Age range: 16+

Controlled by: Henshaws Society for Blind People

Contact for admissions information: Lynne Gilland, Marketing & Transitions Manager

Out-of-term contact: As above

Fees: in accordance with LSC funding matrix

Usual source of funding for students: LSC

Aims: To make a visible difference to all our students by focusing on their abilities. To empower students with skills and confidence to maximise their independence, minimise the effects of their sight loss and to achieve success throughout their adult lives.

Student catered for: Students with learning difficulties (moderate/severe) and physical disabilities, many of whom have sensory impairment.

Premises and facilities

Purpose-built campus on a green-field site on the outskirts of Harrogate, with equal access throughout. All teaching areas are on the ground floor. Sport and fitness centre comprising swimming pool, hydrotherapy pool, multi-gym, sports hall, sauna, steam room.

Student accommodation

Range of accommodation includes en-suite rooms, small houses and self-contained flats.

Student numbers

65 residential.

Staffing

Individual learning-support needs are met by a range of staff with relevant qualifications and experience, including multi-disciplinary team approaches.

Courses

Students have the opportunity to work toward nationally-recognised qualifications delivered on site or through supported attendance at a local public sector college or training provider.

Links

Links with general FE colleges, local schools, employers and training providers.

Other information

The College has its own physiotherapy, occupational therapy and speech and language therapy services.

Application procedure

Prospective students, their family and professionals involved are encouraged to make an informal visit prior to submission of application.

Hereward College

Address: Bramston Crescent, Tile Hall Lane, Coventry CV4 9SW

Codes: A C F H O R

Tel: 024 7646 1231   **Fax:** 024 7669 4305   **Email:** enquiries@hereward.ac.uk   **Website:** www.hereward.ac.uk

Age range: 16+

Contact for admissions information: Lois Benton

Fees: On application

Usual source of funding for students: LSC

Aims: To provide inclusive and integrated further education that allows disabled students to study alongside their non-disabled peers.

Students catered for: Students with a wide range of physical and/or sensory disabilities, complex medical conditions, specific or moderate learning difficulties, communication difficulties, brain and spinal injuries and autistic spectrum disorders. Local disabled and non-disabled students welcome.

Premises and facilities

Situated in Coventry, Hereward is in an urban environment with many local amenities. Learning resources include a vocational business studies centre, fully-equipped TV and photographic studios, a learning resources centre, a large creative studies department, a multimedia suite, and IT labs. Enabling technology is used extensively throughout.

Staffing

The college employs some 250 staff with expertise in teaching and learning, care and enabling, nursing, therapies, counselling, educational psychology and enabling technology.

Courses

The curriculum encompasses business studies, management, IT, art and design, performance and music, media studies (including TV, video, photography and journalism), humanities, sports, essential skills and residential education. Academic and vocational options from entry level to level 4 are available, including GCSEs, AS/A levels, NVQs and Access courses. HND in media is also offered.

Links

The College has close links with its local community and neighbouring FE colleges and 6th forms, enabling residential students to access additional learning and leisure experiences with support as required. There are collaborative links with employers and other establishments, e.g. the National Institute of Conductive Education, Jaguar Cars Ltd and Coventry's Youth Service. The College has a Partnership Agreement with Connexions Coventry and Warwickshire, giving students access to specialist careers advice and a wide range of work experience placements.

Other information

24-hour medical, care and educational enabling services are available. Physiotherapy, speech therapy and conductive education are provided according to need. The student services centre houses careers, employment and HE guidance services, work experience, personal counselling and advice on welfare and benefits. Hereward's ACCESS centre is where students' needs are assessed and appropriate technical and study support needs identified.

Application procedure

Regular visits are offered. Disabled applicants are invited to comprehensive assessment including overnight stay for prospective residential students. Decisions regarding admission are taken by a multi-disciplinary team based on an assessment of the benefit of a placement to the prospective student and the impact of admission on the experience of other learners.

Hesley Village and College

Codes: C N O S

Address: Stripe Road, Nr Tickhill, Doncaster DN11 9HH

Tel: 01302 866906   **Fax:** 01302 865473   **Email:** helen.vanes@hesleygroup.co.uk   **Website:** www. hesleygroup.co.uk

Age range: 16+

Controlled by: The Hesley Group

Fees: On request

Aims: Hesley Village and College provides accommodation, vocational opportunities, education and therapeutic services for young adults with special needs. It builds upon earlier experiences and skills in order to educate, train and support residents in achieving as effective a transition to adulthood and independence as possible.

Students catered for: Residents age 16+ with severe challenging behaviour resulting from severe learning difficulties and/or autism.

Premises and facilities

Hesley Village and College is set in 100 acres and includes a general store, clothes shop, bank, hairdresser, beautician, village hall and bistro. The facilities are used by the residents to practise their skills in a safe and non-judgemental environment. They then have greater confidence to achieve transference of these skills into the wider community.

Student accommodation

Residents are accommodated in single self-contained flats and bungalows and three- and four-bedroomed houses. There are also ensuite bedrooms in the main building, a Victorian mansion house. All are decorated and finished to the highest standard.

Student numbers

Currently 73 places.

Staffing

All residents are staffed at 1:1 as standard.

Courses

Courses are designed (based on the needs of communication and behaviour), planned and implemented to meet the needs of the individual. Learning programmes take place across the 24-hour curriculum. Special 'courses' or programmes take the form of multi-area, cross-curriculum study with the opportunity to complete modular programmes via ASDAN/OCN. Work-based learning is also a significant part of the curriculum.

Links

Links are established and maintained with Doncaster College, Goole College (part of Hull College) and Dearne Valley, and there is a partnership with local retail businesses for work experience placements.

Other information

Pottery specialist; dance and movement specialist; speech and language therapists; beauty therapist.

Application procedure

Referral in writing from the funding authority or telephone the establishment for informal discussion or to arrange a visit.

Hinwick Hall College

Address: Hinwick, Wellingborough, Northamptonshire NN29 7JD

Tel: 01933 312470 **Fax:** 01933 412470 **Email:** haysm@hinwickhall.ac.uk **Website:** www.shaftesburysociety.org

Age range: 16-21

Controlled by: The Shaftesbury Society

Contact for admissions information: Admissions Officer

Out-of-term contact: Admissions Officer

Fees: As set by LSC

Usual source of funding for students: LSC

Aims: The College's overall aim is to educate, train and support young people with disabilities to achieve their potential for as effective an adulthood as possible.

Students catered for: Students with disabilities and associated learning, communication and/or emotional difficulties.

Premises and facilities

Grade II listed building set in impressive and extensive grounds, including a sensory garden. Physiotherapy/hydrotherapy suite. Hinwick Hall Plant Centre on campus.

Student accommodation

There are four areas of student accommodation on the campus, including independence training flats.

Student Numbers

60.

Staffing

The College supports students on their courses and residential experience through lecturers, therapists and support staff who facilitate students to reach their potential.

Courses

The courses are designed so that all students have an equal opportunity to develop personal effectiveness and maintain and extend existing skills and develop new ones.

Courses: Independence, Vocational Preparation and Education (IVPE); Self Care Occupational Preparation & Education (SCOPE); Self Care Advocacy and Education (SCAE).

Links

The students link with local employers, Connexions, social services, advocacy services and local schools and colleges.

Other information

Students have access to physiotherapy/hydrotherapy and speech and language therapy on campus; they have contact with local services via hospital referral or advocacy as required.

Application procedure

Following referral (Connexions, social services, school or direct parental contact) the prospective student is invited for an informal interview, discussion and visit.

Holly Bank Trust

Address: Roe Head, Far Common Road, Mirfield, West Yorkshire WF14 ODQ

Codes: E F G N O Q R S

Tel: 01924 490833 **Fax:** 01924 491464 **Email:** info@hollybanktrust.com **Website:** www.hollybanktrust.com

---

Age range: Post-16 department for students aged 16-19 in full-time education. Supported independent living for 18 years to adult.

Controlled by: Trustees of Hollybank Trust

Contact for admissions information: Helen Clayton (extn 307)

Out-of-term-contact: 08.30-15.00 admin, all other out-of-term times 01924 490833

Usual source of funding for students: LEAs/social services/health authority

Aims: To deliver excellence in education, development and lifelong care for children and adults who have complex disabilities.

Students catered for: People who have physical disabilities coupled with moderate to profound learning difficulties and complex needs. 24-hour nursing cover is provided.

Premises and facilities

School building converted to its present use in 1990. Registered as a children's home since 2002. Purpose-built multi-therapy centre incorporating hydrotherapy/sensory pool, Jacuzzi spa pool, rebound (trampolining) facilities and hippotherapy (simulated horse riding). Innovative IT provision.
All buildings fully wheelchair accessible. Extensive landscaped grounds.

Student accommodation

52-week residential and day provision (5-19 years) within school building and in two on-site bungalow complexes (5-25); four houses in the community (predominantly 25 years+).

Student numbers

Currently 17 learners attend the on-site 16-19 educational provision. An additional 20 residents aged 19-25 access day provision in the community.

Staffing

On-site staff team of qualified teachers, support assistants, development and social care workers, physiotherapists, speech therapists, occupational therapist, team of ICT specialists, nurses, administration, catering and maintenance personnel totalling 330 throughout the Trust.

Courses

Within the post-16 department, learners follow an individually-tailored, independence-orientated course designed to enhance inclusion, autonomy and quality of life. Achievements are applauded in-house and via nationally-recognised accreditation schemes. Post-19 service users may choose from a wide range of courses offered by local colleges, SECs and other community groups. Pre-vocational options and therapies are offered on site.

Links

Young residents have established links with similar schools, local colleges and universities, theatre and arts groups, as well as service providers, e.g. careers and fire service.

Other information

Frequent visitors include entertainers, therapists, medical, dental and optical services in addition to stakeholders.

Application procedure

A prospectus is available from the School or via the website. If you would like to visit, please contact Helen Clayton (extn 307) or headteacher Pam King (extn 128) to arrange a mutually convenient date and time and to discuss assessment procedures.

Homefield College

Address: 42 St Mary's Road, Sileby, Leicestershire LE12 7TL

Codes: C F O

Tel: 01509 815696   **Fax:** 01509 815696   **Email:** enquiries@homefieldcollege.ac.uk
Website: www.homefieldcollege.ac.uk

Age range: 16+

Contact for admissions information: Linda Crump

Out-of-term contact: Chris Berry (Principal) 07702 403106

Usual source of funding for students: Learning and Skills Council (LSC)

Aims: Homefield College is a small, specialist, mainly residential College providing a high-quality, friendly and supportive environment for students with learning difficulties. Day provision is also offered. The College aims to enable students to develop and enhance independent living, social, personal and, where appropriate, vocational skills which match their individual needs and expectations.

Students catered for: Young adults (16+), from across the UK, with learning difficulties, communication difficulties and autistic spectrum disorders.

Premises and facilities

The College is situated in a residential area of the rapidly growing village of Sileby, between Loughborough and Leicester. Sileby has good transport links, including a railway station and bus services to local towns and cities.

Student accommodation

On-site accommodation for 17 residential students, with up to four more students at a College house in a nearby village and a number of other houses in the community for long-term student residents.

Staffing

Homefield College has a variety of appropriately qualified teaching staff who work closely with a large team of support workers. However, all members of staff who have contact with the students are involved in contributing to the students' day-to-day learning.

Courses

All students need a small, highly structured and supportive environment as a precursor to learning and confidence-building. The College is open 38 weeks a year, with three academic terms; up to 45 week provision is, if appropriate, available. The students are, ordinarily, at Homefield for three years. The College curriculum includes independent living, literacy, numeracy and communiciation (LNC), pre-vocational learning and personal/social development. Students have individually-designed learning programmes, in order to fully meet their needs and learning styles. Homefield College is City & Guilds registered and also offers external vocational accreditation, where appropriate. On-site courses are complemented by the use of local generalised colleges.

Links

Students are encouraged to participate as fully as possible in the local community and the College takes full advantage of the many formal and informal learning opportunities provided in the area.

Other information

There is access to specialist support services and medical professionals. Student participation in social, leisure and sporting activities is actively encouraged.

Application procedure

Referrals are welcome from existing schools, Connexions advisers, social workers, parents/guardians and usually involve an introductory visit. If the family wish to pursue the enquiry, a one-day assessment is carried out, which is influenced by information received from previous schools and the family. If the application remains viable, a further assessment takes place over two days, after which places are offered. The funding application process then passes to Connexions and the LSC.

Hope Lodge School and Aspin House

Address: 22 Midanbury Avenue, Bitterne Park, Southampton SO18 4HP

Tel: 02380 634346   **Fax:** 02380 231789

Age range: 4-19

Controlled by: Hampshire Autistic Society

Contact for admissions information: Lucy Wood, Deputy Head Teacher, Post-16 Education. Tel: 02380 766162

Fees: Day — £7,770 per term; residential — £17,750 per term (subject to review and assessed support needs)

Out-of-term contact: Residential always open. Residential Manager: Mike Walsh, Head of Support Services. Tel: 01489 880881.

Aims: The Hampshire Autistic Society is dedicated to improving the quality of life for people within the autistic spectrum.

Students catered for: Hope Lodge School caters for statemented students aged 4-16 with an ASD. Hope Lodge School and Aspin House also cater for post-16 students with ASD and associated behaviours, for whom the School assesses that it can meet their learning and support needs.

Premises and facilities

In September 2004, two new units opened offering tailored packages of care/extended curriculum. Aspin House supports SEN- and LSC-funded learners.

Student numbers

There are 46 students at the school site (28 of these are residential). The residential facility is both weekly and 52-week termly boarding.

Staffing

Basic 1:2 support. Additional support available at increased fee rate.

Courses

Hope Lodge School: KS1 - KS4. Full access to National Curriculum modified to suit individual need.
Post-16: 16-19 curriculum based upon development of lifeskills/lifelong learning skills. National accreditation if appropriate.
Aspin House: 16-19 (LEA and LSC) High-functioning Asperger syndrome/high-functioning autistic students. Access to local sector colleges, work experience and social and communication programmes. Aspin House caters for ten students with ASD who attend local sector college.

Application procedure

Via LEA, social services or LSC.

Horizon School for Children with Autism

Address: Blithbury Road, Blithbury, Rugeley, Staffordshire WS15 3JQ

Tel: 01889 504400　**Fax:** 01889 504010　**Email:** info@horizon-school.co.uk　**Website:** www.horizon-school.co.uk

Age range: 4-19

Controlled by: The Priory Group

Contact for admissions information: The Principal

Out-of-term contact: School office 01889 504400

Fees: Residential — £124,031; Day — £59,535

Aims: To raise standards further in the education of children with autism through a unique approach based on 'Daily Life Therapy'. Aims to allow students to acquire improved levels of emotional stability which will lead to greater opportunity to access the whole curriculum.

Students catered for: Horizon school offers specialist education for young people of both sexes with autism and moderate to severe learning difficulties, and focuses on an active approach to teaching.

Premises and facilities

The school has spacious classrooms with specialist areas for music and art, a fully-equipped medical suite, a large gymnasium and a swimming pool. Outdoor facilities include a basketball court, an adventure playground, playing field with a trim trail round its perimeter and an extensive wooded area.

Student accommodation

Residential accommodation consists of one large Georgian house split into four individual houses with facilities for 24 children, approximately six miles away from school, and two smaller new six-bedded houses adjacent to the school site.

Student numbers

36 residential places and 12 day places.

Staffing

In addition to the school principal, deputy and head of residence there are seven class teachers and school learning assistants, specialist teachers, residential coordinators and residential learning assistants.

Courses

Education is delivered through a 24-hour approach. The curriculum is divided into three main areas: physical education, academics and expressive arts. Students follow courses in the National Curriculum at a suitably differentiated level. Students in Upper School take part in ASDAN and Team Enterprise. The curriculum is specifically designed to target the child's development in five global areas; attention, cooperation, self-awareness, communication and independence.

Links

Students from Horizon School attend Cannock College and Rodbaston Agricultural College. They have links with local primary and secondary schools.

Other information

The school has two speech and language therapists and two school nurses. Horizon has access to the specialist services provided by the Priory Group.

Application procedure

Applications should be made to the school. Referral papers and video footage are then required, following which, if suitable for assessment, the child and parents are invited to the school for a day.

Ivers

Address: Hains Lane, Marnhull, Sturminster Newton, Dorset DT10 1JU

Codes: O F S

Tel: 01258 820164   **Fax:** 01258 820258   **Email:** ivers.college@btinternet.com   **Website:** www.ivers.demon.co.uk

Age range: 18+

Controlled by: Privately owned

Contact for admissions information: Mrs Linda Matthews

Fees: £40,000 to £65,000 dependent on need and weeks in residence

Usual source of funding for students: Social services

Aims: To meet the needs of young adults with learning difficulties in order that they might be able to move on after two or three years to live in the community with a considerable degree of independence. Extended placements can be offered to students who require longer-term support.

Students catered for: Students with moderate/severe learning difficulties. Unrestricted catchment area.

Premises and facilities

Ivers is a small residential establishment for young adults with learning difficulties and/or disabilities. It is registered with Dorset County Council. It provides a homely, caring, personal environment in which young people can mature, develop confidence, learn to relate to other people and acquire skills for life which might enable them to live more independently in the community.

Student accommodation

The large country house, its extensions, large gardens and paddocks are situated in the village of Marnhull, near Sturminster Newton, between Shaftesbury and Sherborne.

Student numbers

20.

Staffing

Each student is assigned a key worker and a personal tutor who form a valuable link between Ivers and home.

Courses

The first term is one of further assessment and when level of support and goals have been determined a detailed care plan is written up. An individual learning plan is also written for each student and an individual timetable set to best meet needs. Careful monitoring of needs and progress towards goals is carried out on a regular basis.

Reviews are held with the student, parents, social workers and any other concerned professionals every six or twelve months, dependent on either need or local authority policy.

Each student follows an individual timetable most appropriate to his or her needs and ability. Emphasis is placed on the acquisition of those life and social skills, which include personal care, laundry, cooking, shopping etc, which will best equip the student for future life. The Ivers curriculum includes the areas of: independent living; animal care/riding; horticulture; art and craft; drama; cookery/healthy eating; IT. Work experience and vocational provision is also offered in addition to a wide range of curriculum areas. If appropriate, accreditation is available through OCR National Skills Profile.

Application procedure

As much written information as possible, from the local authority, school and family is requested. Past history and care plans are taken into careful consideration. Ivers has a policy of visiting a potential student in his/her own home or school environment to make a brief initial assessment. The student's careers adviser, social worker or parents can then visit Ivers. After consideration, a date can be set for an assessment visit of six weeks. During this time the student is observed carefully and given the opportunity to participate in a range of curriculum activities. An assessment of need is made and, if appropriate, an admission date is set.

Jacques Hall (Orchard House)

Address: Harwich Road, Bradfield, Manningtree, Essex CO11 2XW

Codes: M also B I K O P

Tel: 01255 870311   **Fax:** 01255 870377   **Email:** jacqueshall@priorygroup.com   **Website:** www.prioryeducation.com

Age range: 16-18

Controlled by: Priory Group

Contact for admissions information: The Principal

Fees: From £2,900 per week

Usual source of funding for students: Social services (children's services), education and health authorities

Aims: Orchard House is a unique residential unit which offers 52-week residential placements providing a 'higher' education in life development skills.

Students catered for: Young people aged between 16-18 who have experienced emotional deprivation and have conduct and emotional difficulties.

Premises and facilities

A well-designed house on the outskirts of Clacton (Essex).

Student accommodation

The house provides four individual en-suite bedrooms and an adjacent annexe has two independent/self-contained bedsits.

Student numbers

Maximum of six.

Staffing

A professional team of 14 residential care workers, providing 24/7 support, supported by a multi-disciplinary senior management team and specialist consultants.

Courses

Individually-tailored programmes utilising local colleges and work-based training providers, building on interim 'lifeskills' and 'independence' packages (including work experience).

Links

Local further education colleges providing a broad range of academic and vocational courses.

Other information

Visiting professionals include an educational psychologist, consultant adolescent psychiatrist and art therapist.

Application procedure

Contact the Admissions Officer at Jacques Hall (Tel: 01255 870311).

Kisimul School

Address: Acacia Hall, Shortwood Lane, Friesthorpe, Lincolnshire LN3 5AL

Code: S

Tel: 01673 880022   **Fax:** 01673 880021   **Email:** info@kisimul.co.uk   **Website:** www.kisimul.co.uk

Age range: 16-19

Controlled by: DfES

Contact for admissions information: Headteacher, Mrs Margaret Daborn

Fees: Upon application

Aims: To provide a caring and homely environment at all times where pupils can grow and develop their skills, individuality and independence.

Students catered for: Must have severe learning difficulties and challenging behaviour.

Premises and facilities

The school is split so that 16-19 year olds are educated and cared for on a separate site. This is situated at Acacia Hall, within the small Lincolnshire village of Friesthorpe. The school building itself has been purposely built with the 16+ curriculum in mind and there are eight acres of very pleasant grounds comprising playing fields, playground, adventure playground, animal paddocks and menage. The extensive grounds are used for horticulture and animal husbandry.

Student accommodation

The 18 residential places at Acacia are mostly single bedrooms with en-suites.

Staffing

Usually 1:1.

Courses

The 16+ curriculum incorporates vocational studies including horticulture and caring for animals and includes ASDAN qualifications.

Other information

Residential, open all year; only closed for two weeks at Christmas.

Langdon College

Address: Leicester Avenue, Salford M7 4HA

Codes: B C F I J K L M N O S

Tel: 0161 740 5900   **Fax:** 0161 741 2500   **Email:** admin@langdoncollege.ac.uk   **Website:** www.langdon.info

Age range: 6-19

Controlled by: Arthur O'Brien

Contact for admissions information: Arthur O'Brien

Usual source of funding for students: Learning & Skills Council

Aims: To provide further education to young Jewish people who cannot access appropriate provision at their local college because of learning difficulties or any other reason.

Students catered for: The College will strive to provide for any young Jewish person who cannot attend their local college.

Premises and facilities

Main college building; four student houses; two student flats; access to other FE colleges; good community resources.

Student accommodation

Ranging from 24-hour staffed accommodation to unstaffed flats allowing appropriate levels of staff support.

Student numbers

Up to 25.

Staffing

Ratio of 1:3 staff to students on average.

Courses

Literacy, numeracy, communication, self-help skills. Any vocational or academic course required. This range of choice is possible because of formal arrangements with local FE colleges.

Links

Bury College, Manchester College of Art and Technology, City College, Hopwood Hall College.

Application procedure

Visit website www.langdon.info or phone 0161 740 5900.

L'Arche

Codes: C E J K O Q S T

Address: 10 Briggate, Silsden, Keighley, West Yorkshire BD20 9JT

Tel: 01535 656186   **Fax:** 01535 656426   **Email:** info@larche.org.uk   **Website:** www.larche.org.uk

Age range: 18+

Controlled by: Board of Trustees

Contact for admissions information: Secretariat (Silsden)

Fees: Negotiated according to need

Aims: That people with learning disabilities and their assistants share life and work together, living as families rather than as clients and staff.

Students catered for: Provides residential care for adults with learning disabilities in Kent, Lambeth, Liverpool, Bognor Regis, Brecon, Inverness, Edinburgh and Preston.

Premises and facilities

A community usually comprises a number of houses within walking distance of each other. Larger communities have workshop/garden project/therapy facilities.

Student accommodation

Members and assistants live in equal numbers in ordinary houses.

Staffing

Generally 1:1.

Links

Links with local churches, colleges and other social facilities are encouraged.

Other information

Members of the clergy visit regularly. Other 'friends' are welcome.

Application procedure

Initial enquiry to central office at Silsden, then referral to a community.

Larchfield Community

Address: Stokesley Road, Hemlington, Middlesbrough TS8 9DY

Tel: 01642 593688/597800   **Fax:** 01642 595778   **Website:** www.camphill.org.uk

Age range: 21+

Controlled by: Camphill Village Trust Communities

Usual source of funding for students: Local authority — which includes state benefits

Aims: Working urban fringe community first initiated between Middlesbrough Council and Camphill Village Trust. Offers training schemes for people with learning difficulties.

Students catered for: Adults from 21 years with learning difficulties.

Premises and facilities

Larchfield is a land-based community on the southern fringe of Middlesbrough, where ultimately 60 people will live and work together in a therapeutic community based around market gardening, farming, food processing and craft work. Facilities include: Larchfield Foods — butchery and food processing; Larchfield Bakery — production bakery; Wheelhouse Coffee Bar — volunteers manning coffee bar in mornings for community; woodwork shop; weavery; organic shop.

Staffing

Co-workers as part of the community.

Courses

Training places available in car mechanic workshop and all other areas.
Farming and horticulture provide the community with a varied workload as there is much to do to develop the land into a properly working bio-dynamic farm, as well as a market garden.

Links

Middlesbrough Borough Council and Council for Voluntary Service, Middlesbrough Social Services, North Yorkshire Social Services and other social services departments, and other Camphill Communities.

Application procedure

Clinic for residential placements. Local (Middlesbrough) Social Services department for day placements.

Lindeth College

Address: The Oaks, Lindeth, Bowness-on-Windermere, Cumbria LA23 3NH

Code: O

Tel: 015394 46265 **Fax:** 015394 88840 **Email:** administrator@lindeth-college.ac.uk

Age range: 16-25

Controlled by: Craegmoor Healthcare

Contact for admissions information: College Administrator

Out-of-term contact: As above

Fees: LSC fees matrix

Usual source of funding for students: LSC

Aims: Lindeth College is committed to providing quality further education and training for people with learning difficulties and disabilities to enable them to achieve their full potential within a caring, supportive and inclusive residential environment.

Students catered for: Lindeth College has a country-wide catchment area and caters for young people with moderate or severe learning difficulties.

Premises and facilities

A seven-acre campus comprising a main building, office, education buildings and six training houses.

Student accommodation

17 students are accommodated in the main house, some in shared bedrooms. Other students reside in the training cottages which have five students per house.

Student numbers

The College has 46 residential places and six day places available.

Staffing

The College has 50 staff comprising of teachers, residential support workers, learning support assistants and ancillary staff.

Courses

Individual learning programmes are based on independent living skills, literacy, numeracy and vocational skills. The latter includes internal and external work placements, horticulture and catering. Students work towards external accreditation where appropriate. The focus for most students is independent living skills, which are promoted through the extended curriculum in addition to the formal curriculum. The College has an evening and weekend leisure programme in which students are encouraged to participate.

Links

The College has an extensive range of work experience placements provided by local employers.

Other information

A speech and language therapist supports students with communication needs on an individual or group basis.

Application procedure

Referrals are accepted from the Connexions service, families, or social services. Following the completion of an application form suitable applicants are offered an assessment.

Linkage College

Codes: B C D E F H J K L N O Q R S T

Address: Weelsby Campus, Weelsby Road, Grimsby, NE Lincolnshire. DN32 9RU

Tel: 01472 241044   **Fax:** 01472 242375   **Email:** info@linkage.org.uk   **Website:** www.linkage.org.uk

Age range: 16-25

Controlled by: Linkage Community Trust

Contact for admissions information: The Transition Administrator: 01472 372400

Out-of-term contact: Pat Lill: 01472 890339

Fees: Individually determined

Usual source of funding for students: Learning and Skills Council

Aims: The College aims to create a stimulating environment based on a curriculum which provides academic, vocational and social development for young adults with learning difficulties and other disabilities. The College supports every student working towards realising his/her full potential for independence and a happy and fulfilling life.

Students catered for: Will consider applications from people with a wide range of disabilities including moderate or severe learning disabilities, Down's syndrome, speech and language difficulties, autism, Asperger's syndrome, visual and hearing impairments, epilepsy, Williams syndrome and other physical disabilities.

Premises and facilities

Linkage College comprises of two campuses in Lincolnshire. Toynton Hall is situated in the rural town of Spilsby and Weelsby Campus in the urban town of Grimsby. Facilities include realistic environments for vocational and enrichment courses e.g. catering kitchens, drama and art studios. Industrial units separate from the campuses provide vocational courses.

Student accommodation

Student accommodation is of a high standard and is based either within their respective main halls or houses in the community. The majority are CSCI registered.

Student numbers

206 residential places and 20 day placements between two campuses

Staffing

The college has a generous complement of professional, specialist and experienced staff which includes a psychologist, professional counsellors, speech therapist, visual impairment specialist, emotional literacy coordinator, plus a nurse at each campus.

Courses

All students have individually-planned courses which are regularly monitored. Courses include Skills for Life, (which incorporates literacy, numeracy and information technology) vocational and enrichment programmes. There is a comprehensive and progressive programme aimed at developing social and independent living skills. There is a strong emphasis on the integration of students into the community and local facilities, including sports and recreational provision, social and entertainment venues and local colleges, are accessed fully by Linkage students.

Links

Linkage College has further education links with Grimsby Institute, Boston College and First College — Louth. There are good links with local businesses that provide work-experience placements for Linkage College students.

Other information

Linkage College can access physiotherapists, occupational therapist etc where necessary. Linkage College has recently opened 'A Quiet Place' in conjunction with the University of Liverpool which offers a six-week programme on relaxation and stress and anger management.

Application procedure

Visits can be arranged via the College transition team on 01472 372400. Interested parties will be invited to visit the College. Following this a formal application can be made. Prospective students are then invited for an assessment.

The Loddon School

Address: Wildmoor Lane, Sherfield-on-Loddon, Hook, Hampshire RG27 0JD

Codes: C S

Tel: 01256 882394   **Fax:** 01256 882929   **Email:** m.redmill@loddonschool.co.uk

Website: www.loddon-school.demon.co.uk/

Age range: 8-18

Controlled by: The Loddon School Trust

Contact for admissions information: Maurice Redmill, Principal

Out-of-term contact: As above

Fees: Dependent upon need

Aims: To provide education for children with severe learning difficulties and challenging behaviour and autism.

Students catered for: Children with severe learning difficulties and challenging behaviour and autism. London and home counties preferred.

Premises and facilities

The school is situated five miles from Basingstoke in a Victorian country house. Children live in one of two individually-staffed units on a family basis. The School concentrates also on communication, relationship building and the functional lifeskills curriculum.

Student accommodation

Children have single bedrooms.

Student numbers

28.

Staffing

150 staff: teachers, psychology assistants, care workers, occupational therapist, music therapist, speech and language therapist, osteopath, drama therapist.

Courses

The curriculum is individualised and personalised using the School's specially developed Personalised Learning for Life Using Supportive Strategies (PLLUSS) and Positive Approaches: PROACT-SCIPS-UK®, which it delivers nationally.

Links

Parent courses are helpful to families and ensure continuity of management and consistency of approach. Liaise Loddon Ltd is developing houses in the community for school leavers.

Other information

Music therapy, aromatherapy, osteopathy and sensory work are important features used to facilitate communication, reduce stress and encourage relationship building.

Application procedure

Initial contact via School office, followed by sending of data regarding the child. Visits by school staff to assess.

Loppington House FE Unit and Adult Centre

Address: Loppington House, Loppington, Near Wem, Shropshire SY4 5NF

Tel: 01939 233926   **Fax:** 01939 235255   **Email:** office@loppingtonhouse.co.uk

Age range: 18+

Controlled by: Loppington House Ltd (Registered with CSCI)

Contact for admissions information: Main Office

Out-of-term contact: Open 52 weeks a year

Fees: Assessed to the individual

Usual source of funding for students: LSC, social services and health (PCT)

Aims: The mission of the College is to provide further education and training for learners to achieve their full potential.

Students catered for: Young people with learning difficulties, disabilities and associated behavioural problems are accepted, and are referred from all over the country.

Premises and facilities

Loppington House is the main site of a privately-owned establishment which consists of a Further Education Unit and Adult Centre. There are two residential units within the main house, three other units on the main site and further accommodation on the sites sites at Wem town and at Whittington.

Student accommodation

Loppington House offers day services and accommodation for 36 learners. Provision is split. Situated in the main house are 16 young adults aged 18-25. Those aged 25+ are situated in satellite units.

Staffing

Qualified/experienced staff specific to the individual learner. Staff to learner ratio 1:1. Staffed 24 hours a day.

Courses

The curriculum is dedicated to living skills. Learners follow a specific programme related to individual needs (inclusive learning). The Essential Skills Award, literacy, numeracy and communication are taught through: art/craft; projects; lifeskills; gardening; residential. In their last year of study, learners may access the College's own shop and workshop situated within the local town. All learners are supported to take an active role in the learning process

Links

Learners are given the opportunity to attend an external college. Work experience is provided via the College's own shop and workshop.

Other information

Speech and language therapy; community health professionals; gymnastics; horse riding; swimming; music; enrichment activities.

Application procedure

Application procedure can be obtained via the main office.

Lufton College of Further Education

Address: Lufton, Yeovil, Somerset BA22 8ST

Tel: 01935 403120   **Fax:** 01935 403126   **Email:** tess.baber@mencap.org.uk   **Website:** www.mencap.org.uk

Age range: 16-25

Controlled by: MENCAP

Contact for admissions information: Tess Baber, Principal

Aims: Students focus on developing the personal, social and practical skills needed to live life independently.

Students catered for: Students with moderate/severe learning difficulties.

Premises and facilities

Two sites on the rural outskirts of Yeovil, with extensive grounds, including a small animal and rare breeds farm, woodland, gardens, glasshouses and a café open to the public. The community facilities of Yeovil, Taunton and surrounding area provide a wide range of leisure facilities.

Student accommodation

Accommodation ranges from sheltered to self-catering within the grounds. Houses in Yeovil provide progression opportunities for living in the community.

Student numbers

116 students, mixed.

Staffing

130+ staff.

Courses

Students enrol at any time for a two- or three-year course. Following an induction and initial assessment period, an individual learning plan is produced. Students have an individual timetable including: daily living skills; personal care and presentation; community and leisure; numeracy, literacy and communication and practical/ vocational skills. An extended curriculum enables students to enjoy recreational, arts and leisure activities on site and access the community in the evenings and weekends. All students follow Mencap National College Essential Skills Award and receive internal accreditation. Vocational areas offered include: small animal care, agriculture, horticulture, catering, office skills, grounds maintenance and car valeting in a fully equipped workshop. A small number of day students can follow the Mencap Essential Skills Award and a countryside studies course as a step towards study or employment.

Links

Links are well established with local FE colleges for students to access part-time courses. Students from other colleges regularly visit Lufton College as part of link work and delivery of agriculture-based courses. As students progress, opportunities for work experience placements in the community are arranged.

Application procedure

Forms available during pre-booked visits. Full residential assessment period.

MacIntyre School

Address: Leighton Road, Wingrave, Bucks HP22 4PD

Tel: 01296 681274   **Fax:** 01296 681091   **Email:** wingrave@macintyrecharity.org   **Website:** www.macintyrecharity.org

Age range: 10-19

Controlled by: MacIntyre

Contact for admissions information: Adrienne Barnes, Head of Education

Out-of-term contact: Ann Bailey, Head of Admin

Fees: £170,000 p.a.

Usual source of funding for students: Local authorities

Aims: MacIntyre School provides children and young people with a happy and secure environment where they can be challenged to achieve in all areas of their lives. Expectations are high, so that all students learn to make real choices in their lives.

Student catered for: Students with severe learning difficulties, ASD, communication difficulties and challenging behaviour.

Premises and facilities

Six modern residential houses. Classes currently in an old manor house. A new school is being built on the site — proposed opening date January 2007 — which will provide a range of new facilities.

Student accommodation

Six purpose-built residential units housing six students in each.

Student numbers

36.

Staffing

All staff are appointed after an enhanced CRB clearance. Selection reflects individual enthusiasm, qualifications, training and experience appropriate to the level of responsibility.

Courses

Students aged up to 16 are given access to the National Curriculum. It is modified to meet the needs of the students and encompasses a full range of learning opportunities. The Further Education Department follows the Equals Moving On curriculum and will gain accreditation through the AQA Award Scheme.

Other information

Speech and language therapists; art therapists; drama therapist; physiotherapists; clinical psychologist; occupational therapist.

Application procedure

We accept referrals at anytime, usually from local authority education or social services departments.

Mary Hare Grammar School for the Deaf

Address: Arlington Manor, Snelsmore Common, Newbury, Berkshire RG14 3BQ

Code: H

Tel: 01635 244200   **Minicom:** 01635 244260   **Fax:** 01635 248019   **Email:** school@maryhare.org.uk
Website: www.maryhare.org.uk

Age range: 11-19

Contact for admission information: Principal, Mr DAJ Shaw

Controlled by: Mary Hare Schools

Fees: 2006/7: £27,840 (boarding) p.a. and £23,800 (day) p.a.

Aims: To offer a broad curriculum to severely and profoundly hearing-impaired children. The Sixth Form is built upon the belief that deaf young people are just as capable as their hearing counterparts. The school acknowledges that deafness can be a significant disability and it seeks to provide an environment where that barrier can be overcome.

Students catered for: Hearing-impaired children of above average ability. Co-educational. Entry is possible age 16+ subject to GCSE results.

Premises and facilities

The school has excellent facilities: six science laboratories, large library, sporting facilities, design technology suite, computer suites, open access computer rooms for students, media studies facility, large hall, swimming pools etc. New for 2006/7 is an acoustically-treated performing arts centre.

Student accommodation

There is a 66-bedroom centre on the 140 acre site. Great attention is paid to the amplification needs of the students and also to the layout and design of the classrooms which are all acoustically treated.

Student numbers

Currently 220; groups are small — rarely larger than six or seven — and there is great scope for individual help and support. The school believes that students do best if they are taught through spoken language and for this reason sign language is not used.

Staffing

50 teachers in specialist subject areas who are also teachers of the deaf; two nurses; 36 care staff — three large boarding houses each with Head of House.

Courses

All major National Curriculum courses to GCSE and Advanced level, including those in applied subjects. The school also offers a range of full-time NVQs.

Application procedure

Annual entrance procedure in November. Head teachers' reports and local authority recommendations are taken into consideration. Notification of results to head teachers and local education authorities by Christmas.

Meldreth Manor School

Address: Fenny Lane, Meldreth, Royston, Hertfordshire SG8 6LG

Tel: 01763 268000   **Email:** meldreth.manor@scope.org.uk

Age range: 11-19

Controlled by: SCOPE

Out-of-term contact: Administration office at the school

Fees: On application

Aims: To provide for the specialised educational requirements of young people with physical disabilities and severe or profound learning difficulties.

Students catered for: Those with physical disabilities and severe or profound learning difficulties. The school caters for pupils with additional sensory impairments and medical needs.

Premises and facilities

Purpose-built and resourced school situated in the village of Meldreth, four miles from Royston, ten miles from Cambridge.

Student accommodation

Development of supported living in a range of residential accommodation.

Staffing

Teachers, physiotherapists, speech therapists, nursing staff and support workers. Additional support including music and dance/movement.

Courses

Meldreth Manor School has a commitment to provide an education which is supportive of each pupil's individual needs within a caring and stimulating environment. In order to fulfil this aim, the School, through a considered and balanced 24 hour curriculum, provides a high standard of education and social care with an emphasis upon personal dignity and self-esteem for all pupils.

Links

Meldreth Manor School has established good links with several mainstream schools and colleges with whom activities are often shared. The importance of leisure and recreation is given a high priority, pupils attending youth clubs, Scouts, Guides etc in the local area.

Application procedure

Informal visits welcomed. Assessment for placement arranged on request.

Mental Health Care

Address: Head Office, Alexander House, Highfield Park, Llandyrnog, Denbigh, Denbighshire LL16 4LU

Codes: O P

Tel: 01824 790600 **Fax:** 01824 790341 **Email:** placement@ mentalhealthcare-uk.com
Website: www.mentalhealthcare-uk.com

Age range: 18-64

Contact for admissions information: Placement team

Fees: Vary

Usual source of funding: LHB and NHS trusts

Aims: The company, based in north Wales, provides services, managed within the Care Programme Approach, for those with complex needs including learning disabilities and/or mental health problems.

Students catered for: Clients who may be detained, within community based care homes and independent hospitals, under the Mental Health Act (1983). Nationwide catchment area.

Premises and facilities

Environments specially designed to provide gender specific care pathways for individuals.

Staffing

High level nurse to patient ratio to meet the needs of the individual.

Courses

A comprehensive pre-placement assessment of the individual using the HoNOS assessment tool; a comprehensive assessment, completed within 13 weeks of admission, that includes a multidisciplinary approach to risk assessment and management; a realistic approach to resettlement of clients, including creating opportunities for learning and re-establishing the client's place in society.

Links

Local community work-based placements offered. Courses at the local FE college offered.

Other information

Psychiatric and psychology input available in-house, together with OT services.

Application procedure

Completion of MHC's application form to be forwarded to the placement team. Assessment then arranged with appropriate placing authority.

The Minstead Training Project

Code: O

Address: Minstead Lodge, Minstead, Lyndhurst, Hants, SO43 7FT

Tel: 023 8081 2254   **Fax:** 023 8081 2297   **Email:** mtp@milestonenet.co.uk

Age range: 18-30 residential (18+ day)

Controlled by: Peter Selwood Charitable Trust

Contact for admissions information: By telephone or fax

Out-of-term contact: as above (52-week service)

Fees: Residential from £507 pw; day from £196 pw

Usual source of funding for students: Social services, direct payment, health (not LSC)

Aims: To provide and deliver responsive training in work, life and social skills to people who have learning disabilities, thus enabling them to realise their full potential and achieve a level of independence appropriate to their ability.

Students catered for: Students with learning disabilities/difficulties, nationwide. Day students also catered for.

Premises and facilities

Large country house set in 17 acres of land comprising fields, ornamental and kitchen gardens, greenhouse and workshop; a further eight acres comprising public garden/tea room/art gallery/nursery and sales area. Swimming pool on main site.

Student accommodation

14 single bedrooms in small flats with wash basin in each. Toilets, showers, baths and kitchenette in each flat.

Student numbers

14 residential places and approximately 36 day places.

Staffing

Two /three care staff on duty. One sleeping staff (no waking night staff). Training instructors during the day.

Courses

Residential: training in all aspects of life and social skills. Day: horticultural training in fruit and vegetable growing, nursery production, greenhouse work, landscaping and garden maintenance. Woodwork and craft workshop offers creative opportunities to achieve with hand and machine skills. Literary, numeracy and information technology support all areas of practical training. Work experience in real work settings.

Links

Other courses such as music, drama, photography are provided on site by external college. Wide range of work experiences.

Other information

Can access local specialist healthcare team where required.
Domiciliary team supports some community-based houses after students leave the residential accommodation where this is appropriate. Closed for Easter and Christmas periods.

Application procedure

Information request. Individual visit. Application (our referral form, care plan and other external reports). Residential trial stay (small fee is charged). Trial stay report provided.

Motherwell College

Address: Dalzell Drive, Motherwell ML1 2DD

Tel: 01698 232323 **Fax:** 01698 232527 **Email:** mcol@motherwell.ac.uk **Website:** www.motherwell.ac.uk

Age range: 16-60

Controlled by: College Board of Management.

Contact for admissions information: Customer services, student services, Support for Learning Department

Out-of-term-contact: As above

Fees: Various depending on course.

Usual source of funding for students: Bursaries, Scottish Funding Council, Student Awards Agency for Scotland.

Aims: Motherwell College aims to enrich lives. The College closes the opportunity gap by removing barriers to participation and exclusion, and provides lifelong learning opportunities to promote employability, develop personal and employment skills and encourage achievement and progression.

Students catered for: The College, in addition to its mainstream vocational courses, provides full-time/part-time, day-release/link and evening classes for students who are physically disabled, sensory impaired, communication impaired and those with learning difficulties from schools and adult resource centres locally and nationally.

Premises and facilities

Motherwell College is a community college providing further education to individuals of all ages and abilities, both locally and nationally, through a choice of courses at advanced and non-advanced levels.

Motherwell College is within easy reach of the town centre, which has excellent transport links by bus and rail to the rest of Scotland. It is minutes away from Strathclyde Park which has facilities for a variety of leisure pursuits. The College provides easy access for disabled students by means of ramps and lifts. Stewart Hall of Residence is situated on the campus and provides accommodation for 46 students.

Student accommodation

Fully accessible Hall of residence on campus.

Student numbers

1,000 (out of 20,000 enrolled students) have additional support needs.

Staffing

300 academic staff; 200 support staff plus out-sourced support staff.
The College is committed to professional training and development of its staff.

Courses

Extensive range of courses at all levels, pre-vocational to degree level. Courses include vocational, personal development and leisure opportunities.

Links

Partnership arrangements with: 35 secondary schools, 30 schools for students with ASN, 14 social work departments, local authorities and employers.

Application procedure

Students are encouraged to talk to the College about their aspirations and needs.

The Mount Camphill Community

Codes: M O

Address: Faircrouch Lane, Wadhurst, East Sussex TN5 6PT

Tel: 01892 782025   **Fax:** 01892 782917   **Email:** office@mountcamphill.org   **Website:** www.camphill.org.uk

Age range: 16-25

Controlled by: Member of Association of Camphill Communities

Fees: Vary

Aims: To provide education, training and community living for adolescents and young adults in need of special understanding in such a way that the full potential of each member of the community is developed to the full.

Students catered for: A wide range of learning difficulties and emotional disturbances. Students are admitted from the age of 16 to foundation course, to complete their pre-college education, and from the age of 18 to the college. Students from principally South and East England.

Premises and facilities

The estate comprises approximately 20 acres of pasture and woodland and includes a two-acre walled garden and orchard. The facilities also include a sports hall and an area for outside games.

Student accommodation

The main building was formerly a Victorian monastery; in addition there are two houses where a more family-type atmosphere prevails and a fourth house which provides the opportunity for more independent living. Students and staff live together in the community.

Staffing

60 individuals including teachers, craft teachers and other co-workers. Co-workers and students live together in family units, sharing responsibility for the management and upkeep of the houses. Resident co-workers trained in curative education, youth guidance and social therapy work together with younger resident co-workers. Other specialist teachers and therapists work on a daily basis.

Courses

Some day places are available. Pupils receive a full creative schooling based on the Waldorf curriculum of Rudolf Steiner. From 18 students at the college specialise in a particular craft or work area — baking, woodwork, horticulture, pottery, weaving and cooking and catering. Some City & Guilds courses are followed. Individual tuition is given in literacy and numeracy where appropriate. In their final year of college, the students spend three or four weeks in another Camphill Community. Students may remain at The Mount after the end of college and take a more active part in the work of the community as part of their preparation for the transition to adult life.

Links

The Mount works closely with other Camphill Rudolf Steiner Communities and has a number of links with other educational establishments in Kent and East Sussex. There is an active relationship with the local secondary school.

Other information

The cultural life within the community is built around the celebration of the Christian festivals.

Application procedure

Please telephone for a brochure or write to The Admissions Group giving a brief description of your enquiry. A recent report on a student is required before offering an interview.

Nash College

Address: Croydon Road, Hayes, Bromley, Kent BR2 7AG

Codes: O R

Tel: 020 8462 7419   **Fax:** 020 8462 0347   **Website:** www.shaftesbury.org.uk

Age range: 19-25

Controlled by: The Shaftesbury Society

Fees: On request

Usual source of funding for students: Most students are funded by the LSC with help from their social services departments.

Aims: To provide high quality education and training for young adults with physical and learning disabilities.

Students catered for: Physical and learning disabilities with associated communication or sensory difficulties.

Premises and facilities

Nash College is a residential college for young people. The College is situated in a lovely wooded site but very close to Bromley for shopping trips and only 30 minutes from Central London. The College has excellent up-to-date computer facilities and is also a centre of excellence for the use of voice output communication aids.

Student accommodation

Whilst most residential students live on site there is an opportunity for progression to living in the community.

Staffing

A multi-disciplinary team of teachers, classroom assistants, technicians, nurses, therapists, counsellors and carers.

Courses

Courses range from independence skills to City and Guilds courses, catering for the whole range of physical and learning disabilities— provided that the students can benefit from what the College has to offer. Amongst the many subjects on offer are horticulture, business studies, catering and art. Nash College also specialises in teaching young people with no speech to use voice output communication aids.

Links

Many students take some of their courses at local mainstream colleges.

Other information

The College has a visiting GP, medical consultants, orthotists and wheelchair maintenance team. The College also offers respite care for students during the holidays.

Application procedure

To the Principal or receptionist at the above address who will arrange a visit and assessment.

N.B. *This entry has not been updated by the establishment for this edition. Please check details.*

The National Centre for Young People with Epilepsy

Address: St Piers Lane, Lingfield, Surrey RH7 6PW

Tel: 01342 832243   **Fax:** 01342 834639   **Email:** info@ncype.org.uk   **Website:** www.ncype.org.uk

Age range: 5-25

Controlled by: Board of trustees

Contact for admissions information: Mandy Richmond, Admissions Coordinator

Fees: Please contact admissions for further information

Usual source of funding for students: LEA, LSC, health services, social services

Aims: The NCYPE works to increase awareness and dispel the myths surrounding epilepsy. It is the UK's major provider of specialist services and the voice of childhood epilepsy, striving to make a positive impact on the lives of children and young people across the UK.

Students catered for: The NCYPE provides day and residential special education services for students through its St Piers School and St Piers Further Education College.

Premises and facilities

Set in over 200-acres of Surrey countryside, close to Kent and Sussex borders, the NCYPE has its own onsite medical centre, 20 student residential houses and working farm and horticultural complex. It also offers a variety of recreational facilities including a full size sports hall, playgrounds and toy library.

Student accommodation

Accommodation is available onsite for students attending the school and college, including a children's home available 52 weeks a year.

Student numbers

161.

Staffing

Staff include teachers and support staff, paediatric neurologists, nurses, clinical specialists, speech and language therapists, psychologists, occupational therapists, physiotherapists, and administrative staff.

Courses

St Piers School offers the National Curriculum differentiated to meet student needs. Accredited courses at Keystage 4, National Skills Profile, ALL project. The College offers externally accredited programmes including Open College units, vocational entry and foundation programmes, DL and NVQs.

Links

The NCYPE is a member of the Tandridge Consortium for school and colleges, working closely with local sector colleges.

Other information

Europe's first professor of childhood epilepsy — The Prince of Wales's Chair in Childhood Epilepsy — is based partly at the NCYPE.

Application procedure

Informal enquiries are welcome through the Admissions Coordinator. Following a formal application and informal visit, prospective students are considered for a placement visit leading to a potential placement.

The National Society for Epilepsy

Address: Chesham Lane, Chalfont St Peter, Buckingham SL9 0RJ

Tel: 01494 601300   **Fax:** 01494 871927   **Helpline:** 01494 601400   **Website:** www.epilepsynse.org.uk

Age range: 18+

Controlled by: National Society for Epilepsy

Contact for admissions information: Chief Executive: Mr Graham Faulkner

Usual source of funding for students: NHS-funded Assessment Service

Aims: To eradicate epilepsy in all its forms and, in the meantime, to strive for improvements in the medical treatments; to improve the clinical and care services provided to people with epilepsy by NSE and health professionals everywhere; to increase public understanding about epilepsy as a medical condition and how to respond appropriately to a seizure; to get accurate, understandable and relevant health information to all people with epilepsy and their carers.

Students catered for: Male and female, all of whom have epilepsy. People with additional learning or physical disabilities are also accepted. Longer term care and respite care are provided. Catchment area: nationwide.

Premises and facilities

The Society offers a full range of facilities for people with epilepsy as both inpatients and outpatients.

Student numbers

The centre has approximately 200 long-term residents, in addition to NHS assessment unit patients.

Staffing

The centre is committed to a multi-disciplinary approach to the needs of people with epilepsy. There are over 450 staff comprising medical and paramedical, administrative and ancillary, nursing and care, social work, teaching and occupational personnel.

Courses

Work placements are found for residents with local employers. More information about the work of the centre can be obtained from the education department.

Links

College courses, ranging from reading and writing through to GCSE and A levels, are arranged at a local college for residents who wish to take a course.

Other information

The centre runs regular courses on all aspects of epilepsy for staff and external organisations and regular half day seminars covering basic information about epilepsy.

Application procedure

People are generally referred by their GPs or hospital consultants. Waiting time varies.

National Star College

Address: Ullenwood, Cheltenham, Gloucestershire GL53 9QU

Codes: A E O Q R S

Tel: 01242 527631   **Fax:** 01242 222234   **Email:** enquiries@natstar.ac.uk   **Website:** www.natstar.ac.uk

Age range: 16-25

Controlled by: Indep, DfES rec.

Contact for admissions information: Mary Hussey, Admissions Officer

Out-of-term contact: Mary Hussey, Admissions Officer

Fees: LSC Funding Matrix

Usual source of funding for students: LSC

Aims: A specialist community college providing programmes of education, training and personal development for young people with disabilities from all over the UK. Students access further education courses and have the opportunity to learn about living more independently in a range of purpose-built accommodation/facilities.

Students catered for: Students with physical disabilities, acquired brain injury and/or complex medical conditions.

Premises and facilities

In the Cotswold countryside within easy reach of Cheltenham and Gloucester. Excellent road, rail and air links. Specialist and fully accessible facilities include professional design and photographic studios, theatre, life skills centre, Karten CTEC information technology centre, sports/fitness centres, heated indoor pool, computer suites, assistive technology suite.

Student accommodation

Accommodation options exist on main campus and in the local community within the cities of Gloucester and Cheltenham.

Student numbers

148 residential plus local day students.

Staffing

Staff with recognised qualifications and experience in care, education and specialist areas – e.g. therapies, nursing and behaviour management. All staff screened in line with prevailing legislation.

Courses

Students build an individual learning programme from a range of course areas and option units. Courses meet the requirements of a wide variety of students. Students may access vocational courses directly or work through pre-vocational programmes. Skills for Adult Life or Skills for Working Life. Work experience and external links with employers form a vital part of the curriculum experience.

Visit the College website for further information about courses and qualifications.

Links

Good links with the local community. Member of Federation of Gloucestershire Colleges. Employer engagement strategies — work placements for students.

Other information

Regular GP surgeries held at the College during the week.

Application procedure

Contact the Admissions Office or email enquiries@natstar.ac.uk. Book appointment to attend monthly Visit Open Day. Subsequently, if placement is appropriate, book full assessment.

NCW (New College Worcester)

Address: Whittington Road, Worcester WR5 2JX

Code: D

Tel: 01905 763933   **Fax:** 01905 763277   **Email:** kcampbell@rnibncw.ac.uk   **Website:** www.rnibncw.ac.uk

Age range: 11-19

Controlled by: RNIB. Independent Autumn 2006

Contact for admissions information: Kate Campbell, Liaison Teacher

Out-of-term contact: Reception manned 9-12 noon Mon - Fri

Fees: Full boarding £38,349-£40,461; weekly £34,638-£36,534; day £25,974-£28,080

Usual source of funding for students: Fees payable by LEA/LSC

Aims: To be a centre of excellence, providing blind and visually impaired students with the means to develop the knowledge, skills and personal qualities they need to succeed in education, work and life. Students follow a carefully graded programme of mobility and living skills and enjoy sports, music, drama, clubs, outings and every kind of outdoor pursuit.

Students catered for: Blind and partially sighted, associated conditions catered for, ASD, ASP, HI, VI, WA2.

Premises and facilities

Greenfield and spacious site with an open outlook to the Malvern Hills, on the outskirts of Worcester, on the A44 a mile from Junction 7 of the M5. The centre of the city is within walking distance or there is a bus service. Five science laboratories, drama and art studios, extensive music rooms and recording studio, new Learning Resource Centre, wireless network, Independent Living Skills and Mobility departments. 25 metre swimming pool, running track, football, cricket and athletics pitch, gym and multi-gym.

Student accommodation

Three student houses, male, female and mixed supported by a house parent and two gap-year students who live in. 6th form hostel with self contained 'flats' similar to a hall of residence.

Student numbers

75 total: senior 36, 6th form 39; male 42, female 33.

Staffing

23 full-time and 15 part-time teaching staff. Teacher pupil ratio 1:2.5, average class size 4, The College aims never to exceed 10 in a teaching group. Subject specialists and qualified in teaching visually-impaired students.

Courses

Access to the full National Curriculum. Students take eight or nine GCSEs, AS and A level courses. 24 subjects offered at AS and A2 level. 95% go on to higher education.

Links

Outreach programme, low vision clinic in conjunction with South Worcestershire Primary Care Trust.

Application procedure

Informal visit followed by application form. Applicants then invited to a four-day residential assessment which gives a taste of school life. Provisional offer, full report sent to LEA to support funding application.

Nexus Direct (The Hall)

Address: Mill House, Bowl Road, Charing, Ashford, Kent

Tel: 01233 713857   **Fax:** 01233 714974   **Email:** nexusdirect1@aol.com

Age range: 16+

Controlled by: Mr A Rogers

Contact for admissions information: Mr Duncan Cotton (Placement Manager)

Fees: £85,000 pa

Usual source of funding for students: Social services

Aims: To provide care and support to young adults and adults with learning difficulties, who present mild to moderate challenging behaviour. Holistic programme with emphasis on employment, training and competence leading to independent living. To equip residents with a wide range of skills geared towards facilitating their successful integration into community based services.

Students catered for: Young adults with learning difficulties who present mild to moderate challenging behaviour.

Premises and facilities

An old converted church hall set in a village close to the towns of Ashford and Maidstone as well as the ports and coastal resorts of Folkestone, Dover and Hastings. Spacious accommodation, TV and satellite, radio lounges, sport and leisure.

Student accommodation

Single rooms, furnished and fitted with a wash basin.

Student numbers

The hall houses nine service users.

Staffing

Ratio of 1:2; five academic staff, senior team leaders; team leaders; supporters/carers; sleep-in/waking carers.

Courses

Vocational training — college attendance, work experience, employment acquisition, training etc. Life and social skills training — image enhancement, domestic skills training, community access skills etc. Life planning — fulfilment of ambition, personal development programmes, social support programmes, the 'Challenge, Excitement, Fun!' module. Holidays included in fees. Programme runs 52 weeks per year.

Links

The home accesses FE colleges, other special needs schools if required and local employers.

Other information

Psychiatrist, psychotherapist, counsellors, behavioural therapist, chiropodist.

Application procedure

By letter/telephone call/email to the Placements Officer, Mr Duncan Cotton 01233 713857 in the first instance.

Northern Counties School

Address: Great North Road, Newcastle upon Tyne NE2 3BB

Codes: A B C D E F G H K M N O Q R S

Tel: 0191 2815821 (Voice and minicom)   **Fax:** 0191 2815060   **Email:** info @northerncounties.newcastle.sch.uk
Website: www.northern-counties-school.co.uk

Age range: 3-19

Contact for admissions information: Headteacher, Judith James

Fees: Secondary: £17,147 p.a. Secondary additionally disabled students: £30,012 p.a. Secondary-age multi-disabled students: £35,841

Aims: Northern Counties provides all age (3-19) day and residential special education for children within a specialist Total Communication environment.

Students catered for: The School provides education for children with sensory impairment, multiple disabilities, autistic spectrum disorder, and a range of complex special needs.

Premises and facilities

Includes hydrotherapy and swimming pools, sensory room, autistic unit, food technology room, ICT suite and indoor and outdoor play areas.

Staffing

Class groups of four to eight. All teachers have specialist qualifications including Teacher of the Deaf, Teacher of the Visually Impaired or Autism. All staff have minimum Stage 1 BSL qualifications. The School also employs specialist tutors of Braille ASALT and mobility.

Courses

All courses are delivered through a Total Communication approach. Specialised teaching ensures all children can access the National Curriculum individually modified to all abilities. KS4 and post-16 students follow nationally accredited courses including Transition Challenge, ASDAN Towards Independence and Unit Awarded Schemes. Therapy is provided on an individual needs basis and all therapy is incorporated in IEP programmes and delivered by the entire class team.

Links

Northern Counties is part of the Percy Hedley Foundation. The Foundation provides comprehensive services including three schools, residential provision, a college, adult day services, an early intervention service and a Family Support Centre.

Nugent House School

Address: Carr Mill Road, Billinge, Wigan WN5 7TT

Codes: M P

Tel: 01744 892551 **Fax:** 01744 895697 **Email:** jenny@nugent.wigan.sch.uk **Website:** www.nugent.wigan.sch.uk

Age range: 7-19

Controlled by: Nugent Care, Liverpool

Fees: Range from £15319 - £29,189

Aims: The education of children with emotional and behavioural disorders, including some with a history of mental health difficulties.

Students catered for: Boys with emotional and behavioural disorders, some with specific learning and mental health problems.

Premises and facilities

Nugent House is a residential and day special school situated in pleasant countryside midway between Liverpool and Manchester. Close proximity to major rail and motorway networks and also International Airport at Manchester. The School is extremely well provided for in terms of facilities, and in addition post-26 students have access to local FE colleges to further their studies. Both termly and 52-week residential care is provided for according to individual needs.

Student accommodation

Post-16 students reside in small communities in specialist semi-independent houses.

Student numbers

68.

Staffing

18.5 teaching staff; 47 residential social work staff; 21 classroom support staff; domestic, maintenance, secretarial and financial staff.

Courses

Nine subjects taken to GCSE level; NVQ; Entry Level; post-16 students access courses at local colleges. Individual study programmes for those requiring modified curriculum.

Links

The School has links with all local FE colleges, psychiatric adolescent unit at Alderhey Hospital, and other special schools in the region.

Application procedure

In the first instance by telephone contact with the headteacher.

Oaklands Park Village Community

Address: Newnham, Gloucestershire GL14 1EF

Tel: 01594 516551   **Fax:** 01594 516821   **Email:** oaklands@camphill.org.uk   **Website:** www.camphill.org.uk

Age range: 21+

Controlled by: Camphill Village Trust

Contact for admissions information: Cecily Bradshaw

Usual source of funding for students: Social services/DWP/Income Support

Aims: Caring about the environment, work, economic and social life and further education, in communities with adults, some of whom have special needs. Providing real, meaningful work, a shared family life, a rich cultural context.

Students catered for: Adults with special needs/learning difficulties.

Premises and facilities

Oaklands Park is a 130-acre estate set between the Forest of Dean and the River Severn. It is particularly active in farm, market garden, forestry and orchard work, and there is also a woodworking shop and, in the village of Newnham, a coffee shop/gallery/toyshop/bookshop complex and weavery.

Student accommodation

Between five and seven residents live in each family house with co-workers and their children.

Student numbers

47 men and women at present.

Staffing

Co-workers receive ongoing training.

Courses

No courses as such are provided, the Village being a community within which each resident can be assisted to individual independence and social adjustment. Christian festivals are celebrated, and there is a very wide range of evening activities: study groups, lectures, dancing, games, music, eurhythmy, acting, sports, reading etc.

Links

There is considerable contact with other 11 Camphill Village Trust communities, and with the local communities of Newnham and Lydney.

Other information

Visiting professionals include art therapist, nurse and chiropodist.

Application procedure

Applications to The Admissions Group. They can be made at the age of 21 onwards. Being put on the waiting list is not joining a queue. The particular needs of each applicant awaiting admission are considered. Forms are completed prior to interview by the medical adviser at Delrow. The waiting list is only made up of those who have had a successful trial visit for a fortnight initially, then for a three-month period when accommodation is available.

Oakwood Court College

Address: 7/9 Oak Park Villas, Dawlish, Devon EX7 0DE

Code: O

Tel: 01626 864066 **Fax:** 01626 866770 **Email:** admin@oakwoodcourt.ac.uk **Website:** www.oakwoodcourtcollege.co.uk

Age range: 16-25

Contact for admissions information: Admin Department

Usual source of funding for students: LSC

Aims: To provide a safe environment in which young people with learning disabilities and associated behavioural, emotional and/or social difficulties can confidently complete the transition from adolescence into the adult world.

Students catered for: Young people who require specialist further education. Continuous care and training provided beyond 25 years.

Premises and facilities

The College has a number of sites in the South Devon area. Opportunities for developing sporting and leisure interests exist in the locality, and students are encouraged and enabled to make good use of these. There are excellent rail and road links to the major centres in the region and to all parts of Britain.

Student accommodation

Students have their own study bedrooms, some with en-suite bathrooms. The residential accommodation is designed to facilitate the development of independent living skills.

Student numbers

Up to 30.

Staffing

Keyworkers and personal tutor systems ensure an individualised approach to care and education and promote student advocacy. A generous staff to student ratio allows high levels of physical care and individual attention. Review conferences are held annually.

Courses

The College offers a range of courses leading to the Vocational Foundation Certificate award. Students may progress to NVQ courses. Programmes to explore and develop insights into all aspects of personal and social relationships prepare students for either supported living, semi-independence or fully independent living.

Recreation, sport, creativity and self-expression are included in students' timetables. A prospectus is available on request.

Links

The College collaborates with the local college and other training providers to extend the range of qualifications available. Work experience incorporated into courses.

Other information

Counselling and other community-based specialist services are used whenever a need is identified.

Application procedure

Prospective students invited to visit Oakwood for three-five day assessment period. Referrals are usually initiated by specialist Connexions/careers personal advisers, LEAs or social services. First term acts as an extended assessment period. Students attend on either 38 week (term time) or 52 week (extended placement) basis.

The Orpheus Centre

Address: North Park Lane, Godstone, Surrey RH9 8ND

Tel: 01883 744664   **Fax:** 01883 744994   **Email:** enquiries@orpheus.org.uk   **Website:** www.orpheus.org.uk

Age range: Apprentices 18-25, students 18-40

Controlled by: Centre Director, Mrs Megan Johnson

Aims: To offer music and the performing arts to young people through which they will discover and develop new skills, new aspects to themselves and therefore new expectations. The Centre works in a user-led way, providing care services to meet individual needs, and delivering educational programmes in a way that meets individual goals. The Centre also employs the social model of disability to inform practice and the youth-work approach to personal development; encouraging individuals to define their identity and role within their communities.

Students catered for: Young disabled people, within the age range and from the UK and Europe, and who have expressed an interest or talent in performing arts.

Premises and facilities

The Orpheus Centre is an inclusive residential performing arts centre founded by entertainer and musician Richard Stilgoe in his former family home in Godstone in 1998. It has a theatre and a range of rehearsal spaces.

Student accommodation

12 single Centre Court flats all at ground level, each with a fully-fitted kitchen and bathroom. Centre Court houses 'Baseline' — three state-of-the-art technology studios providing young disabled people and other community groups access to new technology, work spaces and tools to broaden their learning and develop new opportunities.

Staffing

Courses are led by three professional tutors and students are supported by a team of residential volunteers and support workers. The support team coordinates a range of day-to-day services including 24-hour personal care, catering or assistance with catering, housekeeping and maintenance (laundry, cleaning, repairs etc), and support with learning, social and leisure activities. The Centre also has an administration, learning and facilities team.

Courses

Short courses run from Easter to the end of September and cover all types of performing arts including music, drama, dance, song, musical theatre and technical production.

Links

The Centre enjoys strong links with its local community and works with charities and educational establishments all over the UK. The Centre facilities are used by many different types of organisations and the Centre aims to be as inclusive and accessible to them as possible.

Application procedure

Applications for apprenticeships need to be made directly to the Centre Director. Student and volunteer application forms can be requested from the Centre or be made through the Centre's website.

Overley Hall School

Codes: C J M S

Address: Wellington, Telford, Shropshire TF6 5HE

Tel: 01952 740262   **Fax:** 01952 740262   **Email:** info@overleyhall.com   **Website:** www.overleyhall.com

Age range: 9-19

Contact for admissions information: Jackie Davenport/Gill Flannery

Out-of-term contact: Jackie Davenport

Fees: On request

Aims: The School acknowledges that each young person should be treated as an individual and may require specific provisions that are carefully planned, recorded and evaluated.

Students catered for: Those with severe learning difficulties, autism, epilepsy and challenging behaviour.

Premises and facilities

Set in 14 acres of garden and woodland. The School provides a consistent approach across all settings. Access to the wider community on a daily basis.

Student accommodation

Single occupant bedrooms, decorated and furnished to individual need.

Staffing

The School environment can provide 1:1 staffing. In house three staff to four or five young people unless risk assessment highlights 1:1 for certain activities. Staff have NVQ 3 in caring and young people, relevant health & safety, first aid, child & adult protection. Team Teach professional development is of paramount importance.

Links

Some students have the opportunity to attend college ½ day a week. 'In -house' students attend Mencap youth clubs — where appropriate.

Other information

The School has a consultant child and adolescent psychiatrist from CAMHS, speech and language therapists, psychologist.

Application procedure

Referral in writing with up-to-date relevant information and statement of education need. Prospectus available on request.

The Papworth Trust

Address: Papworth Everard, Cambridge CB3 8RG

Tel: 01480 830341   **Fax:** 01480 830781   **Email:** info@papworth.org.uk   **Website:** www.papworth.org.uk

---

Age range: 18+

Contact for admissions information: Call front desk on 01480 830341 or email info@papworth.org.uk with applicant's details.

Out-of-term contact: info@papworth.org.uk

Fees: Case-by-case basis

Usual source of funding for students: Various sources; self, social and employment services, Jobcentre Plus.

Aims: The Papworth Trust is a leading charity in the eastern region, helping disabled people to achieve their potential and reach a greater independence by providing specialist services covering training, employment, housing, care and advice.

Students catered for: Depending on eligibility and funding, people with a disability can access a range of our services.

Premises and facilities

In-house in Papworth Everard, or from the Trust's centres and offices in Cambridge, Ipswich, Basildon, Bury St Edmunds and Bishop Stortford.

Student accommodation

All the Trust's progression programmes are available on a daytime basis; residential option is available.

Student numbers

47 at time of printing. The Trust helps over 4,500 people every year across the whole range of its services.

Staffing

The Papworth Trust employs 250 staff, and calls on the expertise of contractors, such as physiotherapists and tutors, depending on the needs of service users.

Courses

Progression programmes cover five main areas: independent living skills training, vocational training, creative and performing arts, team enterprise projects, and community volunteering. Training is available with college tutors supporting people to gain formal qualifications.

Employment programmes support disabled people getting into and staying in work, both paid and unpaid. A client-centred approach is used in the delivery of the service. Specific programmes provide opportunities for workplace evaluation, job searching, support and access to mainsteam Jobcentre Plus programmes where relevant.

Links

The Trust values and works with many organisations and groups. Visit the links page on the website for more information.

Application procedure

Talk to your social services representative or call the Trust's front desk on 01480 830341, or email as above. The Trust will come back to you to discuss your eligibility and to help you apply.

Parkanaur College

Address: 57 Parkanaur Road, Dungannon, County Tyrone, Northern Ireland BT70 3AA

Code: O

Tel: 028 877 61272 **Fax:** 028 877 61257 **Email:** wilfred.mitchell@btopenworld.com
or parkanaur-college@btopenworld.com **Website:** www.parkanaurcollege.org

Age range: 16+

Controlled by: Thomas Doran Trust

Contact for admissions information: Wilfred Mitchell, Chief Executive

Out-of-term contact: Wilfred Mitchell

Usual source of funding for students: DEL H&SS Board

Aims: Within a residential setting, the College aims to provide the opportunity for people with disabilities to bridge the gap and facilitate the transition between schools or the sheltered home environment to employment and independent living accommodation.

Students catered for: A range of learning difficulties and disabilities; autism; Asperger Syndrome.

Premises and facilities

A building over 200 years old specially adapted for disabled people. The College also offers supported living and short breaks. Facilities include classrooms, recreation and conference rooms.

Student accommodation

The College has capacity for 21 residential placements. Individual and shared rooms. There are common, recreational and TV rooms.

Student numbers

21 residential and six non-residential.

Staffing

Friendly and professional staff support a learning environment and realistic working conditions. Staff in the residential area wake at night to observe.

Courses

NVQ training in horticulture, catering and hospitality, assembled and upholstered furniture production; business administration including IT with a variety of packages. Opportunities to take A/AS level courses.

Links

East Tyrone FE College tutors visit Parkanaur and students also attend evening classes. Local employers accept students for work experience.

Other information

Each student/resident who needs additional help is provided with the appropriate professional services.

Application procedure

Initial enquiries by phone or visit. The College will request information about the student. If an application is made by all parties, i.e. student, parent/guardian, social worker, a formal application is made with relevant funding body.

Pengwern Further Education College

Address: Sarn Lane, Rhuddlan, Denbighshire LL18 5UH

Tel: 01745 590281   **Fax:** 01745 591736   **Email:** pengwern.college@mencap.org.uk   **Website:** www.mencap.org.uk

Age range: 16-25

Controlled by: MENCAP

Fees: Fees are based on funding matrix and depend entirely on the needs of the individual. Current funding ranges from £23,000 to £50,000.

Usual source of funding for students: Students are primarily funded by the LSC (Eng) or The Welsh Assembly.

Aims: To provide an educational curriculum for transition to adulthood for adolescents with learning disabilities (including severe and profound) in a variety of facilities.

Students catered for: Learning disability as the primary disability and additionally, behavioural, physical and complex disabilities depending upon each individual's situation and need.

Premises and facilities

Pengwern College is situated five miles south of Rhyl (nearest railway station), close to the A55, within 30 miles of Chester. The campus contains the first residential stages of student's development: the coach houses, education block and garden farm. Assessed development by the student leads to residential stages of increasing contact with the community (e.g. work experience, social interaction) in small houses in neighbouring communities. A bed and breakfast facility offers students real work situations. Students continue to access the educational block and farm park throughout their course. Catering sessions are delivered in a real situation.

Student accommodation

Total of 20 different/varied living and training situations. One house with facilities for students using wheelchairs.

Student numbers

Total capacity 60, both sexes.

Staffing

Total of 74 staff including daytime tutors. Pengwern College is an Investor in People.

Courses

The curriculum includes pre-vocational and vocational education with emphasis on learning essential skills. Functional communication skills, physiotherapy, speech therapy and other services are provided. As students develop the appropriate personal, social and daily living skills, they progress through the residential and vocational units within the College. Teaching continues for 38 weeks of the year, seven days a week. The length of the course is up to three years, dependent upon the individual assessment of each student.

All students work through an individual programme based on acquisition of essential skills. Students can access NVQ qualifications as appropriate in the areas of catering and hospitality, agriculture, horticulture, leisure and tourism and office administration. There are regular reviews of progress and, for the purposes of forward planning and setting objectives, students can also access work experience in community situations.

Links

The College has links with Jobcentre Plus, MENCAP local services, where appropriate; community adult literacy; agencies in student's home community.

Other information

Medical, dental services etc provided locally. Specialist skill input, e.g. communications skills, physiotherapy etc when required.

Application procedure

Initial visit by the student with parents and/or social workers. A three-day assessment period is arranged, followed by a review and a decision made. The initial three-month period is used for further assessment and educational programming according to student's needs.

N.B. *This entry has not been updated by the establishment for this edition. Please check details.*

Pennine Camphill Community

Codes: B C J K M N O P Q S

Address: Boyne Hill, Chapelthorpe, Wakefield WF4 3JH

Tel: 01924 255281 **Email:** enquiries@pennine.org.uk **Website:** www.pennine.org.uk

Age range: 16-25

Controlled by: Independent; DfES rec.

Contact for admissions information: Sue Crouch

Fees: As set by LSC Matrix

Usual source of funding for students: LSC

Aims: Pennine is part of the Camphill Movement. Camphill creates settings where people, many with learning disabilities, can live, work and learn with others in healthy social relationships based on mutual care and respect.

Students catered for: The college is intended for young people who have emotional, behavioural, mental health, maturational difficulties, as well as learning disabilities.

Premises and facilities

There are five community houses within a 10-acre campus together with a number of craft workshops, classrooms, a 25-acre farm and horticultural holding, an RDA registered riding school together with a hall central to the campus. An accessible computer network is available for students throughout the estate.

Student accommodation

Most students have single rooms in one of the five community houses. Each house is organised on an extended family basis.

Staffing

Many staff live in, creating a high level of support for students within a semi-secure environment.

Courses

Pennine offers a hands-on experience in traditional crafts and land-based skills. This can lead to NVQ level 1 in hospitality and catering, horse care and horticulture. Student programmes can be extended between 2-5 years dependent on assessment and funding beyond education funding. Students have individual learning plans covering an extended curriculum including an essential and life skills programme.

Links

Pennine shares premises with a registered riding school and accepts students on work experience from local schools and locally run courses.

Other information

Therapies include horse riding, painting and movement together with massage and counselling.

Application procedure

First enquiries can be made by telephone, letter, email or website. Applications may be made by parents, Connexions, social workers, schools or local authority.

Philpots Manor School

Address: West Hoathly, East Grinstead, West Sussex RH19 4PR

Codes: B C I J K M N(mild) O P(mild) T

Tel: 01342 810268 **Fax:** 01342 811363 **Email:** philpotsmanorschool@tiscali.co.uk

Age range: 7-19

Controlled by: Independent School

Contact for admissions information: The Admissions Group

Out-of-term contact: As above

Fees: From £15,548 per term

Usual source of funding for students: LEAs, social services, health authorities and (rarely) private funding

Aims: To help young people for whom the development of human qualities is judged to be more important than involvement in the stress of today's educational system, with the prospect of re-integrating them into the mainstream whenever possible. A Rudolf Steiner School committed to the Steiner-Waldorf ethos.

Students catered for: Children and young people with special needs and associated behavioural problems, who are emotionally disturbed/deprived, have nervous or anxiety symptoms, habit or organic disorders, borderline autism, controlled epilepsy but not physical disabilities. The majority of our young people are working 6-24 months below average.

Premises and facilities

Situated in rural Sussex, the school is set in 25 acres of gardens, a farm and surrounding woodlands. An old manor house — currently under refurbishment — forms the central building. The school is accommodated in spacious classrooms and has associated technical, craft and recreation facilities.

Student accommodation

Students are housed in small family-based bungalows, one larger house and a designated independence-skills unit for training course students (16-19 years).

Staffing

Approximately 90, half teaching, half residential and comprising several therapeutic specialists.

Courses

The School follows the Steiner-Waldorf curriculum. In addition, eligible students are entered for GCSE courses in English, maths and science. A foundation course in art is taken in class 10 (year 11). Open College Network accredited courses are also available in crafts and riding.

Links

Where appropriate, trainees undertake link courses with local colleges. The College has links with Crawley College of Further Education, Brinsbury College and Michael Hall Steiner School/Steiner Waldorf Schools Fellowship.

Other information

Visiting cranial osteopath and masseuse. Full-time play therapist/counsellor and other therapeutic specialists.

Application procedure

Informal exploratory visits may be made by telephoning the School. Formal applications are made to the Admissions Group and should include a statement and recent relevant reports.

Pield Heath House RC School

Address: Victor Braun Centre, Extended Education Department, Pield Heath Road, Uxbridge UB8 3NW

Tel: 01895 258507   **Fax:** 01895 256497   **Email:** admin@pieldheathschool.org.uk

Age range: 16–19+

Controlled by: Congregation of the Sacred Hearts of Jesus and Mary: DfES recognition

Fees: On request

Aims: To promote spiritual, moral, cultural, mental and physical development. To empower all students to be active participants within their community and prepare the individual for the opportunities, choices, responsibilities and experience of adult life.

Students catered for: Mixed, residential — weekly, M/SLD; pupils with language and communication disorders.

Premises and facilities

A purpose-built centre comprises a reception area, team enterprise centre, hair salon, careers office, science room, art room with built-in kiln, as well as an ICT and food technology centre and kitchen. Facilities allow students to be trained on site and have the opportunity to gain practical experience in a wide range of vocational courses.

Staffing

Teaching staff, ancillary workers, speech therapist and nursing staff.

Courses

The National Skills Profile, the ASDAN Towards Independence Scheme, Equals – Moving On, City & Guilds certificate in Effective Augmentative and Alternative Communication, Milestone/Entry level number and maths. Entry level ICT; art. GCSE art. Tutorial based; individual programmes; pastoral care to develop positive self image and transition. Constant revision and updating of curriculum, delivery and resources to meet the challenges of special education for the future.

Links

Strong links with local schools and colleges. Resource base of contacts with professionals in students' home areas, constantly updated. Active member of the local special education compact and have a Connexions personal adviser. Students are offered a wide range of internal and external work placements as part of their work experience. Links with other schools offering Team Enterprise. Business Advisor visits regularly. Victor Braun Centre student committee meets regularly to plan activities and organise fundraising events.

Application procedure

Visit to school and informal interview.

Pontville School

Address: Black Moss Lane, Ormskirk, Lancashire L39 4TW

Codes: B C F O

Tel: 01695 578734   **Fax:** 01695 579224   **Email:** office@pontville.co.uk   **Website:** www.pontville.co.uk

Age range: 11-19

Controlled by: Witherslack Group of Schools

Contact for admissions information: Headteacher, Mr Ian Sim

Fees: Details available on request from School

Aims: To enable each student to achieve his/her full potential in the academic, social, moral and cultural senses. To provide a happy, secure and supportive environment where pupils are valued and can develop their confidence, self esteem, independence, self discipline, respect and concern for others. To celebrate achievement in all its forms. To prepare pupils for the demands of adult life in order to maximise their opportunities for personal fulfilment and happiness.

Students catered for: Young people with communication difficulties, including ASD, Aspergers Syndrome, specific speech and language impairment and global learning difficulties. Based on assessment of need.

Student accommodation

38-week residential provision attached to School; 52-week provision at the School is linked to residential facilities operated by Witherslack Care.

Staffing

Teachers/instructors, speech and language therapist, educational psychologist and careworkers.

Courses

Pontville aims to provide a curriculum and overall educational experience which is broad balanced. The School offers a wide variety of courses and accreditation including: GCSE, NVQ, Entry Level qualifications, ASDAN network units of accreditation. The School Ofsted report in June 2006 indicated that its unique approach to grouping, curriculum planning and delivery 'opens doors' to learning and the fulfilment of potential. Overall pupil development was judged to be 'Outstanding'. The School builds its curriculum around a central core of social communication skills onto which learning can be developed.

Links

The School aims to develop positive links between home, school and the wider community in order to support pupil learning.

Application procedure

Based on submission of papers and individual assessment of need.

Portland College

Address: Nottingham Road, Mansfield, Nottinghamshire NG18 4TJ

Tel: 01623 499111 **Fax:** 01623 499133 **Email:** college@portland.org.uk **Website:** www.portland.org.uk

Age range: 16-59

Controlled by: An independent college

Fees: LSC funding matrix — range £12,800 to £64,300

Usual source of funding for students: DWP; LSC

Aims: To maximise ability and minimise disability in a residential setting for individual empowerment through employment, education and training, independence and integration.

Students catered for: UK and International; students with physical disabilities, with the exception of totally blind students.

Premises and facilities

Three miles south of Mansfield on the A60 in a wooded setting. Special facilities include side doors, covered walkways, specialist equipment to maximise independence. Leisure centre, recreation hall, outdoor sports including bowling, football, wheelchair games. Youth club through which there are strong links with local community. Specialised transport for off-campus activities.

Student accommodation

Purpose built and single storey buildings accessible to students with mobility problems.

Staffing

Approximately 270.

Courses

Business administration, accounts, information technology, horticulture, computer aided drafting and design, further and continuing education, leading to NVQs where appropriate. External accreditation is used wherever applicable, e.g. City & Guilds, RSA, London Chamber of Commerce and Industry. Specialist equipment available, e.g. Touch Talker, Lightwriter, computers, CCTV.

Application procedure

Interview and assessment prior to acceptance. Applications for LS assessment should be sent to the college for the attention of the Recruitment Officer.

Prior's Court School

Codes: C S

Address: Hermitage, Thatcham, Berkshire RG18 9NU

Tel: 01635 247202   **Email:** mail@priorscourt.org.uk   **Website:** www.priorscourt.org.uk

---

Age range: 5-19

Controlled by: Prior's Court Foundation

Contact for admissions information: Admissions Coordinator, Lauraine Jones; CEO & Principal, Robert Hubbard OBE MEd (Cantab); Head of School, Sarah Sherwood BA ACE (Autism)

Out-of-term contact: As above

Fees: On application

Usual source of funding for students: LEA/social services

Aims: To equip students with the necessary skills to maximise their potential and to lead full and varied lives within the community as independently as possible. High quality specialist provision and a unique approach focusing on structured teaching, communication and language acquisition, managing challenging behaviour, physical exercise and ICT.

Students catered for: All are diagnosed with autism and have severe and complex learning difficulties. Some may exhibit challenging behaviours. Some have additional associated disabilities. National and international catchment.

Premises and facilities

54-acre grounds, well-equipped specialist facilities include education block, speech and language, music and occupational therapy suites, psychology and medical departments, sensory and soft play rooms, library, art studio, independent living skills suite, science classroom, ICT, 14-19 department, gymnasium, sensory swimming pool, track, adventure playground, paddock, greenhouse, kitchen garden, workshops, student-run tuckshop.

Student accommodation

Autistic-specific, welcoming and well-equipped residential houses on-site and an off-site house for older pupils offers the opportunity for greater independence.

Student numbers

Co-educational. Approximately 60 pupils with day, weekly and termly places.

Staffing

High staff:pupil ratio with a team of dedicated, highly-trained staff, therapists and specialists who work together with parents to achieve consistent, coordinated approach.

Courses

In addition to the school curriculum, older students gain national accreditation (eg ASDAN modules).

Training in the Prior Approach is available to both parents and practitioners.

Links

Partnerships with local schools and organisations. Visits and regular use of local community facilities. Local companies support on-site and off-site work placements.

Application procedure

Regular open mornings and visits are held for parents and professionals. Further details and dates from Reception or our website and applications via Admissions Coordinator.

Purbeck View School

Address: Northbrook Road, Swanage, Dorset BH19 1PR

Code: C

Tel: 0800 288 9779   **Fax:** 0207 348 5223   **Email:** enquiries@cambiangroup.com   **Website:** www.cambianeducation.com

Age range: 9-19

Controlled by: Cambian Education Services

Contact for admissions information: Sue Goulding (Head)

Out-of-term contact: School office

Fees: From £120,092.70

Usual source of funding for students: LEA/social services

Aims: Purbeck View School is one of seven schools and colleges for children and young people on the autistic spectrum which, until September 2005, were run by The Hesley Group. At this time they became Cambian Education Services. Total commitment is to high quality care and education.

Students catered for: A specialist 38 and 52 week boarding school for pupils with a diagnosis of autism, communication impairment, associated learning difficulties and many display behaviours that require careful management.

Premises and facilities

The School is in Swanage set on a small hill, with views to the Isle of Wight and the Purbeck Hills. The School has well equipped classrooms, specialist art and craft workshop, science and technology, food technology, creative arts studio, full sized sports hall, sensory room, chapel and many individual garden areas for play, sport and relaxation.

Student accommodation

Young people live in safe, attractive and individual comfortable accommodation, in small houses or living units.

Student numbers

Currently registered for 48 pupils/students.

Staffing

Well-qualified and experienced staff across education and care, who have a wealth of knowledge in working with young people on the autistic spectrum. The School has two full time assistant psychologists, one consultant psychologist, speech and language therapist, music therapist, occupational therapist.

Courses

Individual programmes developed for each pupil. Full National Curriculum entitlements at Key Stage 2&3, access to work related learning and vocational education in Key Stage 4 and in Post 16, extended 24 hour curriculum in Personal Development. Unit accreditation AQA; Transition Challenge ASDAN; Towards Independence ASDAN;Key Skills (Entry Level) ASDAN; OCR CLAIT.

Links

Links to local first and secondary schools, social clubs and youth organisations, Mencap, work experience with local employers.

Other information

Sessional paediatric and psychiatric support.

Application procedure

Funding authorities usually contact School with relevant information, prospective parents are welcome to approach and can visit by appointment. Each child is admitted for an initial period of assessment.

Queen Alexandra College

Address: Court Oak Road, Harborne, Birmingham B17 9TG

Tel: 0121 428 5050   **Fax:** 0121 428 5048   **Email:** enquiries@qac.ac.uk   **Website:** www.qac.ac.uk

Age range: 16-63

Controlled by: Alex Mellor — Principal

Contact for admissions information: Ray Piggott/Sonia Sagoo 0121 428 5041

Fees: On application

Usual source of funding for students: LSC, Jobcentre Plus, Residential Training Unit

Aims: Queen Alexandra College provides opportunities for people with visual impairment and/or other disabilities to learn, live and work independently.

Students catered for: Learners with visual impairment, learning difficulties, physical disabilities, Aspergers syndrome. QAC is a national residential and day college.

Premises and facilities

QAC maintains a campus in the quiet and leafy suburb of Harborne, fifteen minutes from the centre of Birmingham and close to shops, pubs and leisure facilities. Modern learning and residential facilities provide learners with ideal opportunities for progression.

Student accommodation

A range of staffed and unstaffed hostels and houses provides a variety of accommodation. Leavers can progress through levels of independent living.

Student numbers

150.

Staffing

Staff include specialists in residential support, education and vocational training, mobility, Braille, technology and nursing.

Courses

Entry level programmes; BTEC qualifications in business, ICT, health & social care, performing arts, hospitality, travel and tourism. ESOL, Braille, Mobility, Skills for Independent Living. NVQs are offered in a variety of subjects.

Links

Associate students are supported in nearby general further education colleges. There are many links with employers for work experience.

Other information

Learners have access to a counsellor, nursing team, doctors' practice.

Application procedure

Learners are referred by Connexions Advisers, Disability Employment Advisers and incapacity benefit personal advisers. Informal pre-assessment visits are welcomed.

Queen Elizabeth's Foundation Brain Injury Centre

Code: A

Address: Banstead Place, Park Road, Banstead, Surrey SM7 3EE

Tel: 01737 356222   **Fax:** 01737 359467   **Email:** rehab@braininjurycentre.org.uk   **Website:** www.qef.org.uk/braininjury

Age range: 16-35

Controlled by: Queen Elizabeth's Foundation

Contact for admissions information: Business Manager — Valerie Foxwell

Fees: On application — reviewed annually

Usual source of funding for students: LSC, Primary Care Trusts and social services

Aims: To provide comprehensive assessment, rehabilitation and education for young adults with acquired brain injuries.

Students catered for: Young adults with acquired brain damage. All abilities, but cannot accept severe and uncontrollable behaviour problems or students requiring high levels of medical care.

Premises and facilities

Part purpose-built centre half a mile form Banstead village. Sutton and Croydon easily accessible. Extensive use of local facilities. Development of personal independence, social skills, practical competence in everyday living are essential parts of students' courses.

Student accommodation

Single study bedrooms and four independent living units help students acquire and practise the skills of independent living.

Student numbers

28.

Staffing

Principal, teachers, occupational therapists, physiotherapists, speech therapists, senior psychologist and qualified assistants, creative therapists, care staff, recreation staff and an orthoptist.

Courses

Individual courses, based on a neuropsychological assessment, are geared to identification of needs and development of potential. Most stay about 18 months. Cognitive therapies, further remedial education, independence/mobility training including where possible, learning to drive and/or use of public transport, vocational assessment, work experience, social/leisure activities. Many activities are carried out away from the Brain Injury Centre using local facilities.

Links

Students may attend a variety of courses at local colleges of further education — vocational or recreational activities according to individual needs.

Other information

Centre is open for 48 weeks a year, closed at Christmas, Easter and August Bank Holiday.

Application procedure

Enquiries should be made to the Business Manager, who will also arrange any visits. Entry at any time during the year.

Queen Elizabeth's Foundation Development Centre

Address: Oaklawn Road, Leatherhead, Surrey KT22 0BT

Tel: 01372 841300   **Fax:** 01372 843753   **Website:** www.qefd.org/development

Age range: 19-40

Controlled by: Queen Elizabeth's Foundation

Fees: Day care — £40 per day; residential care £39,910-£52,000 per year (2004 figures)

Aims: To provide a stimulating living skills centre with progressive arts and leisure facilities for severely disabled young people, giving the confidence and the skills to move on to a lifestyle of their choice.

Facilities and premises

A purpose-built residential centre providing a comprehensive programme for each individual that will promote personal development, build confidence and achieve a realistic level of independence. The education services department offers comprehensive training to individuals to support their move on from the Centre. The leisure department provides information and works with individuals to access sport and leisure opportunities both locally and nationally.

Student accommodation

Single rooms and apartments suited to individual needs.

Staffing

A personal tutor and key worker system operates across the Centre. A dedicated care team encourages individuals to manage their own care whilst providing a network of support.

Courses

Development Centre provides each student with a two- or three-year programme which develops core skills essential for moving on to greater independence. The education services give students the opportunity to discover new skills and pursue creative interests in the visual and performing arts, plus information and communication technology.

Other information

Physiotherapy is available on site, responding to individual needs.

N.B. *This entry has not been updated by the establishment for this edition. Please check details.*

Queen Elizabeth's Foundation Training College

Codes: O P R

Address: Leatherhead Court, Leatherhead, Surrey KT22 0BN

Tel: 01372 841100 **Fax:** 01372 844156 **Email:** angela.webb@qetc.org **Website:** www.qefd.org

Age range: 18+

Controlled by: Queen Elizabeth's Foundation

Fees: Government funded by the Residential Training Unit (part of the DWP)

Aims: The College is committed to vocational training (work based learning) for people with a wide range disabilities.

Students catered for: Residential and day students — adults with disabilities, mental, physical or learning (regrettably cannot accept applications from those totally blind or profoundly deaf).

Premises and facilities

Near junction 9 of the M25 on the A245 Leatherhead to Cobham road off the A3. Custom-designed classrooms and workshops for training incorporating the latest technology and equipment. Restaurant serving three meals daily (included in the fees). Access to nursing support. Karten Suite (Cyber Club), sports and social club, gymnasium, sports facilities, video and TV rooms and an active students' association.

Student accommodation

Purpose-built and well-equipped hostels with resident staff.

Staffing

Principal, head of training, 26 lecturers, head of trainee support, head of employment development plus three employment development managers, three open learning tutors, job club leader, welfare & benefits manager, leisure manager plus leisure team, facilities/ estates manager and full administrative support.

Courses

14 courses in a range of business and technical studies, and practical subjects. All courses geared to job market and lead to nationally recognised qualifications. Modular training to suit individual needs available upon request. Individual personal development/support, basic skills and IT available to all students.

Other information

The College is one of five centres of the Queen Elizabeth's Foundation for Disabled People, Leatherhead, Surrey.

Application procedure

Applications normally through the Disability Employment Adviser at local Jobcentre Plus. Monthly open days for students by invitation — telephone/email for availability.

RNIB College Loughborough

Address: Radmoor Rd, Loughborough LE11 3BS

Codes: A C D E F H I J K L N P Q R

Tel: 01509 611077 **Fax:** 01509 232013 **Email:** enquiries@rnibvocoll.ac.uk **Website:** www.rnibvocoll.ac.uk

Age range: 16-63

Controlled by: RNIB

Contact for admissions information: Admissions Dept (01509 611077)

Fees: No fees to recipients

Usual source of funding for students: LSC, RTDA, Jobcentre Plus

Aims: RNIB College works with partners so that young people and adults with disabilities can develop the skills and personal qualities needed to progress in life.

Students catered for: Supporting people nationally with sight loss, chronic illness, hearing loss, learning or physical mobility difficulties. Mild to moderate mental health issues or autism including Aspergers Syndrome on a day or residential basis.

Premises and facilities

Modern purpose-built environment designed with people who are blind or partially sighted or with reduced mobility in mind. The College shares a campus with a mainstream college offering learners the best of both worlds, all the support of a small specialist college with the option of supported access to the mainstream.

Student accommodation

A short walk from the College, the Stan Bell Centre has 60 en-suite study bedrooms with phone and internet access.

Student numbers

80 — mixed residential and day students.

Staffing

15 teaching staff plus learning support assistants, nine residential support staff.

Courses

Further education courses for people with disabilities aged 16-25 from pre-entry level to Higher National Diplomas. Some students progress to higher education. In-house programmes are offered for students who are not ready for the mainstream, designed to enhance self-confidence, numeracy, literacy and citizenship skills. All younger learners also take part in independent living skills sessions.

Adult programmes are three days, 12 weeks to one year — and are work focused. Suitable for the unemployed or in employment and wishing to retrain.

Links

The College shares a campus with a mainstream college and supports students at other local colleges within the East Midlands.

Other information

Visiting professionals in physiotherapy, holistic therapy; educational and occupational psychologists, occupational therapists, low vision optometrists, speech and language specialists; hearing impairment services.

Application procedure

Prospective students are recommended to attend an informal visit before making an application. Funding can be applied for by a Connexions Adviser or Disability Employment Adviser.

RNIB Redhill College

Address: Philanthropic Road, Redhill, Surrey RH1 4DG

Code: D

Tel: 01737 768935   **Fax:** 01737 778776   **Email:** enquiries @rnib-redhill.ac.uk   **Website:** www.rnib.org.uk/redhill

Age range: 16-63

Controlled by: RNIB

Contact for admissions information: Steph Upton, Marketing Assistant

Out-of-term contact: As above

Fees: Variable according to individual need

Usual source of funding for students: LSC/RTU/social services

Aims: The College aims to create a centre of high quality learning for learners from a wide age range with complex and varied needs including sensory impairment, with an emphasis upon an entitlement curriculum of basic skills, living skills, music and performing arts. The College is committed to promoting economic activity for its learners, and achieves this through partnerships and community involvement.

Students catered for: Young people and adults who are blind or partially sighted, and/or have a range of other disabilities, learning difficulties and additional needs.

Premises and facilities

The College is situated on a 13-acre site of small residential houses, independent flats, teaching blocks and leisure facilities.

Student accommodation

The College can offer accommodation from 24-hour social care services, to independent flats.

Student numbers

120.

Staffing

In addition to teaching and professional qualifications, all teaching staff have specialist qualifications for teaching the visually impaired. Residential care staff are similarly required to undertake a tailored training course provided by the RNIB.

Courses

The College offers a wide range of courses leading to vocational qualifications. Opportunities exist for training in business administration, horticulture, radio broadcasting, music technology and ICT. A wide range of leisure activities including swimming, fitness training and visits to places of entertainment and interest. The College has a fully accessible gym with adapted equipment to support its learners.

Links

Appropriate learners are supported to access part-time mainstream college courses from within the local area.

Other information

Learners at the College can access the following specialist services: physiotherapy, speech and language therapy, counselling, drama therapy and rehabilitation and mobility.

Application procedure

Informal visits can be arranged upon request. All applications are taken forward and an assessment is arranged to ensure that individuals are matched with the appropriate course.

RNIB Rushton School

Address: Wheelright Lane, Ash Green, Coventry CV7 9RA

Tel: 02476 369500   **Fax:** 02476 369501   **Email:** steve.warren@rnib.org.uk

Age range: 4-19

Contact for admissions information: Brenda Smith, Steve Warren

Out-of-term contact: Brenda Smith (Head of Residential Services)

Usual source of funding for students: Local authority

Aims: To provide care and education for pupils with visual impairment and other multiple disabilities.

Students catered for: All pupils have a visual impairment and any of the following: deaf blind, cerebral palsy, epilepsy, mixed and multiple disabilities, autism.

Premises and facilities

Children's home on site. Access to swimming and hydrotherapy pools. Large classrooms.

Student accommodation

52-week residential care in small units on site.

Student numbers

25 — 19 residential; six day.

Staffing

High staffing ratio, physiotherapy team, speech and language team.

Courses

All students from years 10-14 follow Equals Moving On curriculum.

Links

The School has links with Exhall Grange School and Wheelright Lane Primary School.

Application procedure

Initial visit by carers, parents and/or sponsoring authorities. Contact Brenda Smith or Steve Warren.

RNIB Scotland: Employment and Learning Centre

Address: 24D Milton Road East, Edinburgh EH15 2NJ

Tel: 0131 657 8200   **Fax:** 0131 657 6888   **Email:** sarah.littlewood@rnib.org.uk   **Website:** www.rnib.org.uk/Scotland

Age range: 16+

Controlled by: RNIB

Contact for admissions information: Nigel Townley, Programme Coordinator

Out-of-term contact: Open 50 weeks of the year

Fees: Nil to service user

Usual source of funding for students: Jobcentre Plus, RTDA in England and LECs in Scotland

Aims: To provide blind and partially-sighted people in Scotland and the north of England with the skills, qualifications and confidence that will enable them to remain in work or to obtain employment. The Centre will also facilitate access to work-based learning programmes and further education courses across the UK where appropriate.

Students catered for: Blind and partially-sighted adults. Clients with guide dogs can be accommodated.

Premises and facilities

The Employment and Learning Centre has been specifically designed to provide assessment and training for blind and partially sighted people in a friendly and supportive environment. It is located in the grounds of Jewel and Esk Valley College in the eastern suburbs of Edinburgh. The Centre is five minutes walking distance from Brunstane Station. Large, comfortable lounge with a TV, DVD, video, and pool table; three fully-equipped kitchens and a laundry; music and arts room, internet library, large computer suite, assessment room, low-vision room, multimedia room, three training rooms, conference room and café.

Student accommodation

18 en-suite single bedrooms, each with a shower/bath. Each room has a radio/CD player, TV, PC with internet access and a telephone. A member of staff is on call 24-hours to help develop independent living skills and to support service users as appropriate.

Student numbers

18-40.

Staffing

There are 14 members of staff including a centre manager, rehabilitation officer, work preparation coordinator, programme coordinator, IT tutors, care and catering staff and a handyman/driver.

Courses

Employment Assessment: (Up to five days; start date flexible) — for people who want to explore an occupational interest, identify a new career direction or confirm an existing choice. Based on an assessment of keyboard skills, ICT, numeracy and literacy, Braille and communication skills etc. Work Preparation: (Normally nine weeks; start date flexible) — for people who want to stay in their current job or get back into work. Includes ICT related, business and skills training, action planning and work placement.

Links

Being located on the campus of Jewel and Esk Valley College means that there is access to a wide range of subjects and courses and college facilities. There are also links with Careers Scotland, Jobcentre Plus, employers and various other providers.

Other information

A GP is available on call. An optometrist carries out low-vision assessments on a weekly basis and students have access to counselling and additional psychological assessment, where appropriate.

Application procedure

Contact a Disability Employment Adviser at Jobcentre Plus. To make preliminary visits to view facilities at the Centre, contact the Centre directly.

RNID Care Services

Address: South West Region, Watery Lane, Twerton, Bath BA2 1RN

Tel: 01225 332818   **Fax:** 01225 480825   **Email:** informationline@rnid.org.uk   **Website:** www.rnid.org.uk

Age range: 18+

Controlled by: Royal National Institute for Deaf People

Contact for admission information: Residential Services manager, Roy Woods

Fees: Long term care: Deaf — from £900pw; deafblind — from £1,100pw

Rehabilitation: Deaf — from £976pw

Pennard Court Flats – costs available on request

DWP local limit payments apply to all rehabilitation and long-term care placements and are deductible from fees.

Aims : To provide habilitation and rehabilitation, nursing and long term support for adult deaf and deaf/blind people with additional disabilities.

Students catered for: Deaf people with multiple physical and mental disabilities. Ability range from learning difficulties to above average. Day students accepted in the Education and Day Services Unit. Nursing facilities provided.

Premises and facilities

Pennard Court is situated in the grounds of Poolemead site. Real work opportunities are provided via an off-site workshop. Recreation facilities are provided together with the use of local sport and recreation facilities.

Student accommodation

Warden-supported flats and four group homes situated in the local community.

Student numbers

58 residents, men and women.

Staffing

120 full-time support workers; 12 instructors in Education and Day Services Unit; local consultant psychiatrist and medical officer; access to other medical facilities; speech therapy and hearing therapy.

Courses

Each resident is given an individual programme of habilitation and rehabilitation to suit their needs. Programmes are based on total environmental care therapy.

Application procedure

Intake frequency dependent on vacancies, but throughout the year. Forms from RNID Care Services (Bath). The prospective resident, parents, social workers, teachers etc are fully involved in the admissions procedure. Waiting periods vary.

The Robert Ogden School

Address: Clayton Lane, Thurnscoe, Rotherham, South Yorkshire S63 0BG

Tel: 01709 874443   **Fax:** 01709 870701   **Email:** robert.ogden@nas.org.uk   **Website:** www.nas.org.uk

Age range: 16-19

Controlled by: The National Autistic Society

Fees: Paid by LEA. All new pupils subject to an initial two term assessment period

Usual source of funding for students: Home area LEA

Aims: The vision of the National Autistic Society is of a world in which all people with autism are supported and are able to fulfill their potential in a well-informed and tolerant society.

Students catered for: Nationwide. Pupils with a diagnosis of autism/Aspergers syndrome plus associated conditions including challenging behaviours. Full-time 52 weeks or 38 weeks Mon-Fri term-time only.

Premises and facilities

Facilities include: workshops and kiln for pottery, industrial kitchen for catering, training flat, polytunnel and gardening area, quiet rooms, sensory rooms, library, fitness suite, office practice area, IT suite, student lounge, student common room, classroom and tutorial space, individual workstations.

Student accommodation

A positive, caring environment with emphasis on social and life skills.

Student numbers

Maximum 40.

Staffing

Minimum staffing level of one staff member to two pupils. Pupils on enhanced rates supported 1:1.

Courses

Students follow programmes designed to meet individual needs. Core subjects of literacy, numeracy and PHSE are supported by a choice of vocationally related subjects; catering, pottery, gardening, IT and office skills. Students also participate in Team Enterprise activities. Appropriate lifeskills programmes which include basic self help skills such as personal hygiene, making drinks/ simple meals and household tasks. Accreditation is via ASDAN awards, OCR, OCN and NCFE certification.

Links

Students may access work experience placements with a variety of local employers on both short- and long-term placements.

Access to discrete programmes at local college supported by school staff. Individual students may access college programmes, e.g. GCSE/BTEC.

Other information

Psychologists and two speech and language therapists on staff. School nurse.

Application procedure

Formal application by referring LEA/funding authority. Relevant reports and assessments submitted to school admission panel for decision.

Royal College for the Deaf Exeter

Address: 50 Topsham Road, Exeter EX2 4NF

Code: H

Tel: 01392 215179   **Fax:** 01392 410016   **Email:** college@rsd-exeter.org.uk   **Website:** www.rsd-exeter.ac.uk

Age range: 16-21+

Contact for admissions information: Jeign Craig, Head of College

Out-of-term contact: 01392 272692

Fees: On application to Finance Office

Usual source of funding for students: LEA and LSC

Aims: To create the opportunity for hearing impaired students to achieve their personal, educational and vocational goals; to enable them to develop as individuals personally, socially and morally; and provide opportunities for them to learn with their peers in the wider community.

Students catered for: Full range of hearing-impaired students (including some with additional special needs), mainly from the south west peninsular, London and the Channel Islands.

Premises and facilities

The purpose built College shares a 12-acre site with the School. There are excellent ICT facilities, library, workshops, indoor swimming pool, gymnasium, football pitch, indoor and outdoor recreation areas, and an Audiology Centre. It is a ten minute walk to the centre of Exeter.

Student accommodation

The residential accommodation consists of single study bedrooms and a series of independent flats all with access to kitchen facilities.

Student numbers

Academic year 2006/7 expected to be 70+ students.

Staffing

Students have access to fully qualified Teachers of the Deaf, Communication Support Workers, on-site educational audiologist and speech and language therapist and care staff key workers.

Courses

A/AS levels, GCSEs, BTEC courses, NVQs at various levels. Personal achievement and communication, skills for working life, literacy and numeracy, OCR CLAIT/PLUS, CACDP British Sign Language Levels 1, 2 and NVQ3, PSE and independent living skills.

Links

Students have access to and are supported in a variety of courses at Exeter, Bicton and East Devon Colleges.

Other information

As required, students have access to: physiotherapist, occupational therapist, orthotist, orthoptist, psychiatric services, educational psychology service, cochlear implant services and Connexions.

Application procedure

An initial visit is followed by an overnight assessment visit. Application is then by application form from both the parents/guardians and the current school.

The Royal National College for the Blind (RNC)

Codes: C D E G H I L N R

Address: College Road, Hereford HR1 1EB

Tel: 01432 265725/376621   **Fax:** 01432 376628   **Email:** info@rncb.ac.uk   **Website:** www.rncb.ac.uk

Age Range: 16-65+

Contact for admissions information: Central Admissions 01432 376621

Usual source of funding for students: The Learning and Skills Council and the Residential Training unit

Aims: To provide a range of full-time academic and vocational programmes designed to prepare people who are blind or partially sighted for progression to further education, university and the world of work; but most importantly... independent living.

Students catered for: Blind or partially sighted, school leavers and adult mature students from all over the UK. Students with additional difficulties (e.g. hearing impairment, physical difficulties, Aspergers) also welcomed.

Premises and facilities

Social activity is considered important. On campus, there are a range of leisure facilities.

Student accommodation

Purpose built accommodation. The majority of rooms are en-suite. 24 hour support provided.

Student numbers

Approx. 200.

Staffing

RNC has approximately 175 teaching staff and 60 student support staff. Medical, counselling, residential and student support services are provided by qualified staff. Students have one-to-one support with mobility and daily living skills.

Courses

Royal National College offers a wide range of A/AS Levels and GCSEs, vocational studies and preparation for higher education, sport and recreation and work preparation. Individualised programmes are supported by Braille, Braille technology, communication skills, literacy, living skills, mobility, transitional skills, numeracy, study skills and using assistive technology.

Other information

Other services include: low vision, medical support, careers advice and guidance, counselling service, multi-faith provision, residential support workers, visiting ophthalmologists. Other therapies available.

Application procedure

Individual visits arranged for potential students. Contact Central Admissions on 01432 376621. Potential students attend a 24-hour residential assessment for which no charge is made.

Royal School for the Deaf

Address: Stanley Road, Cheadle Hulme, Stockport SK8 6RQ

Codes : C D E F G H O Q S

Tel: 0161 610 0100   **Fax:** 0161 610 0101   **Email:** headteacher@rsdmanchester.org   **Website:** www.rsdmanchester.org

Age range: 5-22

Controlled by: Non-maintained (Seashell Trustee Ltd)

Contact for admissions information: Principal — Mrs H Ward

Out-of-term contact: As above

Fees: Band A day £37,280 up to Band D 52 weeks £178,658

Usual source of funding for students: 5-19 years local authority; 19 years+ LSC — most students

Aims: To provide high quality education, care and specialist services to individuals with complex learning and communication difficulties whose needs cannot be met in their local environment, and to promote their development, success and participation in the community.

Students catered for: Students who have complex learning and communication difficulties, including combinations of sensory impairment, autism, physical and medical difficulties, severe and profound and multiple learning difficulties.

Premises and facilities

The College is currently undergoing a new build to provide refurbished teaching rooms including ITC, accessible life skills, art, DT, a new student common room and small therapy and sensory rooms.
Sports hall and inclusive fitness suite. An all-weather pitch is in progress. Swimming and hydrotherapy pools.

Student accommodation

Individual bedrooms in eight residential units on site.

Student numbers

80 — 60 of whom are in the College.

Staffing

All teaching staff have additional higher diplomas in hearing impairment, visual impairment, multi-sensory impairment, autistic spectrum disorders, profound and multiple learning difficulties.

Courses

A pre-vocational and vocational course.

Links

Other specialist colleges, other special schools, some links with sector colleges; access into the community via various youth and church groups, scouts and gym clubs etc; supported work placements with a range of local employers.

Other information

The College employs speech and language therapists, physiotherapists, OTs, educational psychologist, audiologists and have visiting CAMHS and adult psychiatrists.

Application procedure

Applications via the local authority or Connexions adviser to the principal.

Ruskin Mill Educational Trust

Codes: B C F I M O T

Address: Old Bristol Road, Nailsworth, Gloucestershire GL6 0LA

Tel: 01453 837500   **Fax:** 01453 837512   **Email:** admissions@ruskin-mill.org.uk   **Website:** www.ruskin-mill.org.uk

Age range: 16-25

Controlled by: RMET

Contact for admissions information: 01453 837521

Out-of-term contact: 01453 837500

Fees: LSC scales or by negotiation with social services

Usual source of funding for students: LSC

Aims: To provide opportunities for specialist further education in the context of creative communities, cultural initiatives and commercial regeneration. These opportunities are designed to enable young people with learning difficulties to engage in activities and social interaction that will help them maximise their potential for autonomy and employability.

Students catered for: Young people who have exhibited challenging behaviour and emotional disturbance, or who have been unable to form meaningful relationships due to conditions such as Asperger's Syndrome; students who have struggled to come to terms with the consequences of suffering abuse or having a specific learning difficulty or a delicate constitution. Each year RMET is able to offer 30-40 new student places.

Premises and facilities

A specialist college on three separate sites in Gloucestershire, the West Midlands and Sheffield.

100 acre Ruskin Mill College consists of two converted cloth mills, a small mixed farm, market garden, trout farm, lake and woodland open to the public. There are craft workshops, exhibition and performance spaces, an organic vegetable shop, coffee shop and restaurant. Glasshouse College is situated on the edge of the Staffordshire and Worcestershire countryside and has a range of high-quality craft workshops, with a visitor trail, a shop and café. Freeman College is located on a range of sites across Sheffield and grounded in the strong craft and industrial traditions of the city.

Student accommodation

Residential accommodation and independent living training are offered in households within the local community, where the students live in the homes of the residential care workers with progression into independent living units with arm's length support available where appropriate. There is college holiday care provision available and some students stay throughout the year.

Student numbers

Ruskin Mill College 95; Glasshouse College 75; Freeman College 30.

Staffing

Teaching at all three RMET colleges takes place in small groups of rarely more than three students, or on a 1:1 basis if this is required, by staff qualified in the appropriate craft, land work, or basic skills area.

Courses

Individual programmes designed to enable students to make the most of their own potential. Therapeutic craft activities, basic and continuing education, work experience within the RMET's own small businesses and vocational training are all available. 1:1 counselling, therapy sessions and social use of language; small intensive groups working together in the craft workshops and on the land; group work in drama, story telling and music; regular educational and recreational visits to the continent. Students can work towards qualifications from OCN, RSA, City & Guilds, NCFE, SEG and AEB. GCSE courses available where appropriate.

Links

Students are able to progress to NVQ or equivalent vocational qualifications through integration into local colleges.

Application procedure

Applications should be made to the Admissions Manager, who will arrange visits if appropriate and discuss the suitability of a placement. Referrals are accepted from prospective students and their carers, specialist Connexions and Social Services departments. Placements are offered for both day and residential students.

St Catherine's School

Address: Grove Road, Ventnor, Isle of Wight PO38 1TT

Tel: 01983 852722   **Fax:** 01983 857219   **Email:** general@stcatherines.org.uk   **Website:** www.stcatherines.org.uk

Age range: 7–19

Contact for admissions information: Sue Betchley

Out-of-term contact: As above

Fees: £32,555–£35,058

Usual source of funding for students: LEA

Aims: Grove Hill FE Centre offers young people with specific language disorders an integrated educational programme which blends vocational, specialist language and independent living skills within a residential setting. The Centre provides an interim period of ongoing therapy and small group teaching between school and a future full-time vocational/learning experience.

Students catered for: Students at St Catherine's have a statement of special educational needs which describes their primary disability as being their speech and language disorder.

Premises and facilities

St Catherine's is situated overlooking the sea in the seaside town of Ventnor. Older pupils attend Grove Hill FE Centre, situated opposite the main school site. The school is set in its own grounds and has pool, football, tennis, basketball, swim facilities as well as its own chapel.

Student accommodation

Students have their own rooms and are supported through the keyworker system to expand their social and leisure experiences.

Student numbers

There are 33 places for students aged 16–19.

Staffing

Multi-disciplinary team including speech and language therapists, care staff and teaching staff.

Courses

OCR National Skills Profile; OCR Computer Literacy and IT; London Chamber of Commerce & Industry (LCCIB) adult numeracy and adult literacy; ASDAN Further Education Award Scheme. Students are given the opportunity to gain accreditation not only for work completed at college and the Centre but also in structured leisure time.

Links

Students with areas of particular ability may also follow some GCSE courses, either at the FE Centre or at local high schools or Isle of Wight College. Also links with local employers.

Other information

St Catherine's has OT on site and school nurses. Local GP is always on call. School has access to a play therapist and psychotherapist.

Application procedure

Formal applications for admissions are normally considered from the LEA. The best way of judging whether St Catherine's is the right place is to go and see.

St Christopher's School

Address: Carisbrooke Lodge, Westbury Park, Bristol BS6 7JE

Code: S

Tel: 0117 973 3301   **Fax:** 0117 974 3665   **Email:** st-christophers@st-christophers.bristol.sch.uk
Website: www.st-christophers.bristol.sch.uk

Age range: 6-19

Controlled by: Independent residential special school. Registered charity

Aims: To prepare the pupils to find their place in the community and become as independent as possible.

Students catered for: Children with severe and complex learning difficulties, some also with challenging behaviour, some with mobility difficulties.

Premises and facilities

Located on the edge of Durdham Downs. Minibus outings and use of the School pool are an integral part of hostel life. A Christian (non-denominational) service is held on Sundays for pupils to attend. A wholefood, additive-free diet is provided where possible. Drawing, painting, modelling and drama enhances the pupil's experience of life. Music sessions take place daily in each class and a weekly school concert is given by teachers and pupils.

Student accommodation

There are seven hostels, of various sizes, catering for the differing age groups and needs. There is provision for pupils on a 52-week placement, when needed.

Staffing

Steiner- and state-educated teachers. High ratio of staff to pupils. Qualified medical staff are on duty day and night to give help and advice when necessary. Homeopathic remedies are used where possible.

Courses

Pupils are educated over a six-term year. The curriculum is based on the principles of curative education indicated by Rudolf Steiner for children with special needs. Pupils also have access to the National Curriculum, independence and social skills and a range of therapies. Pupils aged 14-19 have access to ASDAN accreditation schemes.

Links

Access to local FE colleges, close proximity to local shops and amenities allow safe and convenient participation in community life.

Application procedure

Contact the Educational Registrar at the above address.

St Davids Care in the Community

Codes: C E J N O S

Address: Fairfield, St Davids Road, St Davids, Pembrokeshire SA62 6QH

Tel: 01437 720003   **Fax:** 01437 720175   **Email:** stdavidcare@ad.com   **Website:** www.stdavids.co.uk

Age range: 18-65

Contact for admissions information: Miss Lyn Hall, Director

Fees: Variable according to needs. Rising annually

Usual source of funding for students: Local authority

Aims: St Davids offers continuous support for life for all residents, 52 weeks per year. St Davids is committed to a Christian way of life, recognising the right of all residents to make whatever life choices their ability allows.

Students catered for: People with varying degrees of dependency from independent living with support to high-dependency, specialised care.

Premises and facilities

Seven registered care homes. One community centre with restaurant. Full day-service facilities including working farm with horticulture programme and computer/IT centre.

Student accommodation

Homes registered for three-ten residents. All with single bedrooms.

Student numbers

45.

Staffing

Qualified staff of 40 working in care, education, maintenance, administration, catering and horticulture. Care staff qualified to NVQ level 2/3. Four registered managers.

Courses

IT, literacy/numeracy, art/craft, music therapy, horticulture, drama.

Links

Pembrokeshire College, Haverfordwest.

Other information

Specialist services include aromatherapy, chiropody. Community nurse, dietitian, intensive support team, speech and language therapy, psychology support.

Application procedure

Telephone contact initially to director. Trial visits can be arranged.

St Elizabeth's School

Codes: C F M N O S

Address: Much Hadham, Hertfordshire SG10 6EW

Tel: 01279 844270 **Fax:** 01279 843903 **Email:** school@stelizabeths.org.uk **Website:** www.stelizabeths.org.uk

---

Age range: 5-19

Controlled by: DfES approved non-maintained

Contact for admissions information: Pam Tomkins

Out-of-term contact: 01279 843451

Fees: On application

Usual source of funding for students: LEA

Aims: St Elizabeth's admits young people of any or no denomination according to their statement of special educational need. By integrating education, care, therapy and independent living young people are able to assume greater control of their lives.

Students catered for: Residential/day education for pupils with epilepsy, autism, MLD, SLD, complex needs and communication difficulties.

Premises and facilities

A 68-acre parkland estate with excellent transport links. Buildings are single storey and fully ramped. A new Living and Learning Complex is due to open in November 2006. Small groups of en-suite study bedrooms are built around dedicated fully-equipped learning spaces. A multi-therapy unit was opened in 2003.

Student accommodation

Purpose built easy access single-storey accommodation. The majority of learners reside in single study bedrooms sharing a common and dining room.

Student numbers

68 boarders; 12 day.

Staffing

A team of teachers, therapists, nurses, social workers, residential care workers, waking night staff and learning support assistants work closely with pupils and their families.

Courses

A living and learning programme that takes into account interests and aspirations provides access to the National Curriculum and the Post 16 Framework. Individual Learning Plans (ILPs) are augmented and enhanced by a range of therapies.

The literacy, numeracy, ICT, PSHE and the enrichment curriculum are in the context of life skills and promote confidence and competence in daily living. The extended curriculum in the evenings and weekends supports learning opportunities.

Links

Within St Elizabeth's Centre's campus three Social Enterprises and an FE College operate; they provide structured and supported work-related placements. Achievement is celebrated throughout the year and progress is accredited in different ways.

Other information

Pupils have access to visiting consultant specialists in neurology and the local GP team. This multi-disciplinary approach allows pupils to assume greater control of their lives.

Application procedure

Learners have a statement of SEN. Their LEA consults if they feel multi-disciplinary provision is appropriate. Families are welcome to make initial visits by appointment.

St John's Catholic School for the Deaf

Address: Church Street, Boston Spa, West Yorkshire LS23 6DF

Tel: 01937 842144   **Fax:** 01937 541471   **Email:** info@stjohns.org.uk   **Website:** www.stjohns.org.uk

Age range: 3-19

Controlled by: Non-maintained

Contact for admissions information: Mrs J Butterick

Fees: On application

Usual source of funding for students: LEA

Aims: To provide an oral education to deaf pupils.

Students catered for: Severely and profoundly deaf students who may also have additional difficulties.

Premises and facilities

Acoustically-treated classrooms. All people taught using a group hearing aid system.

Student numbers:

98.

Staffing

Qualified teachers of the deaf, an audiologist, nurse, five speech and language therapists, special needs assistants and care staff.

Courses

GCSEs; entry level courses; vocational courses.

Links

Links with several mainstream colleges for post-16 education and with employers for work experience.

Other information

Various health professionals can be accessed.

Application procedure

An assessment of each prospective pupil must be done before a place is offered: four days for primary-aged pupils and five days for secondary-aged pupils.

St Joseph's Extended Education Department

Codes: D E H N Q R

Address: St Rose's School, Stratford Lawn, Stroud GL5 4AP

Tel: 01453 763793   **Fax:** 01453 752617   **Email:** admin@stroses.gloucs.sch.uk   **Website:** www.stroses.gloucs.sch.uk

Age range: 16-19

Contact for admissions information: Mrs Billington (Headteacher)

Fees: On application

Usual source of funding for students: LEAs

Aims: To consolidate and continue basic education; to prepare students for the next stage which can range from specialist FE to a residential placement; to enable students to appreciate their personal worth and develop their independence.

Students catered for: Students who have difficulties arising from their physical problems (except severe behaviour disorders).

Premises and facilities

Two bungalows separate from main school. Situated in Stroud and close to all amenities. Students access community facilities regularly and benefit from a full extra curricular programme. Facilities to develop personal independence.

Student accommodation

Two bungalows that both sleep six students. Hoisting and specialist equipment throughout. Single or double bedrooms. The newer bungalow has en-suite facilities.

Student numbers

12 residential and day placements.

Staffing

One senior teacher; occupational therapist; physiotherapist; speech therapist; seven subject teachers; 15 teaching assistants/carers; workshop instructor; nurse on site.

Courses

Individual programmes according to need include basic numeracy, literacy, PSHE and citizenship, life skills, all of which can lead to a number of qualifications and accreditation such as GCSE; ASDAN Youth Award Scheme (FE and Towards Independence); City & Guilds Food Studies; National Skills Profile & Accreditation of Life & Living.

Students can attend local schools or colleges for certain courses. Courses last one to three years, according to need.

Links

Close liaison with mainstream schools and colleges. Visits to FE specialist colleges. Work experience organised locally whenever possible and appropriate.

Other information

All therapists on site. GP at local medical centre. Visiting professionals — orthotist; wheelchair services.

Application procedure

Informal contact welcomed. Official application through LEA. For information please contact Sheila Talwar (Head of Dept) or Mrs Frances Billington (Headteacher).

St Joseph's School

Codes: B C F J O S

Address: Amlets Lane, Cranleigh, Surrey GU6 7 DH

Tel: 01483 272449   **Email:** office@st-josephscranleigh.surrey.sch.uk

Age range: 7–19+

Controlled by: Governing Body

Contact for admissions information: Marion White

Out-of-term contact: School office open throughout the year

Fees: 2006/07 residential £42,958; day £29,832

Usual source of funding for students: LA & London Borough funded

Aims: The Extended Education Department aims to achieve a balance between preparation for work, independence, participation in the community including recreation and for adult family life. It offers opportunities to broaden relationships, experience and learn from a range of activities, handle personal spending and explore independence and interdependence in a managed environment.

Students catered for: Students on the whole continue to have their SEN statement met within educational provision. The students abilities range from P6 to NC level 3. Many students have needs relating to ASD. Students who have specific learning difficulties are not catered for.

Premises and facilities

The school is set in 20 acres of landscaped grounds on the slopes of the North Downs, above the village of Cranleigh. The grounds include a wooded area, football pitch, a basketball court, an adventure playground and a heated outdoor swimming pool.

Student accommodation

The students are accommodated in three on-site comfortable house groups and one off-site house in the village of Cranleigh. Accommodation is in single, double and treble rooms and all house groups have dedicated family facilities such as a living room, kitchen diner and shower room.

Student numbers

32 students, however some travel to the school daily.

Staffing

Qualified teachers and tutors including several specialist teachers i.e. art & design, PSHCE and work related learning. The department is overseen by a lead teacher and an assistant headteacher.

Courses

Personalised and individualised programmes for students, of either two or three years duration. Programmes of study work towards the Equals Moving On accreditation, AQA Unit Awards, GCSE art and ASDAN. The programmes offered include community skills, life based skills, work related learning including weekly and block work experience and enterprise, citizenship and PSHE, creative arts, sport and leisure, numeracy and literacy basic skill support and religious education.

Links

24 local employers offer work experience programmes, Cranleigh arts centre, Cranleigh leisure centre, local FE colleges and other KS5 courses in Surrey special schools, RDA and Challengers.

Other information

Physiotherapists and occupational therapists visit regularly; therapeutic personalised music sessions available; intensive speech & language therapy delivered by one of our three therapists.

Application procedure

A copy of the students SEN statement sent to school. The school will then contact the LA or parents to arrange an initial visit. The school does not arrange for assessment visits without confirmation of funding from LA or London Borough.

St Loye's Foundation

Code: Q

Address: Topsham Road, Exeter, Devon EX2 6EP

Tel: 01392 255428   **Fax:** 01392 420889   **Email:** info@stloyes.co.uk   **Website:** www.stloyesfoundation.org.uk

Age range: 18-63

Controlled by: Managing Director, Martin Rich

Contact for admissions information: Viv Johnson, Admissions Administrator; Joan Stirk, Admissions Administrator

Fees: The Foundation operates under a Government-Funded Programme

Usual source of funding for students: The Foundation operates to a Government Residential Training for Adults Programme and is funded by the Department of Work and Pensions

Aims: St Loye's will enable adults with long-term ill health or disabilities to become skilled and valued members of society by resolving the constraints to employment and inclusion and using specialist and focused personal development towards achieving this.

Students catered for: Throughout the UK on a residential/non-residential basis, unemployed adults with a long-term ill health or disability.

Premises and facilities

Based in over 22 acres of landscaped gardens offering a full recreational programme in addition to on-site cyber café, sports hall, snooker and music room, bar, multi-gym and outdoor cricket/football pitch. 24hr healthcare, therapeutic intervention, social and life skills, support with personal development.

Student accommodation

Trainees reside in female/male blocks with well-appointed bathrooms. Their secure study rooms have a TV aerial and washbasin.

Student numbers

Approximately 150 residential trainees and 40 non-residential trainees at one given time.

Staffing

Approximately 115 staff based on a single site.

Courses

Roll-on, roll-off programme of 40-52 weeks duration. Programmes are mainly modular based and cover City and Guilds and NVQ qualifications. A range of short introductory courses is also offered.

Links

Jobcentre Plus, Connexions, Shaw Trust, WTCS, Royal School for the Deaf, West of England for Children With Little Or No Sight.

Other information

Counsellers, psychologists and GPs. Details of a Direct Referral Service can be found on the website along with additional information on short courses.

Application procedure

In general, applications are made through the Disability Employment Adviser (DEA), then approved by the RTU and forwarded. The trainee is contacted direct regarding start dates.

St Mary's College

Codes: B C D E F H J K L N O Q

Address: Wrestwood Road, Bexhill-on-Sea, East Sussex TN40 2LU

Tel: 01424 730740   **Fax:** 01424 733575   **Email:** adm@st-marys.bexhill.sch.uk   **Website:** www.st-marys.bexhill.sch.uk

Age range: 16-19

Controlled by: St Mary's Wrestwood Children's Trust

Fees: On application — generally paid by student's home LEA

Aims: To prepare young adults for the change from compulsory school education to adult life. To prepare the individual student for independent living and working to the highest level achievable by the student. The college aims to provide a balanced curriculum which is both fun and helps the students develop into young adults.

Students catered for: Young people within the MLD range and with particular needs in regard to speech/language difficulties, autism, physical difficulties and complex medical conditions.

Premises and facilities

From St Mary's School and St Mary's College students are able to access shops, activities and facilities in the community, assisted when necessary by College staff.

Student accommodation

Residential accommodation on the main site for less independent students and two living houses in Bexhill town centre for more independent students.

Staffing

Qualified teachers, teaching assistants, speech & language therapists, occupational therapists, physiotherapists, counselling psychologist, art therapist, facilitators/care staff, audiologist, qualified nurses, college transition coordinator and independent social worker. There is close liaison with teachers and facilitators in the College.

Courses

All students attend bi-annual meetings to review their individual learning plan/action plan that targets educational and independence needs. The College offers nationally-recognised qualifications and the ASDAN Life Skills Award and First Skills Profile. Horticulture is accredited to the National Proficiency Tests and art as a GCSE. Key Skills are also used as a guide to assessing religious education, personal, social and health education, diary keeping and budgeting.

Links

The programmes are enhanced by carefully selected college courses and appropriate life experiences. The College has links with Hastings College of Arts & Technology, Bexhill College, Claverham Community College, Plumpton Agricultural College and local schools.

Application procedure

Referral and assessment.

SeeAbility

Codes: D plus A B C E F G H J M N O P Q R S

Address: SeeAbility House, Hook Road, Epsom, Surrey KT19 8SQ

Tel: 01372 755 000   **Fax:** 01372 755 051   **Email:** enquiries@seeability.org   **Website:** www.seeability.org

Age range: 16/18-65

Controlled by: Trustees

Contact for admissions information: Paul Bott (Area Manager **South East**) 01372 389 407 Email: pbott@seeability.org

Janet Dewar (Area Manager **South Central)** 01372 755 047 Email: jdewar@seeability.org

Colin Fletcher (Area Manager **South West)** 01823 448 236 Email: cfletcher@seeability.org

Out-of-term contact: As above

Fees: Assessed according to individual need

Usual source of funding for students: Social services and/or health authorities/PCTs

Aims: To work with adults who have visual impairment and additional disabilities enabling them to explore their potential, develop their skills/independence and enhance the quality of their lives.

Students catered for: Adults who have a visual impairment and a range of additional disabilities including those listed in the codes above.

Premises and facilities

SeeAbility currently operates:

eight registered care homes in Surrey, East Sussex, Hampshire and Somerset; four activity and resource centres in Surrey, East Sussex, Hampshire and Somerset; three supported living/domiciliary care services in Surrey, Hampshire and Devon.

Student accommodation

Residential homes offer individual bedrooms, some with en-suite facilities and shared use of a kitchen, bathroom, laundry, dining and living areas.

Supported living accommodation offers a secure housing right through rental or shared ownership to individual's own self-contained property.

Student numbers

Currently 157.

Staffing

267 full- and part-time staff, who receive full training. Support staff meet NVQ targets.

Courses

No formal education/courses. SeeAbility supports people through everyday opportunities; specialist training from rehabilitation workers for the visually impaired; activity and resource centres; access to community-based resources, to maintain and develop skills which increase their choice, independence and quality of life.

Links

As appropriate, links are made and supported with local colleges and employers.

Other information

Some services have specialist therapists within their establishments, whilst others forge good links with local primary care resources. Additional/specialist services are accessed according to need.

Application procedure

Enquiries are welcomed from individuals, families and sponsoring authority representatives by telephone, email, post, fax. There is no formal application form but a process of individual assessment takes place involving visits to/from SeeAbility.

Sense East

Address: 72 Church Street, Market Deeping, Peterborough PE6 8AL

Codes: D G H

Tel: 01778 382230 **Fax:** 01778 380078 **Email:** enquiries@sense-east.org.uk **Website:** www.sense.org.uk

Age range: 17+

Controlled by: SENSE

Contact for admissions information: Regional Director, Kate Lockett

Fees: £85,000+ per annum

Aims: The education and training of students with Rubella Syndrome and multi-sensory impairments.

Students catered for: Rubella Syndrome. Dual or single sensory impairment, with possible additional learning difficulties, physical disabilities and language delay.

Premises and facilities

52-week residential education and training. Access to sport, leisure and cultural facilities in surrounding towns and countryside. There is a swimming pool, music room and well-equipped teaching rooms, each with a computer.

Student accommodation

Students live in groups of between three and five in ten different houses in Market Deeping, Peterborough, Skegness, Louth, Dereham (Norfolk) and Kettering (Northants).

Staffing

Social tutors (including waking night staff); education tutors; vocational tutors; ancillary and administration staff.

Courses

Vocational training takes place in pottery, woodworking and jewellery-making etc, in craft workshops on local industrial estates. Individually-designed programmes in areas of communication (including, where appropriate, sign-supported English, Braille and other systems), basic skills in literacy and numeracy, science and creative arts, physical education and independence skills and vocational training.

Links

Various courses as part of the training programmes take place at local colleges of further education and other community-based facilities.

Applications/selection

Telephone/letter to Regional Director in first instance.

Sense West

Address: 9a Birkdale Avenue, off Heeley Road, Selly Oak, Birmingham B29 6UB

Codes: D G H

Tel: 0121 415 2720   **Fax:** 0121 472 8449   **Textphone:** 0121 415 2720   **Email:** westenquiries@sense.org.uk

Website: www.sense.org.uk

Age range: All ages

Controlled by: SENSE

Contact for admissions information: Regional Director, Peter Cheer

Fees: Based on individual needs

Aims: To provide advice, support and developmental services for people with dual sensory impairment (who may have other disabilities), or with a single sensory impairment and additional physical and/or learning disabilities.

Students catered for: Deafblind people (both sight and hearing impairments) and sensory impaired people with additional physical and/or learning difficulties. Midlands and south west. No upper age limit. Services open 52 weeks a year.

Premises and facilities

Sense West offers a range of living accommodation in the West Midlands and South West regions, designed to meet individual needs and preferences. Sense West also provides a range of day opportunities for local people who live at home or in other accommodation, including vocational training.

Student accommodation

Accommodation ranges from one-bedroom flats to group homes for up to six people, situated in local communities. Living accommodation is adapted and designed to meet the individual needs of the people living there, including the use of high colour contrasts, tactile surfaces, modified lighting, and aids and equipment to enable people to move around and live as independently as possible.

Staffing

Staff are specially training in deafblindness and communication techniques, and also a range of other relevant subjects such as challenging behaviour. A range of staff work in residential services, education, day and vocational training; advice and support staff.

Courses

No specific courses are offered; individual learning programmes increase the person's independence and develop a range of skills through accessing a wide range of activities and facilities. Development of communication skills is a particular area of focus, and functional vision and hearing assessments enable staff to identify, and so devise, ways to stimulate residual sight and hearing. Specialist in-house facilities are used, specifically designed to stimulate all the senses.

Links

Facilities in the local community are accessed as much as possible.

Other information

One-to-one support can be provided at home or in the community through the provision of Intervenors (for children and adults born deafblind) or communicator-guides (for adults with acquired dual sensory loss). The training and consultancy team also offers a range of advice, training and assessments to families and professionals working with deafblind people.

Application procedure

Contact Krystyna Cieslik. Home visits; visits to services and assessments can be arranged.

The Sheiling Community

Address: Horton Road, Ashley, Ringwood, Hampshire BH24 2EB

Code: O

Tel: 01425 477488   **Fax:** 01425 479536   **Email:** enquries@sheilingschool.co.uk   **Website:** www.sheilingschool.co.uk

Age range: 6-19

Controlled by: Independent

Contact for admissions information: Heidi Hoffman (6-16) 01425 482406, Mrs Nikki McGrath (post-16) 01425 482401, Carol Cheeseman (post-19) 01425 479926

Out-of-term contact: Management Group 01425 482450

Fees: Fee structure on application

Usual source of funding for students: Education authority/social services

Aims: To fill the gap where local and national special school facilities are not appropriate, providing a total environment whereby children can be helped to reach their full potential. The Lantern and Sturts Farm are 'intentional communities' providing 52-week supported living facilities — home life, fulfilling work, social interaction, adult education possibilities.

Students catered for: MLD/SLD pupils/students/adults. No geographic restrictions.

Premises and facilities

The Sheiling Community occupies a 50-acre wooded site near to the market town of Ringwood. Individual houses are scattered around the village green and provide an extended family household situation, together with house parents, their own children and co-workers (carers).

Student accommodation

Students either have individual rooms or share with another student.

Student numbers

49 students aged 8–19 at present.

Staffing

Consists of a variety of teachers, care professionals, therapists and craft specialists.

Courses

Recreational facilities include swimming, folk dancing, courses in arts/crafts and participation in the rich cultural life of the community which includes drama, concerts, etc. All of these are pursued not FOR the special needs people but WITH them, each contributing towards the wellbeing of the community according to ability and experience.

Links

Bryanston School.

Other information

Support from resident medical officer and nurse. Liaison with psychologist and psychiatrist.

Application procedure

Through the Community's medical officer.

Solden Hill House

Address: Banbury Road, Byfield, Daventry, Northamptonshire NN11 6UA

Code: O

Tel: 01327 260234   **Fax:** 01327 263840   **Email:** info@soldenhillhouse.co.uk   **Website:** www.soldenhillhouse.co.uk

Age range: 19-65

Controlled by: Independent Charity

Contact for admissions information: Mrs Delia Thomas, Administrator

Out-of-term contact: As above

Fees: From £695 per week

Usual source of funding for students: Jobcentre Plus and local authority

Aims: An independent residential home for the care and training of adults with learning difficulties, based on the principles of Rudolf Steiner.

Students catered for: Adults aged 19-65 with mild to moderate learning difficulties.

Premises and facilities

Solden Hill House consists of three residential houses — Main House and Apps House are set in 8½ acres of grounds, and Flora Innes House ½ mile away in the picturesque village of Byfield.

Activities include craft workshops, dance and circus workshops, outings and activities nearby — riding, sailing, swimming, college courses and sports.

Student accommodation

Each service-user has their own furnished, single room with hand basin and shares a bathroom with a maximum of three other residents.

Student numbers

Up to 30.

Staffing

A residential management team for each of the houses; other residential and non-residential care staff; waking night care staff; domestic, administrative and maintenance staff.

Links

Daventry Tertiary College, Daventry Gateway Club, 'Sailability', Horse riding with the RDA, sports sessions at Daventry Leisure Centre, swimming sessions at Southam Leisure Centre and Hellidon Lakes.

Other information

Chiropodist visits every six weeks, and any other professionals as and when required by each individual.

Application procedure

Apply to the Administrator for initial details and to arrange an interview with the Manager.

Somerset Court

Address: Harp Road, Brent Knoll, Highbridge, Somerset TA9 4HQ

Code: C

Tel: 01278 760555   **Fax:** 01278 761919   **Email:** somerset.court@nas.org.uk   **Website:** www.nas.org.uk/

Aims: To provide adult development and care programmes for adults with autism centred around the provision of an emotionally secure and structured pattern of life experiences and opportunities. To make life for residents as much as possible like living in their own home, looking after themselves and each day going out to work, as well as enjoying planned leisure activities together.

Students catered for: Adults with autism.

Premises and facilities

Somerset Court is a large house with 26 acres used for cultivation of vegetables and produce/plants for sale in the garden centre.

Student accommodation

Residents live in family groups in five individual units.

Student numbers

Up to 44 adults for the residential service with a limited number of day placements.

Staffing

Residential services offer professional care, domestic and leisure activities and individual skills training. Enhanced staffing ratios, usually an average baseline of 1:3.

Courses

Each resident has a personalised care/activity programme which is determined at annual case conference and subject to ongoing assessment and review through the IPP system. Subjects include: woodwork, horticulture, creative arts, grounds, communication and information skills. Use of information technology computer suite. Full individual service programmes and keyworkers' assessments help in a comprehensive planning and development programme for each individual.

Strathmore College

Address: Florence Villa & Park View Administration Centre, 38/40 Dimsdale Parade, Wolstanton, Newcastle ST5 8BU

Tel: 01782 740034   **Fax:** 01782 714860   **Email:** Strathmore.info@Craegmoor.co.uk

Age range: 16-23

Controlled by: Craegmoor Healthcare Group Ltd

Contact for admissions information: As above

Out-of-term contact: 52-week college

Fees: LSC Matrix

Usual source of funding for students: LSC

Aims: To provide residential training in urban living and independence skills for school leavers and young adults with special needs. Both long-term and short-term residents accommodated.

Students catered for: Most residents have moderate/severe learning difficulties. People with severe physical disabilities are not catered for.

Premises and facilities

Florence Villa and Park View function as residential colleges. Both properties are in pleasant residential areas of the potteries town of Longton. They are within a short walking distance of each other and the town centre. Students are encouraged to use community facilities, swimming baths, leisure centres, youth clubs, special Olympic activities, local cinemas, etc. The College is also able to offer day training facilities and has a retail outlet Jasmine — florist/confectioners.

Staffing

Staff are qualified trainers and care staff are experienced in residential work.

Courses

Students do not take prescribed courses. Individual programmes are devised to meet their needs. Emphasis is placed on independence training. When appropriate, training programmes may include work experience.

Links

Local college of FE, local businesses, registered with Staffordshire Social Services and Staffordshire Association of Registered Homes and ARC.

Application procedure

By application form. Clients/students referred by Connexions/careers personal adviser, social workers, health authority workers and parents.

Surecare Homes (Devon) Ltd

Address: 26 Mills Road, Cumberland Park Gardens, Devonport, Plymouth PL1 4NF

Codes: A B C F M N O R T

Tel: 01752 204598   **Fax:** 01752 218463   **Email:** Surecarehomes@supanet.com   **Website:** www.surecarehomes.co.uk

Age range: 16-25 (can be increased)

Contact for admissions information: Patricia Hawkins

Out-of-term contact: Residential, always open

Fees: £1300+ per week depending on needs

Aims: To provide small, family-type homes, offering clients with varying difficulties and disabilities full support and guidance to reach their full potential.

Premises and facilities
No wheelchair access. Plymouth offers a full range of facilities and is within easy access of Dartmoor, coast and country pursuits.

Student accommodation
Two- and three-bedded homes in pleasant parts of Plymouth, close to all amenities.

Staffing
Mostly on a 1:1 basis

Courses
Wide range of courses available through Plymouth College of Further Education, Saltash College, Duchy College and other providers.

Application procedure
Following referral reports and depending on needs. Transition period.

Taurus Crafts

Address: The Old Park, Lydney, Gloucestershire GL15 6BU

Codes: O P R

Tel: 01594 844841   **Fax:** 01594 845636   **Email:** training@tauruscrafts.co.uk   **Website**: www.tauruscrafts.co.uk

Age range: 19+

Aims: A working community designed to create the opportunity for a broad range of individuals with special needs to gain experience, develop confidence and, when attainable, a qualification, within a commercial environment. Provides work experience and daycare. Taurus Crafts is part of the Camphill Village Trust.

Students catered for: Female and male trainees accepted. They can be people with special needs i.e. learning disabilities, people with mental health problems or people with physical disabilities, although the whole operation is not accessible to people with significant mobility disabilities.

Premises and facilities

Taurus Crafts is a growing visitor attraction and craft centre in the Forest of Dean. The centre is based in an old coach house and farm buildings on the Lydney Park Estate just off the A48 between Lydney and Aylburton. The centre encompasses a café restaurant, pottery, craft shop and other workshops.

Student accommodation

Accommodation can be arranged for trainees with local families or in small residential homes for a fee.

Student numbers

Depending on funding, the centre can provide up to 20 training, work experience and day-care places.

Staffing

Taurus Crafts has a team of staff and volunteers with wide experience in their professional areas and experience of working with people with special needs.

Courses

Taurus Crafts currently offers training and work experience in the following areas: catering, pottery, retail and organic horticulture and is willing to try and organise training around particular craft skills through local craft workers if possible.

Links

The Centre has close links with the Grange and Oaklands, two neighbouring Camphill Village communities. The Centre also works closely with the local FE college and the Forest of Dean Adult Consortium.

Application procedure

Apply direct to Taurus Crafts. If they are in the position to provide a training place, a placement assessment will be organised to confirm the offer of training and develop a customised training programme.

Thorngrove/Mulberry Court

Address: Mulberry Court, Common Mead Lane, Gillingham, Dorset SP8 4RE

Code: E

Tel: 01747 822241/2 **Fax:** 01747 825966 **Email:** mulberry.court@scope.org.uk **Website:** www.scope.org.uk

Age range: 18+

Controlled by: SCOPE

Fees: Based on individual assessment

Aims: To provide residential accommodation for people with cerebral palsy, who also wish to contribute to the running of a garden centre.

Students catered for: Those with cerebral palsy, ambulant or semi-ambulant are accepted for residential care.

Premises and facilities

Thorngrove Garden Centre is pleasantly situated in 50 acres of farmland near the town of Gillingham, Dorset. It has a large and modern glasshouse nursery producing houseplants, bedding plants and shrubs to the general public.

Student accommodation

Mulberry Court provides accommodation for ten people in two purpose-built bungalows which are staffed continually.

Student numbers

17 male and female clients; 20+ for day care.

Staffing

20 staff including care workers, horticultural instructors and other support staff.

Courses

A team of staff offer support using individual plans so that each person can develop in the way that suits them best. Practical help and encouragement for those wishing to live more independently. Leisure activities include swimming, horse riding, yoga, group holidays and outings, and a wide range of hobbies such as photography, sport and cookery.

The Garden Centre gives people the opportunity to contribute to the running of a modern plant centre, producing houseplants, shrubs, conifers and bedding plants.

Other information

There are three other community homes where service users live more independently, but are provided with agreed staff input and 24-hour backup from Mulberry Court for emergencies.

Application procedure

Application in the first instance to the manager. Informal visits welcomed followed by short stay for assessment. Variable waiting times for admission. It is expected that a local authority assessment will have been completed and funding agreed.

Treloar College

Codes: A D E F H K O Q R

Address: Holybourne, Alton, Hants GU34 4EN

Tel: 01420 547425　**Fax:** 01420 542708　**Email:** admissions@treloar.org.uk　**Website:** www.treloar.org.uk

---

Age range: 16–25

Controlled by: Treloar Trust, a registered charity 1092857

Contact for admissions information: Helen Burton, Admissions Officer

Out-of-term contact: Helen Burton

Fees: Day £4,655–£46,476; Residential £14,350–£65,868

Usual source of funding for students: LSC

Aims: To provide education, therapy and independence training for physically disabled learners from pre-entry to A level. A wide range of opportunities enables students to explore their potential and make informed choices. Most leavers proceed to further or higher education, residential accommodation, open or supported employment.

Students catered for: Physically disabled students, possibly with associated medical, sensory, learning or communication difficulties. Majority wheelchair users; all independently mobile. Nationwide catchment.

Premises and facilities

Purpose-built facilities for living and learning, including halls of residence, learning resource centre, business admin, photography and horticulture areas. 24-hour health centre (waking nurses), swimming pool, gym, wheelchair race track. Riding, sailing, competitive and leisure sport, driving instruction.

Student accommodation

Majority ground floor, single rooms or sharing with one. Eight flats for independent living at edge of campus.

Student numbers

168 residential + up to 20 day students.

Staffing

Total of 348 including tutors, teaching assistants, physio-, occupational and speech and language therapists, rehabilitation engineers, nursing staff, medical officer, residential support staff, driving instructor; dietitian, educational psychologist, counselling team, specialist careers guidance, sensory impairment specialists, activities organiser.

Courses

Pre-entry and entry level courses including life skills and vocational elements, and vocational and AS/A levels in a wide range of subjects — plus many at level 3 in conjunction with neighbouring Alton College. Qualifications include City & Guilds, GCSE, RSA, Pitmans, AEB Basic Skills, BTEC and equivalent and the ASDAN Award Scheme.

Links

Teaching partnership with Alton College over past 20 years; recent link with adjacent secondary school over shared sports hall and fitness centre. Beacon College status has encouraged links with specialist providers and general FE colleges in the south.

Other information

Entry and pre-entry level learners share a week's 'outdoor bound' style study trip; optional music and driving tuition; emphasis on independence as well as academic goals.

Application procedure

Initial visit for learner/parents from year 9, followed by application form and interview. Places allocated on basis of 'can Treloar's meet student's needs?'

Vyrnwy Academy

Address: Vyrnwy House, Oswestry Road, Llansantffraid, Powys, Wales SY22 6AU

Tel: 01691 829112   **Email:** admin@vyrnwyacademy.co.uk   **Website:** www.vyrnwyacademy.co.uk

Age range: 18+

Controlled by: Independent (CSI Wales)

Contact for admissions information: Mr Carlo Ferri

Out-of-term contact: As above (50 weeks per year)

Fees: Base £140,000 per annum (50 weeks residential)

Usual source of funding for students: Social services/ health authority

Aims: 50 weeks per year residential placements for adults with autism/ASD/learning difficulty/epilepsy, etc. To provide an individualised service including individual learning programmes.

Students catered for: All types of learning difficulties including autism/ASD. Individual assessment, epilepsy, dyspraxia, EBD and challenging behaviour (non-violent).

Premises and facilities

Detached Victorian property, fully equipped. Large bedrooms all en-suite. Gardens down to river. In-house teaching/learning facilities and leisure facilities. Access to amenities in village/local towns. Safe/calm environment/ beautiful surroundings.

Student accommodation

Large individual rooms all en-suite. Communal areas for dining, food preparation, leisure activities. Large spacious house.

Student numbers

Maximum five: male/female.

Staffing

Two qualified SEN teachers: 1:1 teaching/learning (two); day support staff: five per day; night staff: four.

Courses

Independent Living Programme; National Accreditation through National Open College Network (NOCN); individual assessment and learning programmes. TEACCH. All areas of self-help, key skills, social/emotional, vocational studies, work experience, Adult Literacy/ Numeracy (NOCN).

Links

MENCAP-Countryside Project for gardening/woodwork skills, local adult social clubs, Careers Wales, Local National Autistic Society (NAS), Local FE Colleges, supported work schemes, Twocan — adult literacy group.

Other information

Access to all therapies/specialists — individual provision. Yoga and therapy on site.

Application procedure

Initial non-prejudicial visit by parents/carers, service user, professionals. Staff to visit home/school, etc. (initial needs assessment). Funding arranged with relevant authority. Transition arranged to include minimum two-night stay (no charge).

The West of England College

Address: Countess Wear, Exeter, Devon EX2 6HA

Code: D

Tel: 01392 454245 **Fax:** 01392 430517 **Email:** info@westengland.devon.sch.uk
Website: www.westengland.devon.sch.uk

Age range: 16-19+

Fees: Paid by students' home LEAs or LSC

Aims: The College aims to extend the students' academic education, provide vocational and pre-vocational training, develop the students' personal and social competence and promote independence.

Students catered for: Visually-impaired students, including those with learning difficulties and additional disabilities. South/South-west England & South Wales.

Premises and facilities

The West of England College is purpose-built and caters for blind and partially-sighted students. It is a branch of the West of England School for Children with Little or No Sight and has access to the School's excellent facilities.

Student accommodation

Provision is made for day and boarding students. Boarding is on a termly basis with exeat weekends and half-term breaks. All students are accommodated in single study bedrooms. There is a full weekend leisure programme which students are encouraged to help plan and take part in.

Student numbers

50.

Staffing

The campus has an excellent medical centre with RGN cover. Other services include audiology, speech therapy, occupational therapy and physiotherapy.
The pastoral aspect of the curriculum is delivered by an experienced team of care staff who work closely with individual students, encouraging them to make their own decisions and take responsibility for themselves.

Courses

A wide range of academic and vocational courses. Students may be enrolled on courses at local colleges for their studies, supported by the specialist staff and resources of the West of England College. An 'in-house' programme for students with additional learning difficulties. Independence living skills programme, mobility training and an active leisure programme are vital aspects of the extended curriculum offered to all students.

Links

The College has close links with Exeter College, St Loye's Foundation and Bicton College.

Other information

The ophthalmic surgeon, paediatrician and other specialists visit on a regular basis.

Application procedure

Telephone the West of England College for information and to arrange a visit. Applicants will have an advice and guidance meeting followed by a three-day assessment which is free of charge.

Westgate College

Address: Westcliff House, 37 Sea Road, Westgate-on-Sea, Kent CT8 8QP

Codes: H and also F G M O

Tel: 01843 836300   **Fax:** 01843 830001   **Email:** enquiries@westgatecollegeadmin.co.uk
Website: www.westgate-college.org.uk

Age range: 16+

Controlled by: The Royal School for Deaf Children Margate

Contact for admissions: The Admissions Officer

Out of term contact: The College Secretary

Usual source of funding for students: LEA, LSC, social services

Aims: Westgate College aims to educate deaf people for a positive future; to help students to decide on their goals and ambitions and then realise them. Every student is treated as an individual with the right to make decisions. Students have the right to live as independently as possible, and to be treated fairly and with equal opportunity.

Students catered for: The College provides residential education for a diverse range of learners aged 16-25 years, all of whom have sensory disabilities. Many have additional learning difficulties, physical disabilities and associated challenging behaviours.

Premises and facilities

The College operates from two sites in Westgate-on-Sea, St. Gabriel's House and Westcliff House, which both provide teaching and residential accommodation. The College also makes use of some facilities shared with The Royal School for Deaf Children in Margate such as the swimming pool, medical centre, and their commercial farm at Dargate near Whitstable.

Student accommodation

Residential accommodation is provided in a variety of units including some self-contained flats, and group homes on the periphery of the school site in Margate.

Student numbers

The College caters for 55-80 students of either sex.

Staffing

Skilled and experienced staff including teachers of the deaf, tutors, support and residential support staff, service staff, medical and professional staff (including occupational therapist, audiologist, physiotherapist, speech and language therapist, educational psychologist).

Courses

Education provision includes independent living skills and pre-vocational/vocational programmes. Students may work towards nationally accredited courses including NPTC and NVQs in animal care, catering, horticulture, wood occupations and BSL. Students may also attend local FE colleges as part of their programme. All courses also include a residential curriculum that is planned to increase the students' autonomy, encourage informed decision-making and develop personal and social independence skills.

Links

The College has excellent links with Thanet College of Further Education in addition to a wide variety of businesses, both locally and nationally, and the local community.

Application procedure

In the first instance contact The Admissions Officer or The College Secretary.

William Morris Camphill Community

Address: William Morris House, Eastington, Stonehouse, Gloucestershire GL10 3SH

Tel: 01453 824025   **Fax:** 01453 825807   **Email:** williammorris@camphill.org.uk   **Website:** www.camphill.org.uk

Age range: 16-25

Controlled by: The Management Group

Fees: LSC Matrix

Aims: To continue education and training as a preparation for life. Developing ability, skills and encouraging independence for adult life whether in the community or a sheltered environment.

Students catered for: Those with learning difficulties, also including social and multiple difficulties.

Premises and facilities

A college and training centre in Severn Valley (Stroud four miles, Stonehouse one mile and Gloucester ten miles). Large gardens; pottery; weaving; woodwork and food processing workshops. There is also a farm community nearby for older trainees, offering agricultural training.

Student accommodation

The main house accommodates young people in two separate extended family groups. Two additional houses for eight young people and three independent young people.

Student numbers

17.

Staffing

Residential co-workers, teachers and craft workshop instructors, supported by therapists and artists.

Courses

Those aged 16-19 are offered a three-year further education course each morning and training in a workshop activity in the afternoons. They spend 12 weeks in each workshop to develop a wide range of craft and skill abilities. At 19, further education continues but the emphasis is on craft training and employability skills. Additionally offered drama, music, adventure training, horse riding and education trips.

Links

Courses available at Stroud College.

Application procedure

Application forms and prospectus on request, followed by interview. If applicable, trial visit is arranged. Vacancy situation dictates waiting period.

The Wing Centre

Address: Vicars Hill, Boldre, Lymington, Hampshire SO41 5QB

Code: C

Tel: 0800 288 9779   **Fax:** 020 7348 5223   **Email:** enquiries@cambiangroup.com   **Website:** www.cambianeducation.com

Age range: 16-19

Controlled by: Cambian Education Services

Contact for admissions information: Julia Scrase/Katy Knight

Out-of-term contact: 0800 288 9779

Fees: £2,958.80 (boarding) per week; £1,479.40 (day) per week

Usual source of funding for students: LEA

Aims: The Wing Centre exists to help young men who are experiencing difficulties as a result of a diagnosis of Asperger Syndrome (AS) and other associated difficulties falling within the autistic spectrum. Students usually stay for a period of two years.

Students catered for: Young men with Asperger Syndrome and associated difficulties within the autistic spectrum, whose difficulties have prevented their needs being fully met in mainstream schools or other centres. Students range from a low to average ability, above average, or gifted and able, but demonstrate difficulties in a range of key areas of development affecting everyday life.

Premises and facilities

The main site of The Wing Centre is situated near Lymington in Hampshire. It enjoys a superb countryside setting close to the New Forest. Two other residential units are located in Southbourne and Bournemouth in Dorset. Both units are very close to local shops, main line bus and train stations.

Student accommodation

Each student has a single bedroom with washbasin and shaver unit and some with en-suite facilities, shared bathrooms, showers, a living room, dining room, kitchen and study areas with secluded gardens.

Staffing

All care staff employed directly to the Wing Centre have a qualification range from Cert Ed and Diplomas to NVQs. In addition all care staff work in classes supporting, guiding and encouraging student progress.

Courses

National Qualifications/accreditations are available in C & G Word power, Number power and preparing for employment, OCN lifeskills, ASDAN, Food Hygiene foundation certificate. Individually-tailored timetables include literacy, numeracy, ICT, careers and work experience, citizenship, health, relationships and responsibilities, workshop, money matters, art, cooking, sport and leisure, relaxation techniques and transition issues.

Links

Link provision with three local colleges is in place, where students can pursue particular subject interests academically, vocationally or just for fun.

Other information

Students are registered with a local GP. Other services available include consultant clinical psychiatry, clinical psychology, counselling, speech and language therapy and occupational therapy.

Application procedure

Papers are sent from local authority representatives or parents make a private visit. Ideally, the local authority should indicate an intention to fund, before the process progresses. This is followed up by an initial assessment.

Winslow Court

Address: Rowdon, Bromyard, Herefordshire HR7 4LS

Tel: 01885 488096   **Fax:** 01889 504010   **Email:** donellsmore@winslowcourt.com   **Website:** www. winslowcourt.com

Age range: 18-30

Controlled by: Registered with Hereford LSC

Contact for admissions information: Don Ellsmore

Out-of-term contact: Don Ellsmore

Fees: £1,900–£2,400 per week

Usual source of funding for students: Social services

Aims: To provide an environment in which residents will be able to achieve their full potential — physically, emotionally, intellectually and socially.

Students catered for: Severe learning difficulties and behavioural problems.

Premises and facilities

A purpose-built facility. Besides student accommodation, it has training rooms and recreational facilities to enable staff to offer social activities to larger groups, individual training and therapies. Transport is provided for shopping and off-site leisure pursuits. An activity barn is also available for indoor sports activities and a spa pool.

Student accommodation

The unit has 24 single bedrooms and is single storey. Designed to provide four separate independent units, each having a kitchen, dining room and recreational rooms.

Student numbers

24 at Winslow Court.

Staffing

Residential manager, head of care, four unit managers, two activity coordinators, 48 care staff — waking night on each unit and sleeping night time supervisors in. Psychologist, assistant psychologist, speech therapist, music therapist.

Courses

Two occupational therapy rooms provide opportunities for structured activities and training: artwork, woodwork, pottery, music therapy.
Each resident has their own development plan which is developed to give each young person training in life and social skills.

Winslow Court also uses horse riding, horticultural and local facilities to develop young people.

Links

Winslow Court uses the facilities offered by both Hereford and Worcester Colleges of FE. Residents attend cooking and IT courses at the colleges and the outreach departments from both colleges visit Winslow Court offering courses on IT, gardening, art and sensory.

Other information

Winslow Court will provide physiotherapists, chiropodist etc. as required by the young people. There are also two new homes in Herefordshire, one 5-bed home and one 6-bed home. They have their own manager, staff and transport and are aimed at independent living. These will be stepping stone-type locations for residents to move to more community based living.

Application procedure

Apply to Don Ellsmore — assessment carried out, visit to Winslow Court, develop placement plan, offer of placement and then transition.

Wirral Autistic Society

Address: 2 Grisedale Road, Old Hall Estate, Bromborough, Wirral CH62 3QA

Code: C

Tel: 0151 334 7510   **Fax:** 0151 334 1762   **Email:** admin@wirral.autistic.org   **Website:** www.wirral.autistic.org

Controlled by: Wirral Autistic Society

Contact information: Steve Owen; Director of Client Services

Fees: Fees are determined following individual assessment of the client's needs and the service package offered

Aims: To provide support and continuing development to adults on the autistic spectrum to enable them to live as fulfilling a life with as much independence as they can manage.

Students catered for: Adults over 18 years old who have a diagnosis of having an autistic spectrum disorder.

Premises and facilities

Accommodation includes larger units in spacious grounds for those people who need high levels of support for their complex needs and smaller group living situations in houses/flats in the wider community whose focus is on more independent living. The Society also provides day services in a range of areas including a garden centre and craft workshops. Facilities also include a swimming pool, small gym, multi sensory room and narrowboat.

Student accommodation

All clients occupy single rooms in all of the residential facilities.

Student numbers

Currently residential (inc five days' day services) services to 90 clients. The Society provides a further 15 places for days services only. There is one respite bed.

Staffing

Over 250 staff including residential and day service support. Staffing levels are determined by individual assessment of a person's support needs. There is a communication coordinator.

Courses

A full range of day services including: P.E. (outdoor pursuits, swimming, aerobics etc.), horticulture (including a garden centre), woodworking and furniture restoration, ceramics, printing, IT/computer skills, music and personal and life skills.

Links

Supported work placements are arranged with local employers. Art and drama courses are accessed at a local college.

Other information

Local NHS support, private podiatry and an alternative therapist are accessed as required.

Application procedure

Interested applicants are invited to contact the Society to arrange to view the facilities. Application forms are available from the Head Office. When vacancies arise, an assessment of suitability is undertaken by senior managers of client services.

Womaston School

Address: Womaston School, Walton Presteigne, Powys LD8 2PT

Tel: 01544 230308 **Fax:** 01544 231317 **Email:** womaston@macintyrecharity.org

Age range: 14-19

Controlled by: MacIntyre

Contact for admissions information: Martin Bertulis

Out-of-term contact: As above

Fees: Base £110,000 pa

Usual source of funding for students: LEA/SSO(Health)

Aims: Positive approach to behaviour, developing communication and confidence. Using 'essential skills' to develop independence and vocational skills.

Students catered for: 52-week residential. Students with SLD, autism and challenging behaviour. Students who cannot be accommodated at home and are excluded or close to exclusion from special schools. 24-hour curriculum.

Premises and facilities

Residential houses, ICT suite, café, studio (art/crafts), library/careers room, sensory room, pottery, woodwork area, fitness suite (aerobic), kitchen and sensory gardens, crazy golf, common rooms, independence flat (in construction).

Student accommodation

Three houses for five, five and six students. Individual bedrooms, communal kitchen, lounges, gardens in each house.

Student numbers

Up to 16.

Staffing

Integrated setting with teachers, learning support and some care support workers. Night staff in each house. Management, domestic maintenance and admin staff on site.

Courses

Individual programmes based on the 'essential skills' to develop independence, confidence and self esteem.

Links

Links to Coleg Powys for ½ day – two day accredited courses. Links to Radnor scouts.

Other information

Clinical psychologist, speech and language — both bought in. MacIntyre support services, training, behaviour intervention service/support planning. Yoga, reflexology, art, music therapy, pottery.

Application procedure

Contact School. Visit to School. School assesses student in situ.

Woodlarks Workshop Trust

Address: Lodge Hill Road, Farnham, Surrey GU10 3RB

Tel: 01252 714041

Code: R

Age range: 18+

Contact for admissions information: Moira Woodage

Controlled by: Local Management Committee (member of Surrey Care Association)

Fees: £600+ per week

Usual source of funding for students: Social services etc.

Aims: To achieve maximum independence within the disability in a secure and happy home environment.

Students catered for: Physically disabled adults.

Premises and facilities

An independently run home and sheltered workshop. Workshop activities include a wide variety of handcrafts and gardening. There is also a gym.

Student accommodation

22 single bedsits (including one for respite care).

Student numbers

21.

Staffing

Manager and two assistant managers, head of care, administrator, two full-time and six part-time senior care staff, full-time workshop manager, workshop assistant and four workshop volunteers (part-time), grounds/maintenance person. The Trust employs contract cleaners and caterers.

Courses

Residents may attend workshops up to 4½ days per week, unless participating in adult education courses, social activities etc within the community.

Links

Residents attend local adult education classes, help in charity shops etc in local community.

Other information

Visiting physiotherapist.

Application procedure

All applications considered, to conform with CSCI residential home standards.

Yately Industries for the Disabled

Address: Mill Lane, Yateley, Hampshire GU46 7TF

Tel: 01252 872337   **Fax:** 01252 860620   **Email:** PatMcLarry@aol.com   **Website:** www.yateleyindustries.co.uk

Age range: 16-65

Controlled by: Council of Management

Contact for admissions information: Mrs Karen Palmer

Aims: To enhance the lives of disabled people by providing remunerative employment and residential support.

Students catered for: Must have use of upper limbs and have the potential to live independently, with sufficient mental ability to live and work with minimal supervision. No other restrictions on ability. Cannot accept those with blindness or those requiring nursing care.

Premises and facilities

Village built on three acres in centre of Yateley, producing screen printed textiles for sale. Bungalows are grouped around a pleasant lawn, and the supported factory, gift shop and tearoom are situated on site. Within wheeling distance of most shops.

Student accommodation

Residents live in bungalows in self-contained custom-built village.

Staffing

General manager, production manager, residential support manager, finance manager, administrator, supervisors, sales and support staff.

Courses

Assessment for suitability for employment in specialised packing and assembly, retail and catering. Up to four people live in self-sustaining groups and work in similar groups, each under their own disabled leader. Living skills will also be assessed. Four weeks duration. Intakes throughout the year.

Work and domestic training provided. Employment is offered to those willing to undertake the work and who can make a significant contribution to production. Final desired outcome is to attain mainstream, independent employment and living for those who are able.

Links

Links with Basingstoke FE College and Farnborough College, and local employers.

Application procedure

Visits are welcomed. Apply direct or through DEA or social worker. Waiting period for assessment is dependent on the applicant's county social services department being willing to fund the cost and to give financial support when the applicant becomes an employee. Full training provided.

Appendix 1
Financing of courses

It is essential to clarify the nature and source of financial support for individuals who attend the various establishments described in this Directory. Our intention in this section is to provide some general information on this subject.

Specialist colleges in England

The majority of placements are funded by Learning and Skills Councils. The sources and level of financial support can vary, depending on a number of factors. These include the type of course, the type of establishment, and the nature of the disability.

There may be variations in policy from one area to another, and different possible combinations of financial support. This may confuse the student or parent. It is important that advice is sought at an early stage from the individual's key worker, from the establishment the student hopes to attend, and/or from sources mentioned below.

Students whose needs cannot be met in a mainstream FE college can apply for funding from the local LSCs in England for a place at a specialist independent college. Under the Learning and Skills Act 2000, the LSCs will pay for the education (other than higher education) or training of students with learning difficulties and/or disabilities, whose needs cannot be fully met by a local college, to attend a specialist institution on a residential basis if necessary. Requests should normally be submitted to the LSC by the end of March for admission in September of the same year. Students on courses at specialist colleges can be funded between the ages of 16 and 25, but not necessarily for all this time. The LSC may also, in some circumstances, fund provision for over-25s. The LSCs usually fund people on courses for a maximum of three years, for up to 38 weeks per year. It may be possible to have this extended, but it depends on the circumstances.

For each student for whom an LSC-funded place is sought, local authorities and/or Connexions services are asked to make a recommendation to the LSC. This recommendation includes medical and educational evidence, and confirmation that suitable provision is not available at an FE sector college. The LSC, the referring agency and other relevant bodies will meet to discuss the placement request. The LSC may need to request further information before reaching a decision. Parents or carers may submit supplementary evidence if they wish. If the LSC decides not to fund a placement, they will give their reasons for that decision to the individual, their family and the referring agency. A formal review is then possible.

Details of the application procedure, and the criteria that the LSC uses in deciding whether to pay for a student to attend a specialist college, are available from Connexions personal advisers or the local LSC. This information also includes a list of specialist colleges at which the LSC funds places at present. If an establishment is not on this list, it may take some months to reach a decision as to whether LSC funding will be forthcoming.

The LSCs may, in certain circumstances, expect other agencies to contribute towards the cost of the place, e.g. they may expect the social services department or health authority to part-fund it if the placement is for medical or care needs, as well as educational reasons. For instance, the LSC may agree to fund the day costs of attendance at an establishment, but not the residential costs. Entries for the establishments in COPE include an indication of typical sources of funding for students.

Mainstream further and higher education

Further education

FE colleges are funded to meet the needs of individual students with learning difficulties or disabilities. Students wishing to study at a local college should apply direct to the college concerned. Young people do not normally have to pay fees, and help for living costs is available through Learner Support Funds (Financial Contingency Funds in Wales), which are targeted at students with financial difficulties or who have special needs. Extra help is available for students who have to attend colleges outside travelling distance from home. EMAs are also available for students aged 16-18 from low-income households (see below). Scotland and Wales offer ILA schemes, and parts of England provide Adult Learning Grants for young adults studying for their first level 2 or 3 qualification.

Under the Disability Discrimination Act (DDA), colleges are obliged to make reasonable adjustments to make facilities accessible, and to provide aids and services to prevent disabled learners from being disadvantaged.

For information on further education funding in England, including EMAs, view: www.dfes.gov.uk/financialhelp

For information on student funding in Northern Ireland, see www.delni.gov.uk

For information on further education funding in Wales, see www.wales.gov.uk

For information on further education funding in Scotland, see www.scotland.gov.uk

Full-time higher education

Higher education institutions in England may charge up to £3,000 per year in tuition fees (and most do charge the full amount). However, student loans are available to cover fees and to contribute to living expenses. Loans don't have to be paid back until the student has finished or left the course and is earning over £15,000 p.a. Means-tested, non-repayable Maintenance Grants or Special Support Grants are also available to students from low-income households. Most students should apply to their local authority, although in some areas student support is dealt with directly by the Student Loans Company (SLC). Universities and colleges may also offer extra funding through bursaries or through Access to Learning funds. Students should approach the institution's student support or student services office.

The student loan does not take disability-related benefits into account as income when calculating the loan pay back, even if they are taxable.

Fairly similar arrangements apply to students in Northern Ireland and Wales; Scotland's student funding differs more, but also requires no 'up front' payment of fees. For students resident in one part of the UK studying in another, they usually pay the fees as charged by the host country, with the support offered by where they are resident.

Disabled Students' Allowance

Disabled Students' Allowances (DSAs) are available to meet course-related costs arising from a disability. These allowances are not income-related. Support will be in the form of a non-repayable grant. Disabled students on part-time (50% or over) higher education courses can also claim the DSA. Full details of the DSA are available from the awarding authority or Skill. (See contact details at the end of this section.)

For further information

England – full details are given in the DfES guide *Financial Support for Higher Education Students* and in *Bridging the Gap: a guide to the Disabled Students' Allowances in higher education.* Telephone 0800 731 9133 or textphone 0800 328 8988 for a free copy, or download from: www.dfes.gov.uk/studentsupport/formsandguides

Wales – contact your local authority, phone the bilingual helpline: 0845 602 8845, or view www.studentfinancewales.co.uk

Northern Ireland – see www.delni.gov.uk

Scotland – view the Student Awards Agency for Scotland site: www.saas.gov.uk

Residential training for adults

The Government funds residential training places for people with disabilities aged 18-63, if there are no suitable alternative programmes available locally. There are over 50 vocational courses, many leading to NVQs.

Programmes are tailored to meet an individual's training needs, using a mixture of guidance, work experience and vocational training. Courses last no longer than one year. A number of the providers are establishments listed in this Directory.

Successful applicants receive an allowance as well as residential costs, which can include help towards travel. Your DEA at Jobcentre Plus can advise.

Other sources of financial support

Additional funds for students in financial hardship

Higher education and further education colleges have funds which can be awarded to any student in financial difficulties, not just students with disabilities. These funds are known by different names in different parts of the country. For example, Access to Learning and Learner Support Funds in England are known as Financial Contingency Funds in Wales.

Educational Maintenance Allowances (EMAs)

EMAs are available to 16- to 19-year olds from families on low incomes as an incentive to continue in full-time learning. This includes Programme Led Pathways (leading to Apprenticeships) and E2E programmes. Full details can be found on the DfES website. The learning provider and learning programme involved need to meet certain criteria to be registered with the DfES; in some instances, EMAs can be claimed by students at specialist colleges.

Charities and trusts

Various voluntary organisations, educational charities and trusts may also be able to assist with certain costs, usually in a small way. They would not be in a position to meet the full costs of attending a residential course if the statutory authorities were unable to assist.

For information on bodies which may make awards, refer to the publications – *The Directory of Grant Making Trusts*, the *Charities Digest*, and *Educational Grants Directory* which should be available for reference in local libraries. Also, Skill can advise on organisations that fund students with disabilities.

Further information

If you experience difficulties or confusion regarding finance, the local authority key worker or Connexions personal adviser should be able to advise you.

Skill's Information Service can offer advice about funding entitlements in further and higher education. You can phone on Tuesdays from 11.30am to 1.30pm or on Thursdays from 1.30 to 3.30pm on 0800 328 5050 (freephone – voice) or 0800 068 2422 (textphone) – or ring 020 7657 2337 to save Skill money! You can also contact Skill at the address on page 167.

Skill publishes the information booklets *Funding for Students with Disabilities in Further Education* and *Funding for Students with Disabilities in Higher Education* (free to students with disabilities, but priced for advisers) which can be viewed on their website. There are also books on financial assistance for students published by Skill (£2.50 each for students or £6.50 for advisers) but, at the time of writing, these were due to be updated.

Information on the full range of employment and training services and schemes and on disability-related benefits can be obtained from Jobcentre Plus.

The New Deal for Disabled People can assist in finding relevant training for people with disabilities to help them find employment. Talk to Jobcentre Plus, or phone the New Deal Helpline on 0800 137 177.

Appendix 2

Societies offering advice on specific disabilities

Many of the organisations and societies listed below offer a range of services concerned with assessment, training and employment, as well as general support.

Please note that many of the smaller organisations tend to move quite frequently and keeping up with address changes is thus difficult. If you experience problems contacting the addresses below, check with the Disability Rights Handbook, published annually, which contains a comprehensive list of societies and organisations.

Acquired Brain Injury

BIRT (Brain Injury and Rehabilitation Trust) – 60 Queen Street, Normanton, Wakefield WF6 2BU. Tel 01924 896100. Fax: 01924 899264. Email: director@birt.co.uk Website: www.birt.co.uk

Brain and Spinal Injury Charity (BASIC) – The Neurocare Centre, 554 Eccles New Road, Salford M5 5AP. Tel: 0161 707 6441. Fax: 0161 206 4558. Email: enquiries@basiccharity.org.uk Website: www.basiccharity.org.uk

British Brain and Spine Foundation – 7 Winchester House, Kennington Park, Cranmore Road, London SW9 6EJ. Tel: 020 7793 5900. Fax: 020 7793 5939. Helpline: 0808 808 1000. Email: info@brainandspine.org.uk Website: www.brainandspine.org.uk

Cerebra – Principality Buildings, 13 Guildhall Square, Carmarthen SA31 1PR. Tel: 01267 244200. Fax: 01267 244201. Freephone: 0800 3281 159. Website: www.cerebra.org.uk

Child Brain Injury Trust – Unit 1, The Great Barn, Baynards Green, nr Bicester OX27 7SG. Tel/fax: 01865 552467. Helpline: 0845 601 4939. Email: info@cbituk.org Website: www.cbituk.org

The Disability Trust – First Floor, 32 Market Place, Burgess Hill, West Sussex RH15 9NP. Tel: 01444 258377. Fax: 01444 244978. Email: info@disability-trust.org.uk Website: www.disability-trust.co.uk

Head Injury Re-Education (HIRE) – Email: hire.office@virgin.net

Headway – the Brain Injury Association – 4 King Edward Street, Nottingham NG1 1EW. Tel: 0115 924 0800. Fax: 0115 958 4446. Minicom: 0115 950 7825. Email: enquiries@headway.org.uk Website: www.headway.org.uk

National Meningitis Trust – Fern House, Bath Road, Stroud GL5 3TJ. Tel: 01453 768000. Fax: 01453 768001. Helpline: 0800 028 1828. Email: info@meningitis-trust.org.uk Website: www.meningitis-trust.org.uk

The Neurological Alliance – Stroke House, 240 City Road, London EC1V 2PR. Tel: 020 7566 1540. Email: admin@neurologicalalliance.org.uk Website: www.neural.org.uk

Angelman syndrome

ASSERT (Angelman syndrome Support Education and Research Trust) – PO Box 13694, Musselburgh EH21 6XH. Tel/fax: 01268 415940. Email: assert@angelmanuk.org Website: www.angelmanuk.org

Arthrogryposis

Arthrogryposis Group – Beak Cottage, Dunley, Near Stourport-on-Severn, Worcs DY13 0TZ. Tel/fax: 01299 825781. Email: info@tagonline.org.uk Website: www.tagonline.org.uk

Asthma

Asthma UK – Summit House, 70 Wilson Street, London EC2A 2DB. Tel: 020 7786 4900. Fax: 020 7256 6075. Email: info@asthma.org.uk Website: www.asthma.org.uk

Asthma UK Scotland – 4 Queen Street, Edinburgh EH2 1JE. Tel: 0131 226 2544. Fax: 0131 226 2401.
Email: scotland@asthma.org.uk

Asthma UK Cymru – 3rd Floor, Eastgate House, 34-43 Newport Road, Cardiff CF24 0AB. Tel: 02920 435 400.
Fax: 02920 487 731. Email: wales@asthma.org.uk

Asthma UK Northern Ireland – Peace House, 224 Lisburn Road, Belfast BT9 6GE. Tel: 02890 669736. Fax: 02890 669736.
Email: ni@asthma.org.uk

Ataxia

Ataxia UK – 9 Winchester House, Kennington Park, Cranmer Road, London SW9 6EJ. Tel: 020 7582 1444.
Fax: 020 7582 9444. Helpline: 0845 644 0606. Email: helpline@ataxia.org.uk Website: www.ataxia.org.uk

Ataxia-Telangiectasia Society – IACR-Rothamstead, Harpenden, Herts AL5 2JQ. Tel: 01582 760733. Fax: 01582 760162.
Email: atcharity@aol.com

Attention Deficit and Challenging Behaviour

ADDISS – 10 Station Road, Mill Hill, London NW7 2JU. Tel: 020 8906 9068. Fax: 020 8959 0727. Email: info@addiss.co.uk
Website: www.addiss.co.uk

ADHD UK Alliance – 209-211 City Road, London EC1V 1JN. Tel: 020 7608 8760. Fax: 020 7608 8701.
Email: info@adhdalliance.org.uk

The Challenging Behaviour Foundation – C/o Friends Meeting House, Northgate, Rochester ME1 1LS.
Tel: 01634 838 739. Fax: 01634 828 588. Website: www.thecbf.org.uk

The Henry Spink Foundation – c/o Montgomery Swann, Scotts Sufferance Wharf, 1 Mill Street, London SE1 2DE.
Tel: 020 7228 6272. Email: info@henryspink.org Website: www.henryspink.org

Hyperactive Children's Support Group - 71 Whyke Lane, Chichester PO19 7PD. Tel: 01243 539966.
Email: hyperactive@hacsg.org.uk Website: www.hacsg.org.uk

The Scottish Child Psychotherapy Trust – 5 La Belle Place, Glasgow G3 7LH.

YoungMinds – 48-50 St John Street, London EC1M 4DG. Tel: 020 7336 8445. Fax: 020 7336 8446. Parents Information
Service: 0800 018 2138. Email: enquiries@youngminds.org.uk Website: www.youngminds.org.uk

Autism/Asperger Syndrome

Autism Independent UK – 199-205 Blandford Avenue, Kettering, Northants NN16 9AT. Tel/fax: 01536 523274.
Email: autism@rmplc.co.uk Website: www.autismuk.com

Autism Initiatives – 7 Chesterfield Road, Crosby, Liverpool L23 9XL. Tel: 0151 330 9500. Fax: 0151 330 9501.
Website: www.autisminitiatives.org

National Autistic Society – 393 City Road, London EC1V 1NG. Tel: 020 7833 2299. Fax: 020 7833 9666.
Helpline: 0870 600 8585. Email: nas@nas.org.uk Website: www.nas.org.uk

Scottish Society for Autism – Head Office, Hilton House, Alloa Business Park, The Whins, Alloa FK10 3SA.
Tel: 01259 720044. Fax: 01259 720051. Email: info@autism-in-scotland.org.uk
Website: www.autism-in-scotland.org.uk

Useful website: www.autism-awareness.org.uk

Blindness and partial sight

Action for Blind People – 14-16 Verney Road, London SE16 3DZ. Tel: 020 7635 4800. Fax: 020 7635 4900.
Email: info@afbp.org Website: www.afbp.org

National Blind Childrens Society – Bradbury House, Market Street, Highbridge, Somerset TA9 3BW.Tel: 01278 764764.
Fax: 01278 764790. Email: enquiries@nbcs.org.uk Website: www.nbcs.org.uk

National Federation of the Blind – Sir John Wilson House, 215 Kirkgate, Wakefield WF1 1JG. Tel: 01924 291313. Fax: 01924 200244. Email: nfbuk@rmplc.co.uk Website: www.nfbuk.co.uk

Partially Sighted Society – Queens Road, Doncaster DN1 2XA. Tel: 01302 323132. Fax: 01302 368998.

Royal National Institute for the Blind – 105 Judd Street, London WC1H 9NE. Tel: 020 7388 1266. Fax: 020 7388 2034. Helpline: 0845 7669 999. Email: helpline@rnib.org.uk Website: www.rnib.org.uk

See also Deaf/blind and Retinitis pigmentosa

Brittle bones

The Brittle Bones Society – 30 Guthrie Street, Dundee DD1 5BS. Tel: 01382 204446. Fax: 01382 206771. Helpline: 08000 282459. Email: bbs@brittlebone.org.uk Website: www.brittlebone.org

Cerebral palsy

Capability Scotland – Advice Service, 11 Ellersly Road, Edinburgh EH12 6HY. Tel: 0131 313 5510. Fax: 0131 346 1681. Email: ascs@capability-scotland.org.uk Website: www.capability-scotland.org.uk

The Hornsey Trust – 54 Muswell Hill, London N10 3ST. Tel/fax: 020 8444 7241. Email: info@hornseytrust.org.uk Website: www.hcec.org.uk

SCOPE – 6 Market Road, London N7 9PW. Tel: 020 7619 7100. Helpline: 0808 800 3333. Email: cphelpline@scope.org.uk Website: www.scope.org.uk

Chest and heart

Different Strokes – 9 Canon Harnett Court, Wolverton Mill, Milton Keynes MK12 5NF. Tel: 0845 130 7172. Fax: 01908 313501. Email: info@differentstrokes.co.uk Website: www.differentstrokes.co.uk

Stroke Association – Stroke House, 240 City Road House, London EC1V 2PR. Tel: 0845 303 3100. Fax: 020 7490 2686. Email: stroke@stroke.org.uk Website: www.stroke.org.uk

Cornelia de Lange Syndrome

CdLS Foundation UK and Ireland – 106 Lodge Lane, Grays, Essex RM16 2UL. Tel: 01375 376439. Fax: 020 7536 8998. Email: info@cdls.org.uk Website: www.cdlsoutreach.org

Cystic Fibrosis

Cystic Fibrosis Trust – 11 London Road, Bromley, Kent BR1 1BY. Tel: 020 8464 7211. Fax: 020 8313 0472. Support helpline: 0845 859 1000. Email: enquiries@cftrust.org.uk Website: www.cftrust.org.uk

Deafness

British Deaf Association – 69 Wilson Street, London EC2A 2BB. Tel: 020 7588 3520. Fax: 020 7588 3527. Email: london@signcommunity.org.uk Website: www.signcommunity.org.uk

Deaf Association of Northern Ireland – Suite 3, Cranmore House, 611b Lisburn Road, Belfast BT9 7GT. Tel: 02890 387706. Fax: 02890 387707. Email: northernireland@signcommunity.org.uk

Deaf Association Wales – British Sign Language Cultural Centre, 47 Newport Road, Cardiff CF24 0AD. Tel: 0845 130 2851. Fax: 0845 130 2852. Email: wales@signcommunity.org.uk

Scottish Deaf Association – Suite 222, The Pentagon, 36 Washington Street, Glasgow G3 8AZ. Tel: 0141 248 5554. Fax: 0141 248 5565. Email: scotland@signcommunity.org.uk

Deafplus – First Floor, Trinity Centre, Key Close, Whitechapel, London E1 4HG. Tel: 020 7790 6147. Fax: 020 7790 5999. Email: info@deafplus.org Website: www.deafplus.org

National Deaf Children's Society – The National Office, 15 Dufferin Street, London EC1Y 8UR. Tel: 020 7490 8656. Fax: 020 7251 5020. Helpline: 0808 800 8880. Email: helpline@ndcs.org.uk Website: www.ndcs.org.uk

Royal Association in aid of Deaf People – Walsingham Road, Colchester CO2 7BP. Tel: 01206 509509. Fax: 01206 769755. Text: 01206 577090. Email: info@royaldeaf.org.uk Website: www.royaldeaf.org.uk

Royal National Institute for Deaf People (RNID) – 19-23 Featherstone Street, London EC1Y 8SL. Tel: 020 7296 8000. Fax: 020 7296 8199. Text: 020 7296 8001. Information Line: 0808 808 0123. Email: informationline@rnid.org.uk Website: www.rnid.org.uk

RNID Cymru – 16 Cathedral Road, Cardiff CF11 9LJ. Tel: 02920 333 034. Fax: 02920 333 035.

RNID Northern Ireland – Wilton House, 5 College Square North, Belfast BT1 4AR. Tel: 02890 239 619. Fax: 02890 312 032.

RNID Scotland – Empire House, 131 West Nile Street, Glasgow G1 2RX. Tel: 0141 341 5330. Fax: 0141 341 5352.

Deaf/blind

Deafblind UK – National Centre for Deafblindness, John and Lucille van Geest Place, Cygnet Road, Hampton, Peterborough PE7 8FD. Tel: 01733 358100. Fax: 01733 358356. Website: www.deafblind.org.uk

Deafblind Scotland – 21 Alexandra Avenue, Lenzie, Glasgow G66 5BG. Tel: 0141 777 6111. Fax: 0141 775 3311. Email: info@deafblindscotland.org.uk Website: www.deafblindscotland.org.uk

SENSE – (National Deaf/Blind and Rubella Association) – 11-13 Clifton Terrace, Finsbury Park, London N4 3SR. Tel: 020 7272 7774. Fax: 020 7272 6012. Email: info@sense.org.uk Website: www.sense.org.uk

Down's Syndrome

Down's Syndrome Association – National Office – Langdon Down Centre, 2a Langdon Park, Teddington TW11 9PS. Tel: 0845 230 0372. Fax: 0845 230 0373. Email: info@downs-syndrome.org.uk Website: www.dsa-uk.com

Down's Syndrome Association – NI Office – Graham House, Knockbracken Healthcare Park, Saintfield Road, Belfast BT8 8BH. Tel: 028 9070 4606. Fax: 028 9070 4075. Email: downs-syndrome@cinni.org

Down's Syndrome Association – Wales Office – Suite 1, 206 Whitchurch Road, Heath, Cardiff CF4 3NB. Tel/fax: 029 2052 2511. Email: wales@downs-syndrome.org.uk

The Down's Syndrome Educational Trust – The Sarah Duffin Centre, Belmont Street, Southsea, Hants PO5 1NA. Tel: 023 9282 4261. Fax: 023 9285 5320. Email: enquiries@downsed.org Website: www.downsed.org.uk

Down's Syndrome Scotland – 158-160 Balgreen Road, Edinburgh EH11 3AU. Tel: 0131 313 4225. Fax: 0131 313 4285. Email: info@dsscotland.org.uk Website: www.dsscotland.org.uk

Dyslexia

Adult Dyslexia Organisation – 336 Brixton Road, London SW9 7AA. Tel: 020 7924 9559. Fax: 020 7207 7796. Email: dyslexia.hq@dial.pipex.com Website: www.adult-dyslexia.org

British Dyslexia Association – 98 London Road, Reading, Berks RG1 5AU. Tel: 0118 966 2677. Fax: 0118 935 1927. Helpline: 0118 966 8271. Email: admin@bdadyslexia.org.uk Website: www.bdadyslexia.org.uk

Dyslexia Institute – Park House, Wick Road, Egham, Surrey TW20 0HH. Tel: 01784 222300. Fax: 01784 222333. Email: info@dyselxia-inst.org.uk Website: www.dyslexia-inst.org.uk

Dyslexia in Scotland – Unit 3, Stirling Business Centre, Weelgreen, Stirling FK8 2DZ. Tel: 01785 446650. Fax: 01786 471235. Email: info@dyslexia-in-scotland.org Website: www.dyslexia-in-scotland.org

Eczema

National Eczema Society – Hill House, Highgate, London N19 5NA. Tel: 0870 241 3604. Email: info@eczema.org.uk Website: www.eczema.org.uk

Epilepsy

Epilespy Action – New Anstey House, Gate Way Drive, Yeadon, Leeds LS19 7XY. Helpline: 080 800 5050.
Fax: 0113 391 0300. Email: epilepsy@epilepsy.org.uk Website: www.epilepsy.org.uk

National Centre for Young People with Epilepsy – St Piers Lane, Lingfield, Surrey RA7 6PW. Tel: 01342 832243.
Website: www.ncype.org.uk

National Society for Epilepsy – Chesham Lane, Chalfont St Peter, Bucks SL9 0RJ. Tel: 01494 601300. Fax: 01494 871927.
Helpline: 01494 601400. Website: www.epilepsynse.org.uk

Fragile X syndrome

The Fragile X Society – Rood End House, 6 Stortford Road, Great Dunmow, Essex CM6 1DA. Tel: 01371 875100.
Email: info@fragilex.org.uk. Website: www.fragilex.org.uk

General disability organisations

AbilityNet – General enquiries: Tel: 0800 269545 (from home), 01926 312847 (from work). Fax: 01926 407425.
Email: enquiries@abilitynet.org.uk Website: www.abilitynet.org.uk

British Council for Disabled People (BCODP) – Litchurch Plaza, Litchurch Lane, Derby DE24 8AA. Tel: 01332 295551.
Fax: 01332 295580. Minicom: 01332 295581. Email: general@bcodp.org.uk Website: www.bcodp.org.uk

DIAL UK (National Association of Disablement Information and Advice Lines) – St Catherine's, Tickhill Road, Doncaster
DN4 8QN. Tel/text: 01302 310123. Fax: 01302 310404. Email: dialuk@aol.com Website: www.dialuk.org.uk

Disability Action (Northern Ireland) – Head Office, Portside Business Park, 189 Airport Road West, Belfast BT3 9ED.
Tel: 028 9029 7880. Text: 028 9064 5779. Fax: 028 9049 1627. Email: hq@disabilityaction.org
Website: www.disabilityaction.org

Disability Alliance – Universal House, 88-94 Wentworth Street, London E1 7SA. Tel: 020 7247 8776. Fax: 020 7247 8765.
Email: office.da@dial.pipex.com Website: www.disabilityalliance.org

Disability Wales/Anabledd Cymru – Bridge House, Caerphilly Business Park, Van Road, Caephilly CF83 3GW.
Tel/minicom: 029 2088 7325. Fax: 029 2088 8702. Email: info@dwac.demon.co.uk Website: www.disabilitywales.org

Lead Scotland – Queen Margaret University College, Clerwood Terrace, Edinburgh EH12 8TS. Tel: 0131 317 3439.
Fax: 0131 339 7198. Email: enquiries@lead.org.uk Website: www.lead.org.uk

Haemophilia

Haemophilia Society – First Floor, Petersham House, 57a Hatton Garden, London EC1N 8JG. Tel: 020 7831 1020.
Fax: 020 7405 4824. Helpline: 0800 018 6068. Email: info@haemophilia.org.uk Website: www.haemophilia.org.uk

Learning disability

BILD: British Institute of Learning Disabilities – Campion House, Green Street, Kidderminster DY10 1JL.
Tel: 01562 723010. Fax: 01562 723029. Email: enquiries@bild.org.uk Website: www.bild.org.uk

ENABLE – 6th Floor, 7 Buchanan Street, Glasgow G1 3HL. Tel: 0141 226 4541. Fax: 0141 204 4398.
Email: enable@enable.org.uk Website: www.enable.org.uk

The Foundation for People with Learning Disabilities – 9th Floor, Sea Containers House, 20 Upper Ground, London SE1
9QB. Tel: 020 7803 1100. Fax: 020 7803 1111. Email: fpld@fpld.org.uk Website: www.learningdisabilities.org.uk

MENCAP – 123 Golden Lane, London EC1Y 0RT. Tel: 020 7454 0454. Fax: 020 7696 5540. Helpline: 0808 808 1111.
Email: information@mencap.org.uk Website: www.mencap.org.uk

Values Into Action – Oxford House, Derbyshire Street, London E2 6HG. Tel: 020 7729 5436. Fax: 020 7729 7797.
Email: general@viauk.org Website: www.viauk.org

Voluntary Service Aberdeen – 38 Castle Street, Aberdeen AB11 5YU. Tel: 01224 212021. Fax: 01224 580722.
Email: info@vsa.org.uk Website: www.vsa.org.uk

Mental illness

Mental Health Foundation – 9th Floor, Sea Containers House, 20 Upper Ground, London SE1 9QB. Tel: 020 803 1100. Fax: 020 803 1111. Email: mhf@mhf.org.uk Website: www.mhf.org.uk

MIND – 15-19 Broadway, London E15 4BQ. Tel: 020 8519 2122. Fax: 020 8522 1725. Infoline: 0845 766 0163. Email: contact@mind.org.uk Website: www.mind.org.uk

The Richmond Fellowship – Head Office, 80 Holloway Road, London N7 8JG. Tel: 020 7697 3300. Fax: 020 7697 3301. Email: enquiries@richmondfellowship.org.uk Website: www.richmondfellowship.org.uk

The Richmond Fellowship Scotland – Head Office, 26 Park Circus, Glasgow G6 3AP. Tel: 0141 353 4050. Fax: 0141 353 4060. Email: info@trfs.org.uk Website: www.trfs.org.uk

Scottish Association for Mental Health (SAMH) – Cumbrae House, 15 Charlton Court, Glasgow G5 9JP. Tel: 0141 568 7000. Fax: 0141 568 7001. Email: enquire@samh.org.uk Website: www.samh.org.uk

YoungMinds – 48-50 St John Street, London EC1M 4DG. Tel: 020 7336 8445. Fax: 020 7336 8446. Parents Information Service: 0800 018 2138. Email: enquirie@youngminds.org.uk Website: www.youngminds.org.uk

Multiple sclerosis

Multiple Sclerosis Society – MS National Centre, 372 Edgware Road, London NW2 6ND. Tel: 020 8438 0700. Helpline: 0808 800 8000. Website: www.mssociety.org.uk

Muscular dystrophy

Muscular Dystrophy Campaign – 7-11 Prescott Place, Clapham, London SW4 6BS. Tel: 020 7720 8055. Fax: 020 7498 0670. Email: info@muscular-dystrophy.org Website: www.muscular-dystrophy.org

Physical disability

Bridget's Trust – Tennis Court Road, Cambridge CB2 1QF. Tel: 01223 367706. Fax: 01223 461324. Email: trust@bridgets.org.uk Website: www.bridgets.org.uk

Disabled Living Foundation (DLF) – 380-384 Harrow Road, London W9 2HU. Tel: 020 7289 6111. Helpline: 0845 130 9177. Email: info@dlf.org.uk Website: www.dlf.org.uk

Disability Alliance – 1st Universal House, 88-94 Wentworth Street, London E1 7SA. Tel: 020 7247 8776. Fax: 020 7247 8765. Email: office.da@dial.pipex.com Website: www.disabilityalliance.org

Dyspraxia Foundation – 8 West Alley, Hitchin, Herts SG5 1EG. Tel: 01462 454986. Fax: 01462 455052. Email: dyspraxia@dyspraxiafoundation.org.uk Website: www.dyspraxiafoundation.org.uk

Leonard Cheshire – Central Office, 30 Millbank, London SW1P 4QD. Tel: 020 7802 8200. Fax:020 7802 8250. Email: info@lc-uk.org Website: www.leonard-cheshire.org.uk

RADAR – 12 City Forum, 250 City Road, London EC1V 8AF. Tel: 020 7250 3222. Fax: 020 7250 0212. Minicom: 020 7250 4119. Email: radar@radar.org.uk Website: www.radar.org.uk

The Shaftesbury Society – 16 Kingston Road, London SW19 1JZ. Tel: 0845 330 6033. Fax: 020 8239 5580. Email: info@shaftesburysoc.org.uk Website: www.shaftesburysoc.org.uk

Polio

British Polio Fellowship – Eagle Office Centre, The Runway, South Ruislip, Middlesex HA4 6SE. Freephone: 0800 0180 586. Fax: 020 8842 0555. Email: info@britishpolio.org.uk Website: www.britishpolio.org.uk

Prader-Willi syndrome

PWSA (UK) (Prader-Willi Syndrome Association) – 125a London Road, Derby DE1 2QQ. Tel: 01332 365676. Fax: 01332 360401. Email: admin@pwsa-uk.demon.co.uk Website: www.pwsa.co.uk

Retinitis Pigmentosa

British Retinitis Pigmentosa Society – PO Box 350, Buckingham MK18 1GZ. Helpline: 01280 821334. Fax: 01280 815900. Email: info@brps.org.co.uk Website: www.brps.org.co.uk

Scoliosis

British Scoliosis Society – Royal Manchester Children's Hospital, Pendlebury, Manchester M27 1HA.

Scoliosis Association UK – 2 Ivebury Court, 323-327 Latimer Road, London W10 6RA. Helpline: 020 8964 1166. Fax: 020 8964 5343. Email: sauk@sauk.org.uk Website: www.sauk.org.uk

Speech and language disorder

Association for all Speech Impaired Children (AFASIC) – 2nd Floor, 50-52 Great Sutton Street, London EC1V 0DJ. Helpline: 0845 355 5577. Fax: 020 7251 2834. Email: info@afasic.org.uk Website: www.afasic.org.uk

AFASIC Cymru – 1st Floor, The Exchange Building, Mount Stuart Square, Cardiff Bay, Cardiff CF10 5EB. Tel: 029 2046 5854. Email: clareafasic@aol.com Website: www.afasic.org.uk/cymru

AFASIC Scotland – Gemini Crescent, Dundee Technology Park, Dundee DD2 1TY. Tel: 01382 561891. Email: afasicscotland@btopenworld.com Website: www.afasicscotland.org.uk

Useful website: www.speechlanguage.org

Spina Bifida and Hydrocephalus

Association for Spina Bifida and Hydrocrephalus (ASBAH) – 42 Park Road, Peterborough PE1 2UQ. Tel: 01733 555988. Fax: 01733 555985. Email: info@asbah.org Website: www.asbah.org

Scottish Spina Bifida Association – The Dan Young Building, 6 Craighalbert Way, Cumbernauld G68 0LS. Tel: 01236 794500. Fax: 01236 736435. Email: admin@ssba.org.uk Website: www.ssba.org.uk

Spinal injuries

Spinal Injuries Association (SIA) – SIA House, 2 Trueman Place, Oldbrook, Milton Keynes MK6 2HH. Tel: 0845 678 6633. Fax: 0845 070 6911. Freephone helpline: 0800 980 0501. Email: sia@spinal.co.uk Website: www.spinal.co.uk

Tuberous Sclerosis

Tuberous Sclerosis Association – PO Box 12979, Barnt Green, Birmingham B45 5AN. Tel/fax: 0121 445 6970. Email: support@tuberous-sclerosis.org Website: www.tuberous-sclerosis.org

Williams syndrome

Williams Syndrome Foundation (UK) – 161 High Street, Tonbridge, Kent TH9 1BX. Tel: 01732 365152. Fax: 01732 360178. Email: john.nelson-wsfoundation@btinternet.com Website: www.williams-syndrome.org.uk

Other useful organisations

Association for Residential Care (ARC) – ARC House, Marsden Street, Chesterfield S40 1JY. Tel: 01246 555043. Fax: 01246 555045. Email: contact.us@arcuk.org.uk Website: www.arcuk.org.uk

ARC Scotland – Unit 13, Hardengreen Business Centre, Eskbank, Dalkeith EH22 3NX. Tel: 0131 663 4444. Email: arc.scotland@arcuk.org.uk Website: www.arcuk.org.uk

ARC Northern Ireland – 43 Marsden Gardens, Cavehill, Belfast BT15 5AFL. Tel: 028 9022 9020. Fax: 028 9020300. Email: arc.ni@arcuk.org.uk Website: www.arcuk.org.uk

ARC Cymru – Unit 3A, Mentec, Deiniol Road, Bangor LL57 2UP. Tel: 01248 361990. Email: arc.cymru@arcuk.org.uk Website: www.arcuk.org.uk

SKILL – Chapter House, 18-20 Crucifix Lane, London SE1 3JW. Tel: 0800 328 5050. Fax: 020 7450 0650. Email: info@skill.org.uk Website: www.skill.org.uk

Index of establishments by location

London, South East and East Anglia

(Bedfordshire, Cambridgeshire, East & West Sussex, Essex, Hertfordshire, Kent, London, Norfolk, Suffolk, Surrey)

Acorn Village

Adolphus Care Ltd

Care Kent

Care West Sussex

Chailey Heritage School

Delrow College

Dorton College of Further Education

Doucecroft Further Education Department

The Grange Centre

Grateley House School

The Helen Allison School

Jacques Hall

Meldreth Manor School

The Mount Camphill Community

Nash College

The National Centre for Young People with Epilepsy

Nexus Direct

The Orpheus Centre

The Papworth Trust

Philpots Manor School

Pield Heath House RC School

Queen Elizabeth's Foundation Brain Injury Centre

Queen Elizabeth's Foundation Development Centre

Queen Elizabeth's Foundation Training College

RNIB Redhill College

St Elizabeth's School

St Joseph's School

St Mary's College

SeeAbility

Sense East

Westgate College

Woodlarks Workshop Trust

Yateley Industries for the Disabled

South and South West

(Berkshire, Buckinghamshire, Cornwall, Devon, Dorset, Gloucestershire, Hampshire, Isle of Wight, Oxfordshire, Somerset, Wiltshire)

Burton Hill School

Care Devon

Care Wiltshire

Cherry Orchards Camphill Community

Cintre Community

Enham

Fairfield Farm College

Farleigh Further Education College (Frome and Swindon)

The Fortune Centre of Riding Therapy

George House

Grange Village Community

Grenville College

Hope Lodge School and Aspin House

Ivers

The Loddon School

Lufton College of Further Education

MacIntyre School

Mary Hare Grammar School for the Deaf

The Minstead Training Project

The National Society for Epilepsy

National Star College

Oaklands Park Village Community

Oakwood Court College

Prior's Court School

Purbeck View School

RNID Care Services

Royal College for the Deaf Exeter

Ruskin Mill Educational Trust

St Catherine's School

St Christopher's School

St Joseph's Extended Education Dept

St Loye's Foundation

The Sheiling Community

Somerset Court

Surecare Homes (Devon) Ltd

Taurus Crafts

Thorngrove/Mulberry Court

Treloar College

The West of England College

William Morris Camphill Community

The Wing Centre

Midlands

(Derbyshire, Hereford and Worcester, Leicestershire,
Lincolnshire, Northamptonshire, Nottinghamshire,
Shropshire, Staffordshire, Warwickshire, West Midlands)

AALPS College

Alderwasley Hall School

Bladon House School

Broughton House and College

Callow Park College

Care Ironbridge

Care Shangton

Condover College

Derwen College

Hereward College

Hinwick Hall College

Homefield College

Horizon School for Children with Autism

Kisimul School

Linkage College

Loppington House

NCW (New College Worcester)

Overley Hall School

Portland College

Queen Alexandra College

RNIB College Loughborough

RNIB Rushton School

Royal National College for the Blind

Sense West

Solden Hill House

Strathmore College

Winslow Court

North

(Cheshire, Cumbria, Durham, Greater Manchester,
Lancashire, Merseyside, Northumberland, Tyne and Wear,
Yorkshire)

Beaumont College of Further Education

Birtenshaw Hall School

Botton Village

Care Ponteland

Care Stanley Grange

Community Solutions

The Croft Community

Croft House

The David Lewis School

Deafway

Dilston College

Doncaster College for the Deaf

Finchale Training College

Fourways Assessment Unit

Fullerton House School

Henshaws College

Hesley Village and College

Holly Bank Trust

Langdon College

L'Arche

Larchfield Community

Lindeth College

Northern Counties School

Nugent House School

Pennine Camphill Community

Pontville School

The Robert Ogden School

Royal School for the Deaf

St John's Catholic School for the Deaf

Wirral Autistic Society

Wales

Bryn Melyn Group

Coleg Elidyr

Mental Health Care

Pengwern Further Education College

St Davids Care in the Community

Vyrnwy Academy

Womaston School

Scotland

Beannachar Camphill Community

Camphill Blair Drummond

Camphill Rudolf Steiner School

Daldorch House School

Easter Anguston Training Farm

Garvald Centre Edinburgh

Garvald West Linton

Motherwell College

RNIB Scotland: Employment and Learning Centre

Northern Ireland

Parkanaur College

Index of establishments by disabilities and disorders

This index has been compiled from information provided by the establishments themselves, and entries have been made where the establishment has indicated that it can cater for young people with particular disabilities. It does not necessarily mean that the establishment has particular expertise in a specific disability or range of disabilities. It is by no means an exhaustive list, and further study of individual entries is advised.

N.B. In some cases, the disability listed is only catered for if combined with another – e.g. visual or hearing impairment or a learning disability. Refer to individual entries for clarification.

The following categories are used:

A   Acquired brain injury

B   Attention deficit disorder/attention deficit hyperactivity disorder ADD/ADHD

C   Autism/Asperger Syndrome

D   Blindness/visual disabilities

E   Cerebral palsy

F   Communication, language and speech impairment

G   Deafblind – visual/hearing impairment

H   Deafness/hearing impairment

I   Disadvantage

J   Down's Syndrome

K   Dyscalculia/dyspraxia

L   Dyslexia

M   Emotional disorders/challenging behaviour

N   Epilepsy

O   Learning difficulties/disabilities

P   Mental health

Q   Mixed and multiple disabilities

R   Physical disabilities/impairments

S   Severe learning difficulties/PMLD

T   Tourette's syndrome.

A – Acquired brain injury

Birtenshaw Hall School

Bryn Melyn Group

Burton Hill School

Fourways Assessment Unit

The Grange Centre

Hereward College

Loppington House

National Star College

Northern Counties School

The Papworth Trust

Queen Elizabeth's Foundation Brain Injury Centre

RNIB College Loughborough

SeeAbility

Surecare Homes (Devon) Ltd

Treloar College

B – Attention deficit disorder/attention deficit hyperactivity disorder

Beannachar Camphill Community

Bladon House School

Bryn Melyn Group

Camphill Rudolf Steiner School

Coleg Elidyr

Croft House

Derwen College

The Fortune Centre of Riding Therapy

Garvald West Linton

Grateley House School

Jacques Hall

Langdon College

Linkage College

Nexus Direct

Northern Counties School

Pennine Camphill Community

Philpots Manor School

Pontville School

Ruskin Mill Educational Trust

SeeAbility

St Joseph's School

St Mary's College

Surecare Homes (Devon) Ltd

Vyrnwy Academy

Womaston School

C – Autism/Asperger Syndrome

AALPS College

Beannachar Camphill Community

Birtenshaw Hall School

Bladon House School

Broughton House and College

Bryn Melyn Group

Burton Hill School

Callow Park College

Camphill Rudolf Steiner School

Coleg Elidyr

Croft House

Daldorch House School and Continuing Education Centre

The David Lewis School

Derwen College

Doucecroft Further Education Department

Farleigh Further Education College (Frome/Swindon)

The Fortune Centre of Riding Therapy

Fullerton House School

Garvald West Linton

George House

The Grange Centre

Grateley House School

The Helen Allison School

Hereward College

Hesley Village and College

Homefield College

Hope Lodge School and Aspin House

Horizon School for Children with Autism

Langdon College

L'Arche

Linkage College

The Loddon School

Loppington House

MacIntyre School

Motherwell College

Nexus Direct

Northern Counties School

Overley Hall School

The Papworth Trust

Pennine Camphill Community

Philpots Manor School

Pontville School

Prior's Court School

Purbeck View School

Queen Alexandra College

RNIB College Loughborough

The Robert Ogden School

Royal National College for the Blind

Royal School for the Deaf

Ruskin Mill Educational Trust

St Davids Care in the Community

St Elizabeth's School

St Joseph's School

St Mary's College

SeeAbility

Somerset Court

Strathmore College

Surecare Homes (Devon) Ltd

Vyrnwy Academy

The Wing Centre

Wirral Autistic Society

Womaston School

D – Blindness/visual impairment

Beannachar Camphill Community

Birtenshaw Hall School

Burton Hill School

Chailey Heritage School

Condover College

Derwen College

Dorton College of Further Education

Henshaws College

Linkage College

Motherwell College

NCW (New College Worcester)

Nexus Direct

Northern Counties School

The Papworth Trust

Queen Alexandra College of Further Education

RNIB College Loughborough

RNIB Redhill College

RNIB Rushton School

RNIB Scotland: Employment and Learning Centre

Royal National College for the Blind

Royal School for the Deaf

St Joseph's Extended Education Department

St Mary's College

SeeAbility

Sense East

Sense West

Treloar College

The West of England College

E – Cerebral palsy

Beannachar Camphill Community

Beaumont College of Further Education

Birtenshaw Hall School

Burton Hill School

Camphill Rudolf Steiner School

Chailey Heritage School

Derwen College

The Fortune Centre of Riding Therapy

The Grange Centre

Henshaw's College

Hinwick Hall College

Holly Bank Trust

L'Arche

Linkage College

Loppington House

Meldreth Manor School

Motherwell College

National Star College

Northern Counties School

The Papworth Trust

Queen Alexandra College

RNIB College Loughborough

Royal National College for the Blind

Royal School for the Deaf

St Davids Care in the Community

St Joseph's Extended Education Dept

St Mary's College

SeeAbility

Thorngrove/Mulberry Court

Treloar College

F – Communication, language and speech impairment

Alderwasley Hall School

Beannachar Camphill Community

Birtenshaw Hall School

Bladon House School

Bryn Melyn Group

Burton Hill School

Callow Park College

Chailey Heritage School

Condover College

The David Lewis School

Derwen College

Doncaster College for the Deaf

Garvald West Linton

Henshaws College

Hereward College

Hinwick Hall College

Holly Bank Trust

Homefield College

Ivers

Langdon College

Linkage College

Loppington House

MacIntyre School

Meldreth Manor School

Northern Counties School

The Papworth Trust

Pield Heath House RC School

Pontville School

RNIB College Loughborough

Royal School for the Deaf

Ruskin Mill Educational Trust

St Catherine's School

St Elizabeth's School

St Joseph's School

St Mary's College

SeeAbility

Surecare Homes (Devon) Ltd

Treloar College

Vyrnwy Academy

Westgate College

G – Deafblind – visual/hearing impairment

Burton Hill School

Condover College

Henshaws College

Holly Bank Trust

Motherwell College

Northern Counties School

The Papworth Trust

Queen Alexandra College

RNID Care Services

Royal National College for the Blind

Royal School for the Deaf

SeeAbility

Sense East

Sense West

Westgate College

H – Deafness/hearing impairment

Beannachar Camphill Community

Burton Hill School

Deafway

Derwen College

Doncaster College for the Deaf

Hereward College

Hinwick Hall College

Linkage College

Loppington House

Mary Hare Grammar School for the Deaf

Motherwell College

Northern Counties School

The Papworth Trust

Queen Alexandra College

RNIB College Loughborough

RNID Care Services

Royal College for the Deaf Exeter

Royal National College for the Blind

Royal School for the Deaf

St John's Catholic School for the Deaf

St Joseph's Extended Education Dept

St Mary's College

SeeAbility

Sense East

Sense West

Treloar College

Westgate College

I – Disadvantage

Beannachar Camphill Community

Bryn Melyn Group

Camphill Rudolf Steiner School

Derwen College

Jacques Hall

Langdon College

Motherwell College

The Papworth Trust

Philpots Manor School

RNIB College Loughborough

Royal National College for the Blind

Ruskin Mill Educational Trust

J – Down's Syndrome

Beannachar Camphill Community

Birtenshaw Hall School

Bladon House School

Coleg Elidyr

Condover College

Derwen College

The Fortune Centre of Riding Therapy

Garvald West Linton

The Grange Centre

Henshaws College

Hinwick Hall College

Langdon College

L'Arche

Linkage College

Loppington House

Motherwell College

Overley Hall School

The Papworth Trust

Pennine Camphill Community

Philpots Manor School

RNIB College Loughborough

St Davids Care in the Community

St Joseph's School

St Mary's College

SeeAbility

Strathmore College

Vyrnwy Academy

Womaston School

K – Dyscalculia/dyspraxia

Bladon House School

Callow Park College

Croft House

Derwen College

Garvald West Linton

Jacques Hall

Langdon College

L'Arche

Linkage College

Northern Counties School

The Papworth Trust

Pennine Camphill Community

Philpots Manor School

RNIB College Loughborough

St Mary's College

Treloar College

Vyrnwy Academy

L – Dyslexia

Beannachar Camphill Community

Callow Park College

Camphill Rudolf Steiner School

Derwen College

Grenville College

Langdon College

Linkage College

Motherwell College

The Papworth Trust

Queen Alexandra College

RNIB College Loughborough

Royal National College for the Blind

St Mary's College

M – Emotional disorders/challenging behaviour

Beannachar Camphill Community

Bryn Melyn Group

Burton Hill School

Camphill Rudolf Steiner School

Cintre Community

Croft House

The Fortune Centre of Riding Therapy

Garvald West Linton

Jacques Hall

Langdon College

Loppington House

Motherwell College

The Mount Camphill Community

Nexus Direct

Northern Counties School

Nugent House School

Overley Hall School

The Papworth Trust

Pennine Camphill Community

Philpots Manor School

Ruskin Mill Further Educational Trust

St Elizabeth's School

SeeAbility

Surecare Homes (Devon) Ltd

Vyrnwy Academy

Westgate College

Womaston School

N – Epilepsy

Beannachar Camphill Community

Birtenshaw Hall School

Broughton House and College

Bryn Melyn Group

Camphill Rudolf Steiner School

Chailey Heritage School

Condover College

The David Lewis School

Derwen College

The Fortune Centre of Riding Therapy

Garvald West Linton

The Grange Centre

Henshaws College

Hesley Village and College

Hinwick Hall College

Holly Bank Trust

Langdon College

Linkage College

Loppington House

MacIntyre School

Motherwell College

The National Centre for Young People with Epilepsy

The National Society for Epilepsy

Nexus Direct

Northern Counties School

The Papworth Trust

Pennine Camphill Community

Philpots Manor School

RNIB College Loughborough

Royal National College for the Blind

St Davids Care in the Community

St Elizabeth's School

St Joseph's Extended Education Department

St Mary's College

SeeAbility

Surecare Homes (Devon) Ltd

Vyrnwy Academy

Womaston School

O – Learning difficulties/disabilities

Acorn Village

Adolphus Care Ltd

Apsley Care

Beannachar Camphill Community

Birtenshaw Hall School

Bladon House School

Botton Village

Broughton House and College

Bryn Melyn Group

Burton Hill School

Camphill Blair Drummond

Camphill Rudolf Steiner School

CARE – all establishments

Chailey Heritage School

Cintre Community

Coleg Elidyr

Condover College

The Croft Community

Croft House

David Lewis School

Delrow College

Derwen College

Dilston College

Doncaster College for the Deaf

Easter Anguston Training Farm

Enham

Fairfield Farm College

Finchale Training College

The Fortune Centre of Riding Therapy

Garvald Centre Edinburgh

Garvald West Linton

The Grange Centre

Grange Village Community

Grenville College

Henshaws College

Hereward College

Hesley Village and College

Hinwick Hall College

Holly Bank Trust

Homefield College

Ivers

Jacques Hall

Langdon College

L'Arche

Larchfield Community

Lindeth College

Linkage College

Loppington House

Lufton College of Further Education

MacIntyre School

Mental Health Care

The Minstead Training Project

Motherwell College

The Mount Camphill Community

Nash College

National Star College

Nexus Direct

Northern Counties School

Oaklands Park Village Community

Oakwood Court College

The Papworth Trust

Parkanaur College

Pengwern Further Education College

Pennine Camphill Community

Philpots Manor School

Pield Heath House RC School

Pontville School

Queen Alexandra College

Queen Elizabeth's Foundation Training College

Royal School for the Deaf

Ruskin Mill Educational Trust

St Davids Care in the Community

St Elizabeth's School

St Joseph's School

St Mary's College

SeeAbility

The Sheiling Community

Solden Hill House

Strathmore College

Surecare Homes (Devon) Ltd

Taurus Crafts

Treloar College

Vyrnwy Academy

Westgate College

William Morris Camphill Community

P – Mental health

Adolphus Care Ltd

Beannachar Camphill Community

Bryn Melyn Group

Burton Hill School

Camphill Rudolf Steiner School

Cherry Orchards Camphill Community

Delrow College

The Fortune Centre of Riding Therapy

Jacques Hall

Mental Health Care

Motherwell College

Nexus Direct

Nugent House School

The Papworth Trust

Pennine Camphill Community

Philpots Manor School

Queen Elizabeth's Foundation Training College

RNIB College Loughborough

SeeAbility

Taurus Crafts

Q – Mixed and multiple disabilities

Beannachar Camphill Community

Birtenshaw Hall School
Bryn Melyn Group
Burton Hill School
Camphill Rudolf Steiner School
Condover College
Derwen College
Finchale Training College
Garvald West Linton
Hinwick Hall College
Holly Bank Trust
L'Arche
Linkage College
Motherwell College
National Star College
Northern Counties School
The Papworth Trust
Pennine Camphill Community
Queen Alexandra College
RNIB College Loughborough
RNIB Rushton School
Royal School for the Deaf
St Joseph's Extended Education Dept
St Loye's Foundation
St Mary's College
Treloar College

R – Physical disabilities/impairments

Beannachar Camphill Community
Birtenshaw Hall School
Bryn Melyn Group
Burton Hill School
Camphill Rudolf Steiner School
Chailey Heritage School
Derwen College
Enham
Finchale Training College
Fourways Assessment Unit
The Grange Centre
Henshaws College
Hereward College
Hinwick Hall College
Holly Bank Trust

Linkage College
Meldreth Manor School
Motherwell College
Nash College
National Star College
Northern Counties School
The Orpheus Centre
The Papworth Trust
Portland College
Queen Alexandra College
Queen Elizabeth's Foundation Development Centre
Queen Elizabeth's Foundation Training College
RNIB College Loughborough
Royal National College for the Blind
St Joseph's Extended Education Dept
SeeAbility
Surecare Homes (Devon) Ltd
Taurus Crafts
Treloar College
Woodlarks Workshop Trust
Yately Industries for the Disabled

S – Severe learning difficulties/PMLD

Beannachar Camphill Community
Birtenshaw Hall School
Bladon House School
Broughton House and College
Burton Hill School
Camphill Rudolf Steiner School
Community Solutions
Condover College
The David Lewis School
Derwen College
Fullerton House School
Garvald West Linton
Hesley Village and College
Holly Bank Trust
Ivers
Kisimul School
Langdon College
L'Arche
Linkage College

The Loddon School

Loppington House

Lufton College of Further Education

MacIntyre School

Meldreth Manor School

National Star College

Northern Counties School

Overley Hall School

The Papworth Trust

Pengwern Further Education College

Pennine Camphill Community

Pield Heath House RC School

Prior's Court School

Royal School for the Deaf

St Christopher's School

St Davids Care in the Community

St Elizabeth's School

St Joseph's School

SeeAbility

Strathmore College

Winslow Court

Womaston School

T – Tourette's Syndrome

Bladon House School

Callow Park College

Garvald West Linton

L'Arche

Linkage College

Philpots Manor School

Ruskin Mill Educational Trust

Surecare Homes (Devon) Ltd

Alphabetical index

S

T

V

W

Y